THE BOOK OF FAITH
OF THE OAK HILLS SECOND WARD OF ZION

THE BOOK OF FAITH

OF THE OAK HILLS SECOND WARD OF ZION

Volume I

by Thomas S. Taylor

DORRANCE PUBLISHING CO., INC.
PITTSBURGH, PENNSYLVANIA 15222

The events, people, and places herein are depicted to the best recollection of the author, who assumes complete and sole responsibility for the accuracy of this narrative.

All Rights Reserved
Copyright © 2006 by Thomas S. Taylor
No part of this book may be reproduced or transmitted
in any form or by any means, electronic or mechanical,
including photocopying, recording, or by any information
storage and retrieval system without permission in
writing from the publisher.

ISBN-10: 0-8059-6941-1
ISBN-13: 978-0-8059-6941-2

Printed in the United States of America

First Printing

For information or to order additional books, please write:
Dorrance Publishing Co., Inc.
701 Smithfield Street
Third Floor
Pittsburgh, Pennsylvania 15222
U.S.A.
1-800-788-7654
Or visit our web site and on-line catalog at www.dorrancebookstore.com

Drawing of our Stake Center by Todd Asay

Home of the Oak Hills Second Ward of Zion

Dedication

This book is dedicated to the universal and eternal principle of Faith; first in God and second in mankind. All of us are children of God. As His children, we must learn and practice faith in our daily lives. Through faith and prayer, God performs miracles in our lives. Faith requires action. God is in charge and will prevail against evil.

These wartime narratives are classic examples of numerous miracles. Miracles have visited these "Heroes Among Us" in their peacetime lives. If your faith needs strengthening, and all of us do, start today and exercise your faith jointly with your families.

Our present war against terrorism is a war of good against evil seekers of power. There are no boundaries or battle lines. All of us are warriors. The sanctity of human life is involved.

Let us all earn our freedom through the exercise of faith and actions. Miracles have already been, and will be, performed. You will receive peace of mind in doing so.

This book is further dedicated to the memory of the author's paternal grandmother, Mary Maude Rogers Taylor; and her exemplary lifetime of love, faith, and service to God, her family, and the community.

INTRODUCTION

The World War II veterans herein are sharing an important part of their lives with their families and all who read this book for a very important purpose—to comply with a Commandment of God which is directed to all men everywhere and says, "Write the words which I speak unto them." God speaks to all of us during our lifetime. We must learn to listen and recognize His spirit voice. By writing His words, we become witnesses of Him, strengthen and develop faith in God and share this with our fellow men. We strengthen each other in the process. This in turn gives meaning and purpose to life and brings us joy, both individually and jointly.

These histories demonstrate faith in action and describe a belief that they have experienced divine intervention and preservation.

They believe:

A) Guardian angels protected them.
B) Faith in God is an eternal principle that is basic to a successful life.
C) They have learned guidelines to follow in developing and strengthening their faith in Him and to commune with God.
D) Their families are eternal and are basic in the meaning and purpose of life.

SCRIPTURAL BASIS

In 2 Nephi 29:11 it states "For I command all men—that they write the words which I speak unto them; for out of the books which shall be written I will judge the world, every man according to...that which is written." Bishop Michael Jackson asked me to serve as Ward Missionary Leader. This caused me to feel that the faith-promoting experiences we receive during our lives are "spoken words" from the Lord; that we need to preserve them in written form; that by sharing these faith-promoting experiences, in writing, we are practicing our responsibilities as member missionaries. Bishop Jackson and the bishopric have been leading our ward as a "Ward of Zion," after the concept of the City of Enoch, a city of faith. Our ward is following his leadership toward becoming a true "Ward of Zion." This is evident from the number and quality of contributions made to this compilation of writings, music, and art work.

Scriptural references are an integral part of this Book of Faith. The Lord has commanded all nations, all men, to write words which He speaks to them, as follows:

2 Nephi 29:7 "Know ye not that there are more nations than one? Know ye not that I, the Lord Your God, have created all men, and that I remember those who are upon the isles of the sea; that I rule in the heavens above and in the earth beneath; and I bring forth my word unto the children of men, yea, even upon all nations of the earth?"

2 Nephi 29:8 "Wherefore murmur ye, because that ye shall receive more of my word? KNOW YE NOT THAT THE TESTIMONY OF TWO NATIONS IS A WITNESS UNTO YOU THAT I AM GOD; THAT I REMEMBER ONE NATION LIKE UNTO ANOTHER? WHEREFORE, I SPEAK THE SAME WORDS UNTO ONE NATION LIKE UNTO ANOTHER. AND WHEN THE TWO NATIONS SHALL RUN TOGETHER THE TESTIMONY OF THE TWO NATIONS SHALL RUN TOGETHER ALSO."

2 Nephi 29:11 "FOR I COMMAND ALL MEN, both in the East and in the West, and in the North and in the South, and in the isles of the sea, THAT THEY SHALL WRITE THE WORDS WHICH I SPEAK UNTO THEM; FOR OUT OF THE BOOKS WHICH SHALL BE WRITTEN I WILL JUDGE THE WORLD, EVERY MAN ACCORDING TO...THAT WHICH IS WRITTEN."

In the family history program of our church we have been encouraged as individuals to write our personal journals. Why is this important? To share with our successors important events and what we have learned during our individual lives, including our faith-promoting experiences and what we have learned about the Plan of Salvation. When we do this we become witnesses to God and active member missionaries for Jesus Christ.

When we exercise our faith, the Lord does speak to us in His spiritual voice. The Lord has spoken to all the contributors of this book and during the experiences described herein. We are privileged to receive the enclosed testimonies through writings, music, and art. I have learned that the playing of religious music and the drawing of religious art can be equal and many times more effective testimonies of God than the spoken or written word. Enclosed in this book are excellent examples of this.

Notice the beautiful diversity and variations of the testimonies contained herein. Some are single events, others are a series of events over a longer period of time, different circumstances, and environments. But like the City of Enoch, they "are of one mind" and merge into one greater truth, like the doctrine of synergy does, later described.

Let us now review the subject of faith. Faith is defined as follows: "Now faith is the substance (assurance) of things hoped for, the evidence of things not seen" (Hebrews 11:1).

A very comprehensive works on the subject of faith is found in *The Lectures on Faith* written by the Prophet Joseph Smith and included in the 1876 edition of the *Doctrine and Covenants* but later removed from the *Doctrine of Covenants* and then entitled *Lectures on Faith*. In the 1876 *Doctrine and Covenants* they were introduced thus:

"Lectures on Faith

Lecture First–Section 1

On the Doctrine of The Church of Jesus Christ of Latter-Day Saints, originally delivered before a class of the Elders, in Kirtland, Ohio."

"It is evident that the lectures were held in high esteem by the Prophet Joseph Smith and the early brethren, even as they now are, though they are not currently published in part of the standard works."

A brief sketch of the lectures is as follows.

Lecture First (Definition; A Principle of Power and Action)

1.24 "Faith is a principle of action and power; it is a governing principle which has power and dominion over all things; that without faith both mind and body would be in a state of inactivity and all exertions would cease, both mind and body and faith is a principle of power in both Deity and man."

Lecture Second (The Object on Which Faith Rests Is God; Evidence of the Existence of God)

2.2 "That He (God) is the father of lights; in Him the principle of faith dwells independently and He is the object in whom faith of all other rational and accountable beings center for life and salvation."

Lecture Third (Essentials to Exercise Faith in God Unto Salvation)

3.2 "Let us here observe, that three things are necessary in order that any rational and intelligent being may exercise faith in God, unto life and salvation."

3.3 "First, the idea that He actually exists."

3.4 "Secondly, a correct idea of His character, perfections and attributes."

3.5 "Thirdly, an actual knowledge that the course of life which he is pursuing is according to His will."

3.12 "The character of God."

3.13 "First, that He was God before the world was created and the same God that He was after it was created."

3.14 "Secondly, that He was merciful and gracious, slow to anger, abundant in goodness and that He was so from everlasting, and will be to everlasting."

3.15 "Thirdly, that He changes not."

3.16 "Fourthly, that He is a God of truth and cannot lie."

3.17 "Fifthly, that He is no respecter of persons."

3.18 "Sixthly, that He is love."

3.19 "Knowledge of the above attributes are necessary for your faith to bond you to God for your lifetime."

Lecture Fourth (Connection Between Attributes of God and Exercise of Faith in Him)

Lecture Fifth (The Godhead; The Father, The Son and The Holy Ghost)

5.2 "and these three constitute the Godhead, and are one."

Lecture Sixth (Course of Life to Pursue to Enable Exercise of Faith in God, unto Salvation)

Lecture Seventh (The Effects of Faith)

The above gives us a foundation and background to read about the clear evidence of faith in the following compiled experiences. We are grateful to those who have shared with us their faith-promoting experiences. The writings, music, and art speak for themselves. They all have one thing in common and "in one mind," THEIR FAITH IN GOD. Having preserved the experiences and shared them, they have become witnesses of God and have complied with 2 Nephi 29.

The World War II chapters demonstrate divine intervention and "guardian angels" preserving lives during wartime. The variety in these chapters is truly remarkable. This is an "open book" that enables us to add to and supplement what is now here as additional ones come in. May this book be used as an effective missionary tool.

SYNERGISM: SYNERGY
I recently discovered the two words *synergism* and *synergy*, and their meaning, that in my opinion are an important application to this book. The dictionary defines the words as follows:

"Synergism: THE DOCTRINE THAT HUMAN EFFORT COOPERATES WITH DIVINE GRACE IN THE SALVATION OF THE SOUL.

A cooperating organ, part, or medicine (in medicine)

Synergy: (1) Combined and correlated force; (2) Specific. In medicine. Correlation or concurrence of action between different organs in health or disease or between remedies. (Greek; *syn*. Together, plus *ergon*. Work.)"

It is meaningful to me that this concept and principle is incorporated into the creation and operation of our earthly bodies. It is a truth that teaches us Divine Grace cooperates and works with human effort or work in the salvation of our souls. Our work with faith in God, joins us to Divine Grace which results in the salvation of our souls.

I recently read a description of synergy that came from the book *Seven Habits of Highly Effective People* written by Steven Covey. He illustrated the Synergy Doctrine with a picture of an aspen tree grove. The explanation described the root system of all the aspen trees in the grove were intertwined; that as a result the trees drew strength from each other and prospered better than they would have if alone. A summary formula of the principle was described as one plus one equals more than three. The total sum was greater than the sum of the individual parts. Mr. Covey has applied this doctrine to business management.

This doctrine of synergy applies to this book. All of the contributors to this book have a strong faith in God; each has worked hard to preserve their testimonies and share them with others, including those who read this book. In doing so, they have obeyed the divine commandment to preserve the words they have received from God and in the process have become witnesses of God. In compiling the chapters I have drawn faith from each one and received a spiritual strength greater than the sum of the individual chapters. Like the above definition and the grove of trees, the joint faiths in this book are greater than the sum of the individual faiths. To me, this book has created a synergy. We have created a large joint faith. We have created a Zion community in this book in that we are all "of one mind" through our joint faith, just as did the City of Enoch.

Enclosed is a picture of a painting of ours painted by Floyd E. Breinholt. We call it "Aspen Grove" and consider it an illustration of "Nature's Synergy." This picture helps me to visualize and to better understand the doctrine of synergy.

Note: All citations from the Mormon Scriptures are from *The Book of Mormon, Doctrine and Covenants,* and *The Pearl of Great Price,* published by the Church of Jesus Christ of Latter-day Saints, Salk Lake City, Utah.

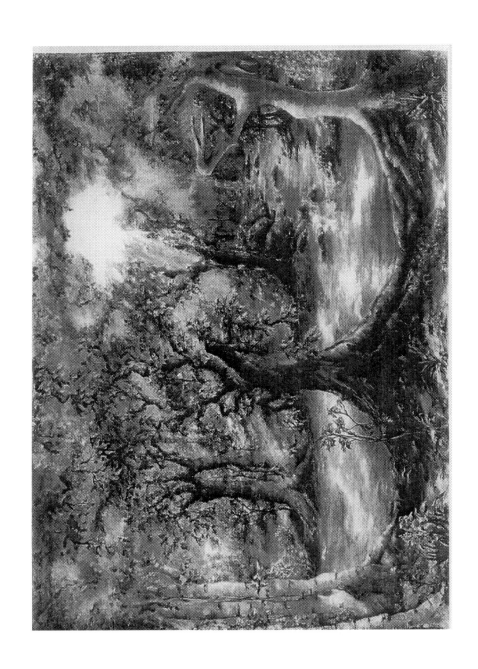

SYNERGY – TREES OF FAITH

by Carole Anderson

In the Book of Mormon (Alma 32), Alma likens faith unto a seed, that when properly planted, nourished, and cared for will ultimately grow into a tree of life filled with nourishing fruit.

Like us, each tree in the painting is an individual—unique, yet each draws on the strength of those around them.

Our lives are a series of circles, touching others around us—becoming intertwined. Just as the trees are in a circle, their roots, branches, and leaves meshing with those around them, they lend strength and stability to their neighbors, families, and friends. The roots, which represent the base (the rock) reach out to incorporate others around them, offering their strength and stability to others. As all these join together they form an almost unbreakable bond, creating a power far beyond what they would have been capable of by themselves.

Alone a tree often struggles simply to survive, but together we and the trees grow straight, sturdy, and strong.

Saplings, and those who are younger and weaker as to the spiritual, depend on those who have more strength and can give protection until they are able to lend strength to another.

Each person/tree creates their own place of beauty around them (flowers, rocks, grasses).

The water represents the living waters (John 4:13-14), the source of constant nourishment around which the trees grow.

Penetrating, far reaching, and shining upon all is the Light of Christ—giving warmth as well as life itself.

7

THE FAMILY—
A PROCLAMATION TO THE WORLD

The Church of Jesus Christ of Latter-day Saints through its First Presidency and Council of the Twelve Apostles, has created and published a document entitled "The Family—A Proclamation to the World." It declares the following concepts:

1. Marriage between a man and a woman is ordained of God; and this family is central to His plan for mankind.

2. All human beings are created by Him and in His image. Each of us is a spirit child of heavenly parents through a premortal, mortal, and eternal plan that God created.

3. God created the earth to enable His children to obtain a physical body, gain experience, and progress and realize their divine destiny.

4. God commanded the sacred powers of procreation to be used only between lawfully wedded husbands and wives.

5. The sanctity of life is vital to God's eternal plan.

6. Members of families each have specific responsibilities within the family and to society, and will be held accountable to God for what they do or do not do.

7. It calls upon responsible citizens and government officials everywhere to promote and strengthen the family for its benefit and the benefit of society.

This Family Proclamation is available to anyone who desires a copy.

STEPHEN B. ELLIS

CAPTAIN STEPHEN B. ELLIS

Written aboard the M/S *World Discoverer*
while cruising the Solomon Islands
March 9, 1987

Qualified in the following aircraft: Steerman, BT-13, AT-17, B-24, B-25, C-45, C-47(DC3), SBD-Douglas dive bomber, P-38, P-47, P-51, and a Cessna 206 which he presently owns and flies.

Areas flown: San Francisco to Hawaii, to Johnson Island, Kwajalein, Eniwetok, Truk, Hawaii, Guam, Okinawa, Manila, Shanghai, China, Korea, Tokyo, Iwo Jima, Saipan, Ponape, and Hawaii.

It all began at Lubbock, Texas, in August of 1942. After having passed the flight exams, I raised my hand and swore under oath—I DO!

As a private earmarked for flight training I was sent home to wait for available training facilities. On February 4, 1943, I was notified to report to the Santa Ana, California, training base for induction and testing to determine what training I was qualified for. From the results of the extensive testing, I qualified for pilot, bombardier, and/or navigator. At that time, the testing could determine within 97 percent of being a navigator, 95 percent of being a bombardier, and only 35 percent of making pilot. I took the long shot and requested pilot training. At Thunderbird Field near Phoenix, Arizona, I was trained to fly Steermans and was the first to solo out of our class 43-K of two hundred and fifty cadets.

Next came basic training at Minter Field near Bakersfield, California, flying BT-13 (Vultee). Night flying and formation flying were included along with cross-country flying.

At twin engine advance training near Marfa, Texas, I flew AT-17s with instrument flying included. The day of graduation I was offered an instructor pilot assignment. Wanting to see the world, I went to B-24 (Liberator 4 engine bomber training) at March Field near Riverside, California. We were assigned into ten-man crews which consisted of pilot, co-pilot, navigator, bombardier, crew chief, radio operator, and four turret gunners. The radio operator and crew chief also manned .50 caliber machine guns during any enemy attack.

We were sent to Hamilton Field near San Francisco and checked out a brand new B-24. A fuel check flight was made prior to our flying non-stop for fourteen hours—destination: Wheeler Field, Hawaii! Here we received gunnery, navigation, bombing, and formation flight training. Being declared combat-trained, we were sent to Kwajelein atoll in the Marshall Islands and assigned to the 27th Squadron, 30th Bomb Group, 7th Air Force.

During a night mission over Truk—takeoff 6:30 P.M.—bomb run at 18,000 feet—we ran into a highly charged electrical storm and for four and a half hours the navigator was unable to use celestial navigation, so we flew dead reckoning because the magnetic compass was spinning like a top. Static electricity (called St. Elmo's fire) was everywhere, along all edges of the plane. Each propeller had a four-inch band at the tips, very colorful.

As we climbed through eleven thousand feet altitude I put on my oxygen mask. Soon I could not see clearly so I took off my mask and gulped fresh air. As my vision cleared, I put my mask on again and the same problem of distorted vision returned. About that time the other crew members started calling on the intercom. All were experiencing similar problems. A decision to make the bomb run at 12,000 feet without oxygen was made. On returning, it was determined that someone had put acetylene gas in our oxygen system by mistake.

As our ETA (estimated time of arrival) approached, the clouds opened up for a few seconds and the navigator obtained a fix and corrected our heading, and shortly the Truk atoll appeared straight ahead. The navigator was off by only thirty seconds on his ETA.

All was dark but the second our bombs were released the anti-aircraft guns commenced firing. Numerous searchlights turned on to light us up so the ack-ack guns could be more accurate. Using violent, erratic, evasive action, we got away and flew back to Eniwetok.

On July 7, 1944, we were scheduled to bomb Truk during the daylight along with twenty other B-24s. The weather was clear and as we entered our bomb run the ack-ack was extremely heavy. Also, several fighters (Jap Zeros) made dives through our formation after dropping phosphorous bombs that exploded above us, causing pieces to fall that were burning at 4500°F. This looked similar to bursting Fourth of July fireworks. We dropped our bombs on a fuel storage tank and were doing evasive action when an ack-ack shell ripped through our left wing midway between our #1 and #2 engines, cutting the fuel lines and tearing one gas tank. I feathered (shut off) the #1 engine and the flight engineer transferred what gas was left into the tanks on the right wing. It was now impossible to fly the five hours needed to get back to Eniwetok due to lack of fuel. My next concern was to nurse the plane as far as possible before running out of gas.

I improved the situation the best I could by (a) trimming the plane to fly on three engines, (b) throttling back to conserve fuel, (c) throwing out (jettisoning) everything we could to lighten the plane, and (d) taking advantage of our 18,000-foot altitude and stretching out our descent.

We all decided that, rather than attempting to parachute, we would try ditching (land with wheels up in the ocean). We broke radio silence and reported the approximate latitude and longitude where we would have to ditch and requested a rescue boat be dispatched to pick up the survivors. Up to that time ditchings had lost half of the crews involved and the planes would break up.

We had plenty of time to ponder and think as I nursed the crippled bomber along. One of the crew had brought a five-pound brick of cheese along. Not knowing how long we might be floating in the water after ditching, should we be lucky enough to survive the crash, it was decided that each one would eat as much cheese as possible. We also sang songs. The airman sang "I've Got Sixpence," which required time to sing, and we sang it several times.

> 1st Verse
>> I've got sixpence, jolly sixpence.
>> I've got sixpence, to last me all my life.
>> I've got twopence to spend and twopence to lend
>> and twopence to send home to my wife—poor wife.
> Chorus
>> No cares have I to grieve me.
>> No pretty little girls to deceive me.
>> I'm happy as a king, believe me.
>> As we go rolling home.
>> Rolling home, rolling home, rolling home, rolling home
>> By the light of the silvery moo-oo-oon.
>> I'm happy as a king, believe me.
>> As we go rolling home.
> 2nd Verse
>> I've got fourpence, jolly, jolly fourpence.
>> I've got fourpence to last me all my life.
>> I've got twopence to spend and twopence to lend
>> and no pence to send home to my wife—poor wife.
> Chorus
> 3rd Verse

> I've got twopence, jolly, jolly twopence.
> I've got twopence to last me all my life.
> I've got twopence to spend and no pence to lend
> and no pence to send home to my wife—poor wife.

Chorus

4th Verse

> I've got no pence, jolly, jolly no pence.
> I've got no pence to last me all my life.
> I've got no pence to spend and no pence to lend
> and no pence to send home to my wife—poor wife.

Chorus

After four and a half hours the three engines coughed and it was now time to ditch. The B-24 stalled at 135 miles per hour. With seven-foot waves, the plane stopped abruptly as it hit the solid wall of water. The force of the impact pulled the pilot seat loose from the floor and I was thrown through the plexiglas and aluminum windshield into the water with the seat still strapped to me. The Army Air Corps had not developed, nor did they furnish, flight helmets. We were issued the infantry trench helmet. Prior to ditching, we all put on our infantry trench helmets. I'm sure that the helmet saved my life by protecting my head as I crashed through the windshield.

I had a broken right arm above the elbow and a chipped left elbow but I was able to undo the seatbelt and get rid of the seat so that I could surface for air. I came up underneath the plane, not knowing just where. If I had been at one wing tip and proceeded under the wing it would have been 104 feet before I could surface and be able to breathe. Fortunately, I came out from under the left wing to the rear. Turning on my back and putting my feet against the wing, I shoved off. The life jacket (Mae West) had two air compartments that would inflate by pulling a string that in turn punctured a CO_2 cylinder. The first compartment was torn and the air just hissed away but the second half of the Mae West held, even though it also had a slow leak. Every few minutes I would have to blow in a hose and replenish the air.

The waves were washing over my head and the GI issue combat boots were awkward to tread water with. I thought about taking the boots off but then decided that any shark that wanted a bite of my foot would have to pay for it with GI boot indigestion. I could hear the other crew members but, because of the high waves, never did see any of them until the minesweeper arrived and picked us out of the water.

Other than the broken bone I was in fairly good condition. Nine of the ten crew members survived and the plane stayed intact. After about an hour it finally sank. The minesweeper picked us up after about three or four hours and I was transferred to a navy hospital ship that happened to be in the Eniwetok harbor. From the hospital ship, I was air-evacuated to Tripler

14

General Hospital in Honolulu, Hawaii. After some time and physical therapy I was able to return to flying.

My next assignment was as a personal pilot for General Thomas, who was the island commander of Ie Shima (next to Okinawa). I flew him throughout the Northern Pacific, including Korea, China, and Japan. It was just after the two atomic bombings, at Hiroshima and Nagasaki, that I flew to Japan and saw the total destruction firsthand.

Later, I was standing nearby and witnessed the transfer of ten Japanese dignitaries en route to the Philippines to arrange for the surrender ceremonies. They deplaned from two Jap twin-engine Betties that were painted white with large green crosses. I'll never forget the look of bewilderment on their faces as they boarded the C-54 that was towering above the Betties. They didn't realize we had such big aircraft. Each Jap held a large bouquet of flowers that was to be presented to General MacArthur upon their arrival at Manila. In Manila the arrangements for the formal surrender were made by General MacArthur and were scheduled to take place aboard the battleship *Missouri* back in Japan at Tokyo Bay.

The military set up a point system for the returning of GIs to the United States. Because of the large number returning versus the available ships, the men with high points went home first. Points were determined by length of time overseas along with decorations and letters of commendation, etc. On December 16, 1945, my time arrived for getting aboard a converted cargo ship for the sixteen-day voyage to good old U.S.A., my dear wife Hazel, and our three-year-old son.

THE UNITED STATES OF AMERICA

TO ALL WHO SHALL SEE THESE PRESENTS, GREETING:

THIS IS TO CERTIFY THAT

THE PRESIDENT OF THE UNITED STATES OF AMERICA

AUTHORIZED BY ORDER OF

GENERAL GEORGE WASHINGTON, AUGUST 7, 1782

HAS AWARDED

THE PURPLE HEART

TO

CAPTAIN STEPHEN B. ELLIS , ARMY AIR CORP.

FOR

WOUNDS RECEIVED IN ACTION

7 JULY 1944 OVER TROCK ATOL , CENTAL PACIFIC THEATER

GIVEN UNDER MY HAND IN THE CITY OF WASHINGTON

THIS   19th   DAY OF   July   19 49

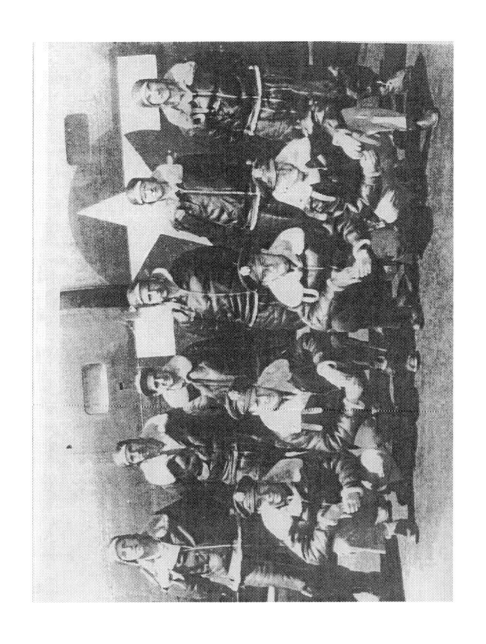

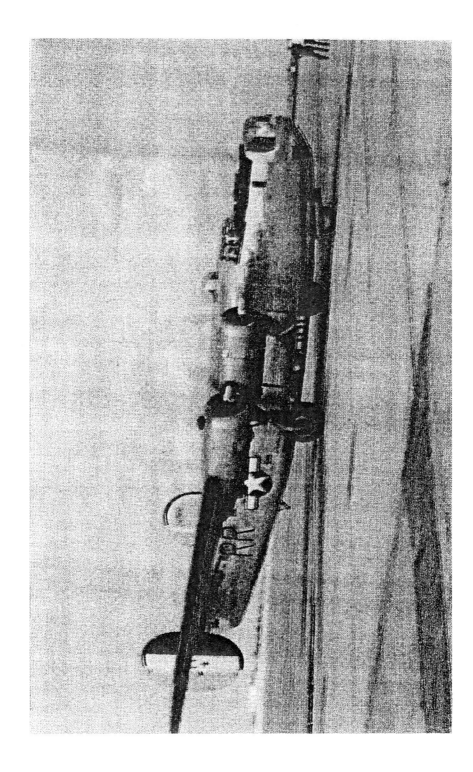

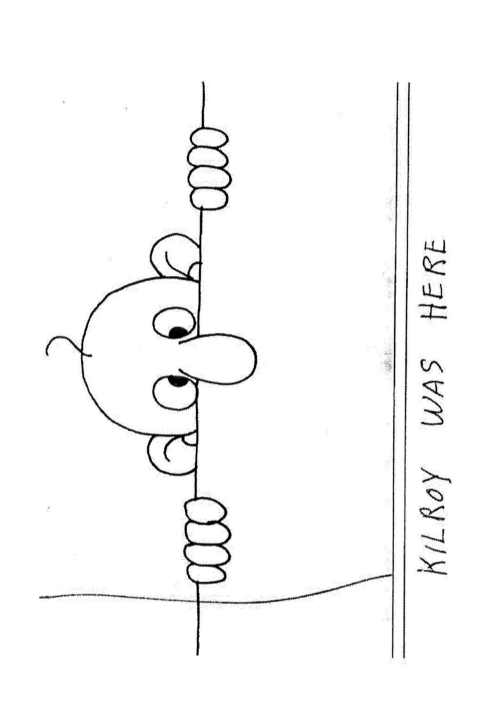

JESSE L. (LARRY) DAVIS

In Memorium

Jesse L. (Larry) Davis lost his battle with a long-term deteriorating disease and died March 14, 2006. His entire life is a classic example of devoted service to his family, church, community and country; all to a degree of excellence.

This hero among us has left a legacy of love and service to his wife, four children, 37 grandchildren, 20 great grandchildren and four step grandchildren.

A legacy of freedom to all mankind. He is now serving in eternity.

JESSE L. (LARRY) DAVIS

L.D. Do not read this if you are a little squeamish about some of these listed things: Times when you are extremely busy; anytime you have not had a bath, changed clothes, or shaved for a few weeks; when you have shot down our own planes filled with paratroopers; you are bombed by the Allied troops; you have been short of equipment to do your work in the early stages of the war; you have to eat English food rations.

If you ever saw planes in the first few months, they were not ours. Generals made mistakes. We made mistakes. We did not know what was going on in the world. We did not know what was happening right next to us. We moved camp twenty-two times in sixty days after working all day. These are a few of the trials and tasks that we had to put up with.

I was a graduate, a civil engineer from the Utah State Agricultural College. I had worked for just over a year on the Deer Creek Dam for the Bureau of Reclamation in Provo. My friends and neighbors caught up with me one afternoon as we were finishing work. My boss drove up and said that he had forgotten to tell me that I was to take a physical yesterday; he had fixed it so I could report that day. I went to the doctor and came out with flying colors. When I was in my senior year of college, the Navy had a team come through the school recruiting fliers. They said I was exactly what they wanted and did I know of any reason why I could not pass the physical. I said that one time I was looking at a *Look* magazine and saw some dots, that was all, and he thanked me for coming. I tried the Air Force. No, they couldn't use me. Same with the Corps of Engineers. I said, "Well, they'll just go ahead and draft me, so they did." My Uncle James was a major. I told him. He said no Davis was ever drafted. I said, "Well, no one wants me."

I was drafted on November 13, 1941, and sent to Fort Douglas, Salt Lake City, Utah. Boy, they pumped up my arms with shots, and they issued us

23

olive drab uniforms. The people who issued the uniforms weren't too particular about how they were supposed to fit. They started having us march. I was fortunate enough to have had some military training at the citizen's military training camp and for two years at Utah State College. I had been having trouble with knowing which was my right hand and which was my left hand, and that's definitely a hazard in the army. So I made a few directional mistakes during my training.

We loaded on the train and went off to Fort Lenardwood, Missouri. The first night on the train, I had an earache and the sergeant said they could do nothing for it. I was aching and stayed up all night, and in the morning it quit. I had never had an earache before.

We finally arrived at Fort Lenardwood. It was in the middle of the woods and made up of two-story wooden barracks. Each would hold fifty men plus one corporal. I was the squad leader of the fourth squad because I was the tallest of the ten men. We were in squads, and four squads were a platoon. The corporal was with us in our barracks, and we had a captain over four platoons that made up our company.

We did the things which the army does: police the area, marching drills, solve the aerial pictures, rifle marksmanship, K.P., and scrub the barracks. I did not leave the site of camp the whole time I was there. I was on K.P. once. I found out that if you came down a little earlier than the rest of them, you got the job of taking care of the tables before the rest of the company arrived. Then after they had eaten, you could eat, and then you were given an easy job for the rest of the day. The sergeant in charge saw me at the easy job and when the men finished eating, I sat down to eat and another sergeant walked in. He saw me sitting there by myself and pointed to me and said, "Pots and pans." I tried to tell him that I was already assigned a job and that I was the first one there. "Pots and pans" was the response. If I ever wound up with him in my command, I would have him do pots and pans for a week.

The lye in the army soap would take the skin right off your hands and you were never finished with the job. Pots and pans went on until midnight.

After three months of this we were ready to be shipped out. Moving in the army is about as fast as snails. "You're going here. You're going there." Friday, the captain told us we were going to Panama on the rail. I learned of Pearl Harbor lying on my bed on Sunday.

Maybe I'd make thirty dollars instead of twenty-one dollars. I took life insurance of ten thousand dollars; it cost me $6.70 a month. Laundry cost us $2.50, so we didn't have too much to spend. A picture show and a quart of ice cream didn't cost me too much on the weekend. I don't remember having a chapel so I didn't attend church, but I read my Book of Mormon and was the only Mormon in our company.

The day came for us to ship out, and the captain called about eight of us out of the ranks and asked if we wanted to go to officer training school at a fort in Virginia. I volunteered and so did the others and we were on our way again on a train. It was about eighteen miles out of Washington, DC, and had a lot of brick buildings. We were the fourth class there at the college.

We were taken to the captain's office when we arrived. First the sergeant told us what we were to tell the captain and showed us how to salute. He corrected us about how our fingers should be, how our arms should be, did everything under the sun, and then sent us in to the captain. I went in to the captain and stated what the sergeant had told me and the captain corrected me. He corrected my salute, he corrected my stance, he corrected what I had said, and told me to go back outside and report in again. That was the first thing that they would do just to try and make you break down, and see if you were capable of taking a lot of stress. Some of the soldiers who were sergeants and above decided they didn't want to take that, and the minute they got in went back to their old outfits.

We stayed with it and were given a rifle and were sent down to the basement to clean that rifle up before we had inspection in the morning at eight o'clock. Our whole group of fifty went down, and there were two big pails of hot water and four or five rags. The rifles were full of cosmoline, which is a kind of grease that they use to keep them from rusting, but it's hard to get out. The next morning we filed out and they had a rifle inspection. Most of us passed that all right.

The one thing that they did do at that school was try to get your goat. They tried every way under the sun. They would file you out in dress uniform. Get you out, and just get you there and say, "File back in and come back out in your fatigues, full field pack, and report back out in ten minutes." At first it was pretty hard on us to get back there in ten minutes and change completely. As time went on, we got to where we could do it, and do it pretty easily. It had just become an easy thing for us to do, and I think that's what the army was trying to show us—that we could budget our time and be able to do things. The platoon had a lieutenant over it and he was sent out each day. He had something to do each day, some major thing, and the officer would have one of the men see the paper and tell him to go ahead and do it.

Well, he had to choose some men out of the ranks and put them together and go ahead and do whatever he was supposed to do, and they graded us on it. Well, the day I was to take charge I was handed a slip of paper that said I was to put up a camouflage net. I'd never seen one. I looked at the print that they had on the paper and it showed about six posts around the camouflage net, which was a flat one about seven feet high, and with these posts were guide-backs so they couldn't be pulled over. I lined up the men with sledgehammers and told them to start putting in the posts, and I didn't yell at them or do anything else. Time passed, and it came time to stop and I was about a third of the way through on the camouflage net. I just knew I had failed it.

I expected to be called in any minute after we went back in, but nothing happened until about two weeks after that. The lieutenant called me in and said, "I guess you know that you failed the test," and I said, "Yes, I did miserably." He wanted to know what I'd done in my background and everything else. I told him that I was a graduate civil engineer, that I'd been in charge of the stake young men in my home town, and there were a lot of men involved. I said "I don't go around yelling at someone to do something when I don't know what they are doing, or what they are supposed to do. I can tell you that I can get it done if I know what I'm doing." I told him that my grades in all of the subjects that we'd gone through were pretty good, and they were, they were excellent. I didn't have any drawbacks, like not doing the things that I was supposed to do, like lining our clothes up, and fixing our bed so tight a quarter would bounce on it.

He said, "Well, go on out and watch the bulletin board and one of these times you'll see your name on there with the drilling that you are supposed to do to make up for this." I waited for that letter to come out on the board, and it never did come. I started sweating it out more. What they did was they waited to almost the very last day and then they would flunk you out, and that made everyone keep on their toes.

I certainly was. I was mainly concerned that I hadn't passed the test, but I also couldn't pass the colorblindness tests. I wanted to know what kind of a test they had. I was afraid I'd get to that and I wouldn't make it, and they'd wash me out.

I looked down the line. One day we were having a test on it, and they had a box of socks you had to match. They'd stir them up and around and then you had to match them. Well, I breathed a sigh of relief because I knew I could do that. I hadn't had to pick out the numbers in the red dots so far.

We got down to where we were very good at what we were doing at the officer's training school. It was for three months that you went through that misery, and we finally got used to it so it didn't bother us too badly. We were given our marching papers, made it to the "second lieutenants, gentlemen, and scholars."

I was sent, of all things, to Fort Ord, a camouflage battalion. I couldn't believe it. I wanted to get out and get with a construction outfit, but that's where I had to go. I got to go home for about ten days before I had to report.

We went down to California, and the camouflage battalion didn't have too many men. They had four officers who came in with me, and they were getting some enlisted men in. We were there for about two weeks and they got a request from the Nineteenth Engineer Combat Battalion for the men and the officers to fill out their cadre end ranks because they were going to ship them overseas. They were located at the Rose Bowl, so I and the four others and about ten other men were sent down to the Rose Bowl.

You know what happens when you are asked to send ten men somewhere away from what you are doing? You don't pick the best ones, you pick the worst ones, and they are the ones you send. That's just human nature. Well, that's what happened. I got down there, and the platoon that I had were going everywhere. I was having problems with them. They were going AWOL. We tried to get them in, and finally got it done. I went out to pay some of the men that were in hospital. The captain gave me some pay envelopes to take out to them and it was south of the Rose Bowl. I found my uncle was down there having a meeting with some officers out on the reservation course. I had the driver drive down there and I met with them, and enjoyed it very much. I came back and the captain wanted to know where I had been. I told him and everything seemed to be all right. We trained a little bit there but not much, but we loaded on a train and went back to Camp Kilmer, New Jersey. We got back there and everyone knew that we were headed overseas, but we didn't know just when. So we stayed. The boys were anxious to get out of camp at night and go see some of the sights that were close. We always had somebody AWOL.

The time came when we were to go on the ship. We went to New York City and what was the ship we were loaded on? The *Queen Elizabeth*, the biggest ship at that time. We got to the gangplank and the captain said, "Davis, you are Officer of the Day. You take care of the men. They are supposed to be out on the deck of the ship." I got up to the gangplank and took a look and there were men everywhere with their bags, and rifles, and there just wasn't any room. I turned to the captain and said, "There's no room," and he said, "They're supposed to be up here, take care of them." So we finally got all of them lying down, and they were down for that night.

The next day was payday for all the soldiers. I never saw so much gambling going on in my life. I had some of the boys in my platoon come to me and say, "Hold this money for me and don't give it back to me. If I beg or anything else don't give it to me." Well, it wasn't long till they were back begging for the money again to take it back, so I gave it to them and they lost it. While we were on the ship there was gambling going on and I think four or five men there of that fifteen thousand that were on that boat ended up with all the money that the men had. They didn't have anything else to do but gamble.

The bunks in the cabins were about five high, so every other night we were on the bunks and then we were on the deck. It worked out pretty well and then everything got shipshape again, and there was enough room for all. The weather got a little rough and the plates started sliding across the table. They had little edges put on the edge of the table so they couldn't slide off, but they were sliding across the table. I got seasick, and was seasick for about a day. I sure hated that, but there it was.

We left the harbor and to help us out and to be our eyes they had two planes fly over us. They just flew out as far as they could go and then they went back and we were all alone on that ship. We were zig-zagging and they claimed that every time they turned unless a U-boat was right straight in our way they couldn't sight on us, and get time enough to get everything taken care of and fire and hit us. So we went through zig-zag, zig-zag, zig-zag across the ocean. We heard a rumor of some U-boats around so we had to turn south for a time and than turn again and go east which cost us another day.

We came into Scotland and we unloaded and were put on a train and taken across to Ireland. There we were supposed to train some more, which we did, backpacks and hikes to get us back in condition after being on the boat.

The men went into town and problems started. Our men had plenty of money and the men in town didn't have so much money, so the girls were flocking to our men. So what happened? The girls were flocking to the men who had money and the British soldiers didn't like it. It made for a little enmity there.

I had to go into the port, which was about seventy miles away, and bring in our trucks in a convoy; I took some of the drivers with me. I had about fifty vehicles there, so I had quite a convoy. One thing the English had done was that they had taken down every sign, in every city, signs in the windows, and everything that mentioned the name of the town where they were. They did this so if paratroopers dropped in, they wouldn't know where they were. Well, I was in the same fix there when I started off; I didn't know quite where we were. I just had to tell them my recollections of what we'd done when we were coming in. I had tried to keep some notes, but they didn't help too much. But I got them back within a mile and a half of our company, and then to where we were. We got out of our vehicles and then they took us out to the port. We had to go out to the ports to load on the ships to go on the invasion.

We got to the ship and found out it was a freighter that we were on, my platoon and I. It was carrying oil in the bottom of it for the ships that were out on the ocean. We sailed out and got down somewhere off Gibraltar in about four days, and then we spent two weeks going around in a circle down there waiting for the troops from the United States to come and join us to go in on the invasion. They were to go in at Casablanca. We were to go in at Arzew through Gibraltar. In two weeks the troops got there and we went through Gibraltar at night. The flares went up and planes went over us, but nothing happened. We knew that come morning we would be ready for the invasion.

There were ships everywhere. We started off in the morning; the first ones to be out there would be the rangers and then the rest of us would go out a little later. We were to have a grand breakfast, eggs, and what-not. And so we'd awaken at night with the shells going off, big guns, the ships were shelling the shore. Evidently the rangers had gone in. As it got lighter, we put our glasses on and looked there and we could see the soldiers there and the tanks that were going and unloading. We couldn't tell whether there was much resistance or not. There was a lot of firing going on, but they just seemed to be shooting at the bank. We waited.

We were supposed to get off, but it was one o'clock before we got off. We didn't have any breakfast and we went off. The coxswain in our LST was steering us in on the boat and had the platoon there. I finally found a junction where we would meet that I could see with my glasses. I told him where we were going in.

The sea was kind of calm and he let down the front of that LST, which was wide and heavy, and said go, and I went. I hit the water and it was waist-deep. I was right before the bow ramp that had been let down, and it was pushing me under. I just happened to slide off to the side or I'd have been pulled under and drowned.

A sergeant did the same thing on the other side as I'd done. We were wet all over, but the rest of the platoon only got their feet wet.

We picked up and assembled all of the equipment in the assembly area, about three hundred yards from the beach. We caught up with the captain and stopped there, dispersing. Our company was alone. My men found a fifty-caliber machine gun that somebody had left. They picked it up and began marching down the road. We were loaded heavily and the marching was kind of ragged. We came into Arzew and camped in an old brickyard for the night. After dark there were still bullets flying around.

The captain showed me a spot on the map and said, "Take your machine gun and five men out and post them there. Then go beyond there, the rangers are there, and locate them."

Gee, I was scared. We started out in the dark with the dogs barking. We had to go into the hills and all I could do was guess where I was going. I had orders to try and contact the rangers. After the second try, I found the right position for our machine gun. The first time a corporal and I left the crew and went out ahead, but I was still scared.

We found out that I had left them in the wrong spot, so I went back and got them and took them to the right spot. Then we went out for the rangers and couldn't find them.

When I got back to camp, I had just gotten back to sleep, and three shots went off in a hurry. Somebody yelled, "Attack!" I grabbed a gun and ran outside, and no one ever found out who fired the shots, but it was morning before we settled down.

November the ninth we marched down to the docks to unload the ships, and did we ever unload them. We saw a dead sniper and a ranger. Shots continued throughout the day. We worked really hard. At about three we were called back to camp to move out. We were all in the building when a shot went through the roof. Everyone ducked. One boy fired his rifle while loading it and another fired his Tommy gun while he was loading it.

The captain told me to take my platoon and go get the snipers. I got the platoon and started off through the gully. I was in the lead. We didn't know where the shots were coming from, but there was banging all around. I headed for some houses. When we finally got there we started kicking in some doors. I believe that it was just American troops firing at each other.

We hiked out and it became dark. We were going up somewhere where the enemy was strong. We walked until we were so tired we could hardly move another step. Finally we stopped to lie down after we had gone ten miles at a fast pace.

Then at 1 A.M. I posted a machine gun. He fired the gun and just missed me and also another unit we didn't know was there across the road, and neither did they know that we were there. Some of the fire just went over their heads.

In the morning two colonels came up and arranged transportation for us up to our new position. We loaded up at four o' clock and rode up to the village. I went ahead on foot to see the lieutenant whose positions I was to occupy. I came to the lieutenant on a little bank and he showed me his positions. They were behind an eight-foot railroad bank. He also said there was considerable sniping up there in the daytime and that they had sent out parties to drive the snipers away. Also, a battalion of enemy troops had been there that day. That kind of keyed us up.

They withdrew and left us there. Morning broke, and I started looking for snipers. Nothing moved, and I set out to establish an outpost on a sandhill a hundred yards away. We got there and as we got there, we were fired on by a first platoon man who was down on the beach. I had the first platoon sergeant man with me, so they signaled the men down there. The bullet hit the sand about nine feet from my boys. We signaled to them who we were and established an outpost there.

The second platoon of men had a road to go to, about a quarter of a mile away. The captain sent me out on a scouting party. I asked for volunteers and I got five. We started up the road in an extended X formation. When we'd gone about a mile or so, we saw a man coming down the road about a third of a mile away. He turned and started to run, and I told the boys they could fire on him. They fired, but he went on and they were in my line of fire so I didn't fire.

Suddenly shots rang out from above us on the hillside. I realized there was an outpost on the hill and that he was trying to cover us. I was sure glad they had missed the man as they had because he was probably innocent as anything.

We kept going around in a circle. We met friendly natives and they gave the boys a drink. All of the natives we had met so far were friendly and just a little scared of us until they found out that we meant no harm to them. They all wanted clothes worse than anything else. The country around where we were was slightly sandy.

We pushed up ahead, and the next day started to relax. Civilians came down by the road and we tried to talk to them. It was sure funny to hear them jabber away and not understand a word they said. We could say anything we wanted back to them, too. We had an Egyptian American in our outfit who understood them very well and some of the boys who talked Spanish. It was hard but we got along okay. We found a couple of dead drabs the infantry boys before us had killed.

Life settled down to a pleasant pastime of swimming at the beach, learning, and trying to make the food taste better. The English rations weren't so bad at that. Meanwhile, our trucks were back in Arzew running day and night hauling the supplies out of the docks and to where they were needed. I did a lot of scouting and enjoyed it quite a bit.

The captain got word to go ahead and look over the coast, ahead of us about twenty miles. We took a halftrack and a squad of my men went. We encountered no opposition at all and came back. An interesting side note is that the C Company's captain was captured the next day by the French while he was trying to contact the second battalion. They took him to the barracks and treated him royally until the next day. They were sure glad to see him. The first day ashore two planes strafed close to us but we missed them and they missed everything, too.

The next day the whole company moved out to take over the port. We were the first Americans in there and prepared for trouble. The natives gathered all around us and it made you feel as if you were a performer in a three-ring circus with thousands watching you. They were curious and some of them got in our way. All we did was guard the port and attract natives. Some of the boys got all wined up and made life miserable for a while. They had so much to drink that it drove them crazy.

I went to a French church and became acquainted with a Frenchman who had been to America. He warned me to be on the watch because there were a lot of people in there who didn't like us, and the rest didn't know quite which way to turn. There were a lot of *legionnaires* in the town, and they all couldn't be trusted.

Finally after a while when nothing happened at all we moved back to Lamacta, where all was peaceful. We guarded the shore and listened to the rumors. Rumors sprang up everywhere and traveled like wildfire. It got to where we didn't believe them and we got along all right.

Finally we moved to Oran where the regiment was and went back to some training, which had no end. Oran turned out to be a pretty nice city, but it can't lose that stinky Arab smell. The Arabs use the street for latrines. I went to Oran about three times with a truckload of boys for sightseeing and then gave it up.

After being there a month we were moved down to Tiemoon. The people there hadn't seen soldiers; again we were a curiosity; the same everywhere we went. We were to guard the railroad bridges against enemy paratrooper attacks, which never did come, despite the false alarms. Quite a few of the people in this town spoke English.

We were finally quartered in an old theater. The officers stayed across the town at the hotel. It was really nice to get into a bed after being in a tent so long. We had never dug in yet, because we hadn't seen any planes. The hotel was cold and the only hot water we ever had was on Saturday afternoon, and once when the commanding major general came into town.

In all the time we were in Tiemoon, I never stayed a third of the nights in the hotel that I paid for. Just offhand I'd say we were there a month. The boys had quite a bit of wine. My platoon went out to a marina near Oran and guarded a six-hundred-foot-long, two-hundred-foot-high railroad bridge, and a thousand-foot-long tunnel. We liked the camping out so much better than staying in Tiemoon that we all wanted to take B Company's turn rather than go back to Tiemoon. However, we took turns.

We got eggs, chickens, and vegetables while out there and really enjoyed ourselves. It was plenty windy with a lot of rain, but we enjoyed it. The first week out we had some French-Moroccans with us and we learned a little bit of their language. They were guarding the other end of the tunnel. It snowed about four inches one night while we were there, about December twentieth.

I took some men and played the French basketball on the dirt. They darn near ran us to death using their rules, and about made us look silly. However, we managed to beat them. I spent Christmas reading some of our mail that had finally come in. We had American beer rations we had had since getting over here. We'd always eaten English rations.

On New Year's I stayed up till eleven-thirty and then went to bed. It was getting so one day wasn't any different from the next. Sundays didn't matter and neither did the date, we just went right on working.

The French were really kind to us, and took a lot of the boys into their homes for dinner. A common thing when the army came up, the French leader gave an order to the French to invite the Americans to their homes for dinner at Christmas, and then an army order came out restricting officers to camp. It kind of hurt the relations; however we let a few men go.

On January first we packed up and left for the Lournel to build a huge airport runway, which had to be done in two weeks. It was to be made of stone. January second we got settled in at another theater and we were ready to go to work. January third we put in half a day of hauling stones to the airport. That afternoon we were informed that we were to start on something. That night the kitchen tarp caught fire and burned up before we got to it. They were cooking an early breakfast on the stoves when it had caught fire.

January fourth we left and headed for Tebussa. We didn't know where we were going, but we knew it was a long way east. We made the several-odd-mile trip in four days. We detoured past Algiers, but were close enough to it at night to hear the bombing of the enemy.

All of this time over here we didn't have a command car or any jeeps yet. The captain rode a motorcycle around almost everywhere he wanted to go. We had to drive back out the last night, and I slept in the truck cab when we'd finally stop, which wasn't for long. The next day we camped at Boulchedka, which is midway between Tebussa and Feriana. We found that our big transports went over every day and took supplies up to Telepta, which was about sixteen miles ahead. They started some training and camped there in the pines.

My platoon was out on a demonstration one day and I let a man fire a rifle-grenade. The grenade never left the end of the rifle, but exploded. The firer was hit near the temple and in the mouth. Five others were hit. The firer was dead before we got him to the hospital. The other five went and after one week one came back. The other four were transferred, and after three months two of them came back. One was shipped to the U.S. with a bad leg, and the other, I don't know where he ended up.

That was the tough part in the army. Once you sent a man to the hospital, you lost all track of him. He went from one hospital to another and was lost, and left almost for good.

That death still sticks in my mind very much. I was the first one to him and he crumpled in my arms. He asked whether he was hurt badly and then lost consciousness. The board is still investigating it to find out if it was my fault or negligence that caused the death.

After a week at Boulchedka we moved ahead to Kasserine. When we were moving by the Telepta airport, I heard an explosion and then another. I told the driver to stop the truck and we all scattered from it. An air raid was going on. The trucks in the convoy ahead kept going and didn't even know about the raid. The munitions train was about a mile ahead of us. The big ninety-millimeter guns of the British cut loose on the Germans. The Americans always kept two planes in the air above the airfield on patrol. I ran back to the truck and got my field glasses. I then laid on my back and directed my machine gun on the truck to what were enemy planes. He put out a burst, very close according to the traces. A stream of stray bullets landed on the ground where some of my men were running, and did they ever. A plane was hit over the airport and the pilot came down on the field. There was a strong wind blowing that dragged him to death on the ground. He was an American pilot. The two enemy planes crashed in the hills when we reached Kasserine twenty miles further on, and everyone dug a deep fox-hole in the sandy soil. It was our first baptism by enemy airplanes at close range, and did we ever dig in.

The camp was located in a cactus patch, and we were pretty well hidden. Later that day, the Germans came over again, and nine of their bombers were knocked down. Two of them were really close to us. We went to work on the road between Kasserine and Sbeitla, filling up holes. The German bombers came over at night and flew around a lot. They dropped two bombs near our waterhole, which was really a ditch, but missed it. They seemed to be poor bombers. They bombed almost every day. We sure threw up a lot of shells at them. Some of them were shot down after they were partway back to their base.

We still worked on the road. I was sent out on a reconnaissance after I came to the territory that might be held by the enemy. My mission was to investigate the road. We went out and saw six trucks, Italian and French. We cut off on a road, which turned out to be just a trail. However, a half-track can go almost anywhere. We explored all over the flats and completed our mission.

The next day we went out again, only this time it was into the hills. The round trip was to be only forty-five miles, so we only took rations for the five of us at noon. We went past the mountain where German paratroopers had landed and then the road turned into a path and it started to rain. I had to get out and pick a path through the gullies and around the rocks. I only had a field jacket on and got plenty wet. A halftrack is the roughest driving thing there is. We kept on going over those flats and around the hills until darkness overtook us. We got stuck and the four of us were soaking wet before we got out. About dark, an Arab came down to us and wanted us to go stay in his tent. I didn't want to and we moved a little further on and parked the halftrack in the gully.

The reason I didn't want to, was if we'd have gone in his tent, we'd have got fleas on us and that would've been it. We'd have had them all the time. We had two overcoats between the five of us and four of us were wet. I didn't dare let them turn on the light or start the motor. I walked about four miles that night trying to keep warm and trying to find a good way out. At dawn we started again and at about ten o' clock we had a good road again as I figured we would. It was good navigating with just a map to go by. We ran into a one-and-a-half-ton truck that was coming out to look for us. A day and a half was a long time to go just about forty-five miles. It was plenty tough country and a ton-and-a-half truck would have never gotten to where we were.

My platoon was given a road job from Sbeitla to a flat twenty miles ahead toward Fayette Pass. Two German planes came over at breakfast and everyone left to try to find a foxhole. I was more interested in trying to find a gun to fire at them. My .45 wasn't too good for that. I got a carbine from the supply sergeant and religiously carried it after that.

One day six English ammo trucks came right on our road, loaded with 150-mm ammo. One of these trucks blew up and threw shells everywhere. The trucks were left in millions of pieces. Shells were lying everywhere. The truck drivers got away first before it all happened. They had a road from that which was called Messerschmitt Alley because it was struck so much.

A few days later a plane struck one of our trucks with five men in it, killing three and wounding one. They also got five French men in their trucks and headed for a truck carrying seventeen of our men. This truck stopped and a machine gunner stayed with it and his machine gun. Three times the man drove those two planes off that had twenty-millimeter cannons. Finally they gave up and left. The private won a Distinguished Service Star for his merits. Out of all the men in the company to win it, I would have picked him to be last. But that just goes to show you how you can underestimate these quiet, reserved American boys. He had a court martial facing him for being drunk. This was dropped.

The fellows really watched for airplanes now; they spotted everything in the air. We had fellows there that were deathly afraid of planes. They died a thousand deaths every time a plane went over. When a plane would come, humans evacuated and would scatter so fast some of them would run too far but they figured it was safer.

I went to the funeral of my boy who was killed by the grenade. He was the first one buried in the American cemetery at Tebessa. He didn't even have a coffin.

We moved back to the cactus patch at Kasserine and still worked on the road. One night I was sent out into the hills to put in mines with one squad. It was the first time that any mines had been laid by our company. We did it at night with almost a full moon. I and another boy scouted out ahead on foot, but found nothing. Some rangers moved in behind us that night, and I couldn't get their officers to come see where the mine field was, even though they were only two hundred yards from it. They didn't want to have anything to do with any mines and booby traps. I left my squad to guard the field and went back to Kasserine.

Meanwhile, all the American forces kept shifting back and forth. Tanks were moved around the front as the Germans would strike one point and then another. We Americans didn't have enough equipment to guard the whole line at once, and we had to shift equipment back and forth a hundred miles, so they were worn out from moving around.

The Germans had taken Sbeitla and were within fifteen miles of us with tanks. We just kept on putting mines in with all kinds of equipment going by. We finished at 4 A.M. and went in to hear what was going on. I was sent out and took up the mine field we had just put in. I was then told to take my platoon and go to a pass about thirty miles away and mine it. A platoon of infantry would join us there. We were to guard and defend that pass until further notice.

We finally got started with three one-and-a-half-ton trucks and one two-and-a-half ton truck loaded with mines, a halftrack, and two tank destroyers. The tank destroyers had seventy-five-millimeter guns on them. It was raining hard and we had a big wadi to cross and no road to cross it.

We had proceeded about three miles down the road when a fellow caught up with us and said that the two-and-a-half-ton truck had turned over. I went back to find it, and found three of my men all covered by mines. They had been trying to sleep on top of them.

I went back to camp and reported in. They gave me a new two-and-a-half-ton truck and told me to load up the mines and go on. I did that and tried to cross the wadi just as dawn broke. I never thought we would make it, but I had orders to go on. I used the halftracks and finally towed all the trucks across and kept on going through the mud on the road. I had to tow the trucks across quite a few gullies. Finally I had a good road to go on.

We then had to go out on the trails again. I was just going by map, never having been there before. Finally at 5 P.M. we got to our destination and there was the infantry platoon just ahead of us. It had taken them two days to get in, and only one for us. There we were, two platoons, one infantry and one of engineers with two tank destroyers trying to hold a pass one mile wide. I sent my halftrack back for rations and water, and the infantry radioed out first thing. The next day we mined a small portion of the pass and took our positions. My halftrack never came back, but a halftrack from C Company came in with rations for the infantry. They had news that Kasserine Pass was under heavy fire. The enemy was breaking through, and one of my best friends, an officer in the C Company, had been killed. They left us and went back. We had orders to hold the pass so we stayed there, one hundred men altogether.

We were very short on rations and water, but we all shared. The next day we were sent back after water and I went along. We ran into a British patrol that reported that no one knew we were in the pass, and that Kasserine Pass had fallen and the Germans were almost behind us. We went back up to our pass with water. That night my guard picked up ten men who were wandering through the hills after escaping from Kasserine Pass. The first sergeant was leading them and they were tired out, but didn't want to stay in there with us. They told us our regiment was all gone and wiped out at the pass. The next morning our planes flew over, and guns of all sizes were firing from all over everywhere. They had one down one road where the planes, the P38's, and others flew back. Some of our men got back from the water point, a big, filled waterhole ten miles behind us, and said the P38's had been fired on from around them.

It was then that we realized we had enemies on three sides of us and a range of high mountains on the other side. We couldn't get any message out by radio because of interference, and the radio wasn't strong enough to cover the thirty-mile distance in the hills. The Germans were jamming all the radio programs over there that could be picked up by the Frenchmen's radios in their homes. Hardly anyone slept a wink that night. The next day at two o' clock, one of my outposts reported a tank had pulled in below us.

They were about two miles down the canyon, which was actually a small valley. We had killed a stray beef during the night to get something to eat; we were pretty hungry. I sent two men out to scout this tank, and they got back about five o' clock with a report that there was a battalion of enemies down below, and they were coming up towards us.

Then at about six o'clock a couple of shells, it sounded like 88s, hit the small knoll behind my outpost. The infantry lieutenant and I gave orders to pack up quietly and try to get out. During the day I had had chains put on all my trucks because the roads were wet and almost impassable. The infantry had three two-and-a-half-ton trucks and one jeep with a radio in it. We piled up the mines we had left, three piles, because we couldn't take them with us. It was dark and we loaded up. Then the convoy took off except for the two tank destroyers and one of my ton-and-a-half trucks. They had not been ordered to start and they left us, three lieutenants, two firsts and one second, waiting for the rear guard to come in.

I set TNT fuses in the mines and the rear guard came in. One of my men lit the fuses and we were off in the dark and mud. I had a new driver that night in my ton-and-a-half truck because the other had gone off in a half-track after food. When we were about a quarter of a mile away the sky lit up like day and an explosion was heard. It turned out that two of those fuses didn't light those mines. The first trucks finally waited for us when they found out we weren't behind them. It was muddy and dark so we had to use the lights on our ton-and-a-half truck because of the inexperienced driver. The two halftracks got stuck in one gully and I had to go back and guide the drivers out at a new angle.

We finally all got together and went along. I had fully expected to be ambushed at any time. I had a map against my skin, two bars of chocolate I had saved from the ship on the ocean when we landed, a 45 in my pocket, and ammunition. I fully intended to walk out of there. I had instructed my men where I would meet them in the morning in case we had to walk out.

After ten miles, it looked as if lights were coming from behind us through the hills. I stopped the last tank destroyer and laid five mines in the road. It later turned out that the flashes were gun flashes shelling the positions and the road we had been coming out on.

We kept on until we reached the point where a signal flare went up about a quarter mile ahead of us. I switched from the rear tank destroyer to the one in the lead and turned off on a road away from the flares. We stopped at a Frenchman's house and he told us that the Germans were camped two miles ahead and couldn't tell us whether or not there were Germans between us and Thala. We went on ahead ten miles farther and the sky lit up ahead of us, so we figured that Thala was about ten miles ahead. We stopped for two hours and tried to get on the radio to find out the situation. We couldn't get it worked out, and we were practically sure the enemy was ahead of us.

We turned around and went back to the Frenchman to see if he knew of a way out through the hills. He did, but said that he didn't believe any vehicles could make it out. I got in the lead tank destroyer and we took off through the mountains on camel trails. After traveling about fifteen miles, we crossed a small valley and came to some trees in a pass. We stopped there at 4 A.M. and I went ahead on foot to see if we could get through the pass while the others slept. I got back at six with the information that we could make it. Back up in the pass, the planes had gone over us every day.

At six-thirty the guard came in and said that about forty men were following our tracks across the valley. I went and looked and finally made them out to be Americans. It turned out that ten of them were Englishmen from tanks that had been knocked out three days ago. They included one captain and two lieutenants. We loaded them on our trucks. They had been wandering for three days and had heard us go by their hideout in the middle of the night, but had not dared stop us for fear that we were Germans.

We kept going with me in the lead tank destroyer and the booming in the distance started coming from one side of us instead of from in front of us as it had been. At noon that tank destroyer threw a track in a gully and we spotted some American recon cars.

During the day we found out that we were in the clear now and that the Germans almost had Thala. The recon cars were out looking for passes in the mountains through which tanks could counterattack. We fixed the track and went on.

At 2 P.M. we finally reached Kalhadjerda where the infantry headquarters were. We took off our chains because we were on the good roads once more. The convoy had consisted of three one-and-a-half-ton trucks, four two-and-a-half-ton trucks, two tank destroyers, and one jeep. We had come through where never before a vehicle had been nor probably would ever go again. We had got out where they didn't think it was possible.

We left at 5 P.M. for Tebessa after getting fed to find out what was left of our regiment. We had had to travel seventy-five miles at night and we went right by the regiment. We camped near Tebessa until morning and then tried to find them. It was noon before we finally got to them. They were sure thrilled with us and started celebrating. We had been thought missing or dead three days ago.

It turned out that we had been sent a radio message five days ago to burn our trucks up in the pass and to try to hike out because we were surrounded. We never got the message. It turned out that only one man had been killed in the company and all the rest got out of Kasserine Pass.

The other companies didn't fare so well. The infantry battalion and our engineers had pulled out of the pass because of the heavy artillery fire and they had just left the engineers on the side. The whole middle of the pass was open. The one side regiment suffered heavy losses, but they stood up against three days of attack before retreating.

While we were coming out through the mountains, leaving the infantry, after we got on good road, it was dark. We had on the cat's eyes on the trucks. They didn't give much light, but they did tell somebody that you were coming. We were rolling along pretty well until I saw a dark spot in the road. I stopped the truck. We got out and looked and the bridge was out, and it dropped about fifteen feet where the bridge had been taken out. We looked around and there was a bypass around the bridge. I decided that the trucks could pass through the mountains where it curved back and forth and no airplane could get a sight on us and no one could shoot at us, so I said, "Turn on the full lights—bright lights." And that's how we traveled until we got through and went on past our battalion.

It was winter. We moved to Kalaat and started working on the road. It was then I got on a motorcycle to go back to Kasserine Pass to see if I could find my stuff that I had lost while chasing the Arabs. It was raining and I didn't make it. I hurt my knee when I ran into some ruins.

Two days later I took a halftrack and went back, but it wasn't there. The Germans had been driven back quite a while ago. There were tanks, fifteen or twenty of them, knocked out between Thala and Kasserine on the road. We had tried to get out of there fast.

We moved to Hidra where my platoon built a concrete fort, which took three hundred barrels of cement. It was a beautiful thing to see and look at, and it will probably be there for years and years to come. I got the cement from Kasserine by just going and getting it from the French storage shed. We built a bridge and then we got to a place twenty miles beyond Thala to make a new road. We heard bombing and saw all kinds of equipment moving up our roads.

We had to have one officer up all night, and they'd arranged it so that I was up at least every fourth night and usually more often. It really got to be tiresome, but orders were orders. The orders were given by General Patton; he was the one who said that his guts and our blood were going to win the war.

We finally moved to Gafsa about the twenty-eighth of March. There was heavy fighting going on at El Guitter, fifteen miles from us. The flares lit up everything. We dug in deep that night, and sure enough here came the Jerries dropping flares. This was when you'd really start to pray.

We were crouching in a hole with planes going back and forth overhead. Down came the bombs but they looked to be quite a ways away. They kept it up all night, and we got little sleep. We could hear the thunder of the guns and see flares.

The road was sandy and hard to keep up, but we did a pretty fair job of it. Gafsa had palm trees in it and was the first real town we had stayed in.

Along came the bombers the next night to bother us. We had moved in during the daytime. When the flares lit up, the guns started. They were shooting all over the sky. Some were trying to put out the flares, which they didn't do. The sky was vivid with flashes and flares. I looked, and we never got close to the planes with the shells. The bombs never hit anything.

Back when we joined the regiment coming out of the pass, I got a message at 4 A.M. to go see the general commanding a certain division. I took off and when I arrived he told me that a captain had been killed and a lieutenant wounded when a jeep went through the minefield I had put in. I had neglected to hand in a drawing and location to the corps.

My driver and I in a one-and-a-half-ton truck led a battalion of infantry back up into that pass to defend it, and I was supposed to point out the minefield. We got back almost to the minefield and ran into where the jeep had blown up. The Germans had planted some of our mines in the road. On investigation we found that our one-and-a-half-ton truck had run over two mines before we could stop, but they hadn't gone off; we had gone just to the side of them and we were very lucky. A mine would blow a jeep to pieces and it would cripple a ton-and-a-half truck badly.

The fighting was still going on close to us, and one night we were ordered to hold an intersection in case the enemy broke through. We spent one day out there and then came back into Gafsa. One night the bombers came over and dropped butterfly bombs on us. I saw the flashes go off on the gun and thought maybe our shells had fallen and exploded. One of my men started calling for help. A bomb had hit just outside his tent as he was coming out to head for a foxhole. He was wounded in the leg and was plenty lucky to be alive.

In the morning we found eighteen bomb craters in our company area. One had landed in the palm trees above me and gone off, putting two holes in my shelter half. Most of the shelter halves had holes in them. The one-ton truck just in front of my tent had two holes in it. A medic had one land beside his cot and not go off; lucky boy. A company just across the street had four killed.

That day everyone's foxhole went down deeper. We had been taking up a lot of enemy minefields, which was very ticklish work, especially as most of them were booby-trapped. Some of our men were injured, but another company wasn't so fortunate.

I saw my first P51 on April tenth; it was escorted by P38s. On April eleventh I played hooky and sped down to (?). The sea was beautiful, and the Eighth Army was scattered all over. I saw eight Allied planes down two German planes there. On April twelfth I took forty Arabs to start to clean up inside this detour around Guitter.

What a detour. I'd rather have done it myself than try with all those Arabs around. All those Arabs got for a day's work was a can of C rations, and they were glad to get that. The young kids just watched all the time, trying to get any food that we threw away when we finished eating. We found a lot of American stuff and not too much German. I went to see if they had passes in Maknassey. There sure was a lot of German and Italian stuff there. We went almost to Sfax and then came back.

The Germans had dug in in the rocks and our artillery shells had covered the hill just like a blanket, making it look as if it had smallpox. April fifteenth I ran into forty enemy trucks in an area a hundred yards square. The airplanes had sure fixed them. All were burned and blown up. A lot of German ammunition was around, which I hauled in the next day. One of my two-and-a-half trucks ran over a mine, with a load of mines on it, and seven of my men. It blew the wheels off, but thank heavens it never set the load of mines off. My boys were shaken up and slightly deafened. I was only a hundred yards away when it went off, and my heart stopped. I raced the jeep back and saw my men running out of the smoke and dust for the hills. It wasn't until then that my heart slowed down. I thought they had all been blown up.

The next day at Gofsa a truckload of mines went off, setting the whole salvage camp on fire. Three two-and-a-half-ton trucks were completely demolished and about twelve soldiers and an unknown amount of Arabs. The explosion was terrific, a straight column of smoke about five hundred feet in the air. I was one and a half miles away in the bivouac area at the time they went off and it about knocked me off my feet. We wondered what was going on.

Gofsa had a hot water spring where we went swimming. It sure was nice. April twentieth we had moved three hundred miles up to Beja along the coast. All the American troops had moved up there for the final drive. We started fixing roads again, and we replaced a blown-up bridge within one mile of the enemy front lines. We could hardly tell where the front was. I saw eighteen German tanks knocked out, six of which were giant Tigers. Boy, were they massive and big. Six English tanks were knocked out too. The country was very hilly and tanks could not be used.

The infantry had to take every foxhole. Our artillery was firing ceaselessly. I never saw so much artillery in my life. Captured Germans wanted to know if our artillery fired automatically. German graveyards were everywhere. I will say one thing, they made some very beautiful graveyards and some real nice wooden crosses for them.

The planes still bombed us at night and dropped "butterflies" also. These butterflies had kind of a little plane tied to them with bombs underneath, and they sort of fluttered down, turning round and round, coming down fairly slowly. Seventeen landed in C Company and never hit anyone. It sure paid to dig in very deep.

On Easter Sunday we moved ahead to within six miles of the line. My platoon had the job of fixing the roads with the grader. We got in so close that the drivers refused to go further. Stakes came over in lots of twenty. They didn't come close to us. They were was the first Jerry planes we'd seen in days. Our cubs were up in the air; those guys sure were brave, going out over the lines in something that a rifle could easily bring down. The hills were very hard to take but we were making beautiful roads with a patrol and a D7.

We had been seeing quite a lot of prisoners go back. One day they shelled two hundred yards behind us while we were working on the roads. Then another burst a hundred yards in front. I gave the order to get out of there. We did in a hurry and a minute after that a shell hit where we were working. It was lucky that the enemy didn't get the range in the first two shots.

All of a sudden the enemy gave way and we Americans were at Mateur. We moved ahead twenty miles and went to work. Prisoners were coming back by the thousands. They were driving their own trucks and guarded by no one. I went into Bizerte on May ninth and saw a city that had been knocked flat. The harbors and ships were a shambles and the city was at least half gone. On the road were long convoys of German prisoners who were coming in by themselves, only guarded by a handful of MPs. They drove their own vehicles and seemed quite giddy for someone who had just been beaten.

That day, May ninth, the bombers continuously shuttled back and forth across the sky. Somewhere the Jerries caught mass destruction.

May tenth I went to Tunis. It reminded me a little of Los Angeles. It had suburbs and everything. The city was intact, but the harbor was gone. People greeted us with open arms everywhere. There were a lot of English troops in there but no Americans. One Frenchman who could speak a little English found out that I was from Utah and asked if I was Mormon. I was really surprised when he asked me. I told him yes but could see no reaction from him.

We started building barbed-wire stockades for prisoners. We had about thirty-three thousand men when we got through. They had all brought most of their equipment with them and seemed quite happy. Our fellows got some good cameras from them for a pack of cigarettes. The prisoners helped us build the stockades. They were pretty good-looking soldiers. Quite a lot of them spoke English and expressed a wish that they would be sent to the USA. They still thought Germany would win the war. They were eating food that they had captured.

A few days later I built a fence around their vehicles and guns. The vehicles were mostly V8s but just a lot of junk. They looked like commercial trucks. Our vehicles were ten times as good as theirs, but on the other hand their ammunition was in beautiful cases of art and workmanship. They made them too darn well.

Since then we had been repairing roads, playing softball, football, and volleyball, and swimming. At night we had outdoor shows and boxing. A word about the French: for an enemy having no equipment or vehicles, they had done a remarkable job. To get anywhere they had to walk, even when they retreated. They used mules quite a lot. Then they got quite a lot of American equipment and were becoming a fine army. Things had slackened up now and life was becoming kind of dull without some excitement. We wished we could get started again and get it over with.

Two companies, A and B, loaded on boats on June twenty-sixth at the African port of Arzon where we had landed for the invasion of Africa. Then we went up and sailed back to within one mile of where we had started on our mad seven-hundred-and-fifty-mile jaunt to get on the boats. One hundred of our men were on an LCI with Lieutenant Rosco and myself. There couldn't be a much smaller ship made. We disembarked at Tunis for a day in a hot wheat field. Then we sailed for parts unknown and landed at Sousse for a day. We must have been trying to fool the enemy, but enemy or not, we fooled and mystified ourselves a lot. We didn't know what was coming or going next.

Then we were really off. The next day was a really memorable one. When dawn broke there were ships everywhere I looked. The transports and LSTs had balloons above them. The sea was so darn rough it about keeled us off the boat. We were all seasick that night. I spent nine-tenths of the day in bed. We saw the Isle of Malta as we passed by it. All of our equipment, trucks, dozers, etc., were on an LST with the rest of the company. That boat of ours would roll over to a thirty-five-degree angle. I thought we were going right on over. That night it calmed, thank goodness.

Saturday found us about a mile off the shore of Sicily. Navy boats were steaming along pumping shells into the shore. It was marvelous to see the shells landing in the same spot while the boat was moving through the water. Our boat was designed to go right into the shore. At nine we came in fast. They dropped an anchor out in the deep water so they could pull themselves off the beach when they were unloaded. I was the first one down the gangplank with my hands clear full of stuff. I got off in about a foot of water and went ashore. Soon we were all off. One fellow lost his rifle and we went through the barbed wire and minefield to a spot in a little ravine. I might add that this island of Sicily was literally covered with the most extensive barbed-wire entanglements, fences, and pillboxes that you could ever imagine. However, the Italians and Germans made very little use of any of these. It was sure fortified in that respect. Every foot of beach had barbed-wire fences and mines on it.

My job was to contact the rest of the company and the colonel the minute they started to unload. I walked two and a half miles down the beach and never saw such a mess in my life. All along the shore were LCAs and LCTs. The boats would bring in infantry and tanks. The boats that capsized filled with sand and water and were being battered to pieces by the waves. The waves were high that day, making landing almost impossible.

There were no roads away from the beach. Sandhills extended inland for three quarters of a mile and the good coastal road was a mile and a half inland. Vehicles were bogged down everywhere, in the water and the sand. Engineers were trying to lay steel track for a road but had difficulty with the vehicles bending it as they went over it. Ack-ack guns were put up all along the shore. Tractors were stuck in the water. Trucks were out in three feet of water. Men and vehicles were trying to go in all directions.

One of our reconnaissance seaplanes flew over and everything cut loose at it. That shows what boys fresh from home do. We were landing with a division that had just come in from the States. They shot at everything in the sky for the first two days. Most of the planes were Spitfires flown by American pilots. They shot this seaplane down which was not over a quarter of a mile from us. It fell into the sea. Every time the enemy planes came in, the Americans never even fired a shot until they had dropped their bombs and were out of range, but just let one of our planes come cruising over on a straight level course and they tried to blast it out of the sky. I wouldn't have blamed the pilots if they had come down and strangled our men for shooting at our planes. They even fired rifles and thirty-caliber machine guns at planes so far out of range it was silly. I bawled out plenty of gunners, and even men in charge of small boats started shooting their pistols, just for the fun of it, I guess. They were making things dangerous all around for everyone.

I wandered up and down the beach waiting for our LST to land at 3 P.M. Then I went back to join up with Lieutenant Rosco and the men. We offered our services to the shore party, but they didn't have anything for us to do except unload a few ducks. Those amphibious two-and-a-half-ton DKWs were our best thing we had yet for water. They went through water at ease and sand couldn't stop them at all. They went out and drove right up to the LST; then they were loaded and came out into the water and went up on the shore. Waves didn't bother them much. They just rode up on the shore and took off to wherever their load was needed.

They had mines on the shore, all marked off by barbed wire, but these green drivers didn't know what they were doing and just up and ran over them. I saw at least six vehicles that were blown up needlessly that day. Our colonel came ashore from the LST at six that night and told us to move inland to a bivouac area. The first grader, ours, off from his LST turned over in the water. They sure were having a sweet time unloading B Company and its equipment from that last LST.

Meanwhile, I went to bring up the stragglers hiking down the beach. They were about worn out. We hiked until twelve o'clock and hadn't reached our destination so we quit. In the morning I went partway back to bring up the stragglers. We were about two hundred yards from the beach when the B Company LST was bombed. The bomb hit fifteen yards away from the boat in the water. A piece of it flew and came whistling down where we were, hitting one of the fellows in his ankle, where it stuck. He was under a trailer that he had crawled under for safety. He was sent back to the States. We hiked until that afternoon and we got so tired we couldn't find a B Company bivouac. We quit.

We wound up only one mile from where we had started from in the beginning. Activities were nil the first night, but from then on it was one continuous nightmare. Our job was to get out into an airfield at Comiso and have it fixed by the D+2, D-day landing day, which meant the morning of the third day on the land. The D+1 night we had to have a field ready by the morning. We had a patrol out on our LST with all our equipment on it; it hadn't even landed to our knowledge. B Company got theirs off and had the field ready by morning. That day sure was the most memorable one in my memory. The movies would give a million to see what we did.

Enemy planes would come over and drop flares on our ships and then circle back and drop bombs. Guns were firing up where they thought the planes were. The tracer was cutting through the sky like ribbons. It just went on hour after hour. We had a battery of forty-millimeter Bofors within two hundred yards of us where we were bivouacked. They just shook the ground. You could hear fellows digging in and getting deeper.

Suddenly there came a loud roar of engines. Two hundred feet above us was a formation of three planes. Those Bofors were practically shooting three feet above us in the trees. The next group came over, and the Bofors got one. It flared up right above us and three of us saw the white star on the wing. It was our own paratrooper plane.

We saw two chutes blossom before the plane hit a third of a mile away. It burned up with all the shells going off in all directions. I saw one more plane catch fire and its tail was blown off from another above us.

I don't know how many planes our men and the ships and the shore batteries brought down that night, but I would estimate that six came down. They're more accurate when they shoot at our own planes. Only two of the nineteen paratroopers in that first plane got out alive. It was very unfortunate that they came in the midst of a bombing raid and that our gunners didn't know they were coming.

Our colonel came by in the morning and gave us orders to stay where we were and tell the rest of our company. We had patrols down by the beach all night long looking for our LST to land. We looked up at a plane and saw it hit a balloon. It came hissing down where we were camping. We thought it was paratroopers that were landing and we were being pushed off from the shore. That sure worried the boys for a while. We stayed at the bivouac all of that day and three quarters of the next before we found out that our LST had landed down on the beach on D+1 or two days before. We were sure mad at being left there for so long.

Our trucks moved us to the company's bivouac near Comiso and then we went to work. My platoon worked all that night. We could see Mount Etna way off in the distance, smoking. We worked filling in bomb holes and craters on an airfield. I didn't know the size of them because I hadn't seen them in the daytime.

Almost at dawn I came upon a sentry standing in the middle of a taxi-way. He stopped by my jeep and told me not to run into the bomb he was guarding. I asked him "What bomb?" and he pointed to it. I went over and picked up that belly tank of aluminum and threw it off the road. He stood there and gawked. He belonged to a green unit, and wore a suntan outfit. I guess his captain had told him to guard the bomb. We all got our laughs at the expense of the green boys from the States.

The next day my platoon rested and I went back to look at the airport. It was about sixty acres of ground with about a seventy-five-yard strip of asphalt for a mile-long runway. The administration buildings were bombed to pieces, but there were about a hundred and fifty planes around them in shelters with about half of them being planes which were practically in shape to fly.

The first night we worked there, the enemy was only about one and a half miles away. The airport turned out to be the best souvenir-hunting place we had ever been to. We really got some good souvenirs from there. We fixed up all the runways, taxi stops, and plane shelters, cleaned out the buildings, and removed the planes. We also picked up the shrapnel off the ground because it is very damaging to any tire that hits it.

The Sicilians greeted us okay. When we passed through the towns at night, I never saw so many military-aged men in the streets anywhere else. They were deserting from the Germans and putting on civilian clothes to remain in their towns. We could tell them by their hob-nailed army boots, but they knew nothing about it. When prisoners were taken, there would usually be some in civilian clothes that insisted upon being taken also because they were also soldiers. This left some pretty unhappy because they *wanted* to be taken prisoner and sent to the United States. All of the prisoners wanted to go there.

After about two days there, my platoon was sent to another airfield at Biscari to fix it up. We took mine detectors and went up. I never saw such a ruined field in all my life. There were at least two hundred and fifty big bomb craters and about twenty acres of airfield proper. We started to go over it with mine detectors, but the large quantities of shrapnel made it hard because the detectors would sing over every piece. It took one day to detect the whole field. Then we started picking up all the shrapnel in our steel helmets. We had four days to get the field in shape and the rest of the company moved in to help us.

Then I discovered places in the field where bombs had landed and not exploded. My platoon was assigned the job of digging down to them and blowing them up. The boys really started to shake when they started that. None of us knew anything about bombs. They dug and discovered them at a depth of about six feet. Then my staff sergeant and I would place TNT (eight blocks) on them and use safety fuses to blow them up. We would clear the whole field of men and then each of us would light three or four fuses and then take off. Shrapnel would fly three quarters of a mile from these bombs. In total we blew up seventeen of these two-hundred-and-fifty-pound babies. We had a D7 filling the bomb craters back up and three motor graders smoothing off a runway two hundred yards wide and a mile long. Our dump trucks were hauling dirt in from an overhead loader to the bomb craters. In four days we had the runways fixed and were starting on the edges when we received orders to move to the coast near Palermo. We left the field and I doubt if they even used it except in an emergency. The British used the one at Comiso with their Spitfires at D+3.

While we were there two Stuka dive-bombers came in to land. They thought the field was still theirs because of all the German planes around. Our ack-ack got them both. One landed at the end of the runway upside down and the pilot and a gunner were dragged to death. One man got out of the plane and said that six started out. All of them were shot down. Pretty nice going. We convoyed up to the coast thirty miles east of Palermo and camped there about ten miles behind the front lines.

From there on we were used as a third line of engineers. The rest of our regiment still hadn't landed. We were now through with airports. We had division engineers and a Corps of Engineers regiment ahead of us. All we had to do was fix up what they had done and then build some more passes when they got too swamped. Our primary mission was to build any bridges that were needed because we were the only ones who knew anything about Bailey bridges.

Just before we moved up to the coast, we were near Kaltenisetta fixing detours and roads. My platoon had the job of building a Bailey bridge across a blown-out bridge, and we had to do it at night. We went out with all our equipment and unloaded it. We were just starting to build it when word came to tear it down, load it up, and move it down a hundred miles to where it was needed more. We did this, working all night, and at dawn we arrived at the new site. We ate and then had the bridge up and traffic going over it in three hours. Most of the men were so tired they just dropped where they were.

Then we drove back to camp and started the road work again. My platoon was filling eight-foot-deep tank-traps in the road near Enna just after it had been taken. An interpreter soldier came up and said that there were some important Germans hiding out in some old sulfur mines in the mountains near there. I asked the company commander if we could finish and go after them and he went with us.

When we got there, we made the owner and the interpreter go in with us. We had Lieutenant Shumack, Rosco, our company commander, and myself. Just five of us went in and I was kind of scared; however, we were in no danger. It was a very old tunnel, half filled with soft spots and six hundred feet long, nice experience anyhow. We found no one there.

The rest of our regiment arrived and we moved from the coast to join them at Randazzo. The first battalion had been in the front all during Africa, so the second battalion was put in the front this time. All we did was fix the roads back about sixteen miles from the front. We sure got tired of that in one quick hurry. We stayed in the rear until the war ended in Sicily.

The mines blew three of my officer pals up when a jeep hit one. The Germans had left mines everywhere. I had the privilege of watching some alien prisoners march down the hill one day. One of them hit an S mine, called a bouncing baby, and it went off, killing two of them and wounding three. Two days before that I was assigned the job of improving the bike paths on the coast. I got out to the bridge and found six civilians putting up an awful fuss. An S mine had gone off and killed one of them. The others were afraid to move. I coaxed them back up onto the road and then went down beside the bridge and railroad track where they had been. I pulled out six S mines with my detector. The engineers that had built the bypass had already pulled out about twenty-three while making it.

Near Randazzo the lava made it very hard for the mine detectors to pick up the mines. I was in Randazzo the next morning after it had been taken by the Americans and just as the British were arriving. It was one big mess and a mine had just gone off, killing three Englishmen and wounding nine. It was all bombed to pieces.

The war ended in Sicily and the regiment all got together again. My captain and the battalion commander had gone back to the States during the campaign, two very good men. The Germans had blown up almost every one of the numerous bridges on the island, but with our equipment we had done the impossible.

Back at Kasserine Pass our casualties were one in four. An estimated three hundred were killed, three thousand wounded, and three thousand missing or captured. The army also lost one hundred eighty-three tanks, one hundred four halftracks, two hundred eight artillery pieces, and five hundred twelve trucks and jeeps. The Americans were pushed back about fifty miles. The Germans lost one thousand men, killed, wounded, or missing, and twenty tanks. The Germans had better guns and training. The eighty-eight-millimeter guns on their new Mark 4-6 tanks could fire from out of the range of the seventy-five-millimeter US Sherman tanks. In one suicidal try to stop the Panzers only four of fifty tanks of a battalion of the First Armored Regiment survived.

The bombers had perfected air ground support, and the German infantry had a terrible new weapon called a *Neblewarfer* (multiple launched rockets). The "Desert Fox" of the Afrika Korps led their commanders. The Americans had only thirty-seven-mm guns for artillery. They were called "paintscratchers" and were removed from the U.S. arsenal. So were some of the armies. So were some of the generals.

We were now set up in bivouac areas for a period of time. The Germans had gone back across the Straits of Messina and had gone up the boot of Italy. The reason for this was they figured out that they could get behind the mountain ranges when they got up near Naples. The mountains run across the island and that would set them up with beautiful places for defense.

The Italian army was about to surrender and we took them and put them in the lines when we got into Italy, and in one day we lost what we'd gained in two weeks. So they took the best ones out of the best infantry and took them out of the lines and gave them to us engineers to go out and build roads at night. We'd go out at night and start building some roads between the lines to get our tanks going on it, and the German artillery would start firing at us. The Italians would take off and we'd have to go to where the MPs were, about a mile. We took them up and put them back to work. They weren't much good.

It was rumored that the Germans were using the Italians in front of them and they would have a sergeant in back with a pistol. If the Italians didn't want to fight, the German sergeant right there took care of them. Those were the rumors that were going around.

We finally went up the coast and landed there. Our soldiers had crossed over Messina and had gone up through the Germans, who had not offered much resistance because they were back in the mountains. Farther up the coast, we finally got to where they were and started fighting again, and winter came. It was miserable.

The roads were fair, at least the main roads were fair. The side roads were terrible. They would go out and they were terrible, and after we got through with them they were worse. Our heavy trucks would come by with ammunition, would turn off from the main road, and would sink almost out of sight. We'd have to go out with our Cats, hook onto them, and pull them out and over to where they were going, to where the artillery was up under the trees, help them unload, and then pull them back to the road so they could go. That's how we were doing this.

We were called every time to move the artillery and the trucks, and it was cold, freezing. We were still in shelter tents. We'd get up in the morning and go by the cook tent where they cooked the food and put it all together in our mess kits. They gave the boys their hot coffee. I had cold water, which didn't help much to get me going. We suffered that for a while and we were making no headway at all.

The really tough part was that only the infantrymen could go out there trying to go up the mountains where the Germans were looking down on them. They'd dig a foxhole there and stay in it. Food might get to them, and might not get to them. More of them got frozen feet and had to be taken out of the lines than got shot and killed at that time. It was a terrible time as far as the men were concerned trying to go on fighting, but that's what we had to do.

We pushed the Germans back finally, back towards Monte Cassino and the Repido River. I and another lieutenant got and "R and R." We got to go back to Naples, get in a hotel, and get into a nice warm bed, with warm water to bathe in. We wanted to go over and see Sorrento.

The Air Force had taken over Sorrento as their R and R area, but they would let us go over during the daytime to look at it. We went over and it was all they said it was. It was just a little village going up the island and then they had a cave with the water coming in. We enjoyed that very much and then we had to go back up and join the company again.

By this time they were getting closer to the Rapido River, and that was going to be the Germans' main line of defense, along the Rapido River. We knew it and they knew it. They had brought a German Panzer division in there to help fortify it.

Meanwhile, one afternoon, the major called me and said, "We've got a job for you. There are four tank destroyers and four M4 tanks out there in the gully in front of this hill that the Germans are on, and they are stuck. They can't get out. They're sitting in the mud. I want you to take a Cat and go out and get them out." So by the time I got the Cat and the men ready to go it was dark. I had never been out where these tanks were stuck in the mud. I had a map that showed me where, and I'd seen it from a distance. So we had to travel and I had a flashlight to guide the Cat. It was a little D4 Cat.

I was walking backwards, guiding the Cat along. We came to a canal bank and went on the canal bank. We got partway along the canal bank and then all of a sudden the Cat tipped over into the canal, which was dry. The Cat operator was not hurt, thank goodness, but the Cat was down there tipped over. So I went back with one of my men to the major and told him what had happened. He gave me a D8, which was much more reasonable to start thinking of getting tanks out with a Cat. So we started out with the D8, got back, pulled the little Cat up on the bank, and went on and got to where the tanks were stuck at just about daylight.

There were some trees around the gully. The gully was around twenty feet deep. Four tanks were lined up in a row and all they did was spin their wheels when they tried them. Four tank destroyers were behind them, and the same thing. The tankers had dug a hole back in the bank on the enemy side, so that the enemy couldn't see them during the daytime. We parked the D8 behind some trees to make it hard to see, and went back down with the tankers there in the little cave that they had. They had several of them along where they were. We went to sleep.

Night came and it was raining. It got dark, so we went out on the Cat and started over. And the first thing we had to do was get down into the gully to get to the tanks to even do anything, so we started pushing from the side there and making a road in front, down in front of the tanks. We got that done all right, but once we got down in and started to run towards the tanks, we got stuck without the dozer. We had to get some trees and such to put in front and back and fortunately we got back out again. So we sat there and put the winch cable out and got hold of some trees. When we'd get hold of the trees, we'd put some trees in the back so the Cat wouldn't sink in so far. We backed up very close to the lead tank and hooked it on, started the winch going, started the tank going, and started the dozer going; nothing moved except it just pulled the line taut. We sat spinning wheels on all three, with the dozer spinning, and the tree was pulled over. We pulled over several trees trying that and it didn't work. So we took the trees over and we cut them up into lengths and we laid kind of a tree path in front of our dozer so it could travel on those. We went back to the tank and took a tree about ten inches in diameter, and took about ten feet of it to the front of the tank. We then laid the tree up against the tank tracks, put some chains around the tree and in and through the track and back out, and put a pin through the cable that would hold it tight, and put a nut on both sides of the tank on each track. We had this tree laying right on the tracks. We started the Cat going, and started the tank going, and we started to move a little and when that tree came around and started to go under the tank, it started to lift the tank up and we started to move ahead. We went about half the length of the tank and had to stop because it was starting to sink again. So then we took another tree trunk and did the same thing, put it in front. We were doing all of this in the rain, in the mud, in the cold, and it took time. We'd put it on and then we'd start the tank and start the dozer and pull up and it worked. The first tree trunk would go back to the back, and the one we just put on would go back to the middle, and then we'd have to take the chains and the tree off from the back, go around and put it on the front again and tie it down. It just took time and was miserable. It wasn't long before daylight came so we went back into the holes in the bank and spent the day sleeping and trying to stay warm.

We got word from the general who wanted to know where his tanks were. I sent word back that they were mired in the mud and we were trying to get them out. We spent the next night trying to get it, and we got that one tank out, by working till three or four that night. We got it to where it could get on those trees that we had put there to keep the dozer up. So we drove it up and out. We put it behind some trees so that they couldn't see it and went back. Then it was daylight again, so we went back and got in our caves.

I just decided that we were not getting anywhere—one tank out in two days, and we had seven more of them to go. We couldn't be fooling around at night. They hadn't shot at us particularly, so I decided we were going to work in the daylight. So that is what we started doing; working in the daylight, we could see what we were doing and we made a lot better time. We started to pull the tanks out and get them up under the trees and behind the trees. Then we'd cut some more trees and take all of them back there and still go at it. In a day and a half we got all of the tanks out. We started the tanks rolling back, and they got stuck again in another gully. We had to start over again and do the same thing to get them out of there. After six days we got those tanks out. Everybody was pleased. Then we went on back to our company.

There was still some fighting going on and we were trying to get the trucks up with ammunition, with supplies, and with food, while the fighting was going on on the mountain. We had to deliver some of this to the soldiers who were fighting in the front lines and gave them food and ammunition. That was tough. The Frenchmen were using mules and that was a lot better way of packing the stuff up. They really knew those mules, and I don't know, but some of those mules weren't very nice to all persons who tried to handle them. They could be as stubborn as all get-out.

The fighting was going on and was starting to get a little fiercer because it was starting to get a little like spring. We pushed back to where we thought they were, at Monte Cassino, where they were behind the Rapido River.

The Rapido River ran down through kind of a little valley that was about half a mile wide and flat on the bottom. It would rise to about thirty feet and it was level on the top on each side. The Germans were in front of the hill, and Monte Cassino was on top of it. They were dug in and they were veterans. They had the field of fire all set up with machine guns. The troops had tried once to get across and hadn't made it. We went back to practice with some infantry, crossing the river in rubber boats. We put four infantrymen in the boat and one engineer. The engineer's job was to guide them across and keep them going straight across and then to bring the boat back for the next load.

The infantrymen didn't make very good paddle men. Paddling on the boats, the first thing that happened was that the boats started going 'round and 'round. When they got that straightened out they were going downstream and we had to turn them slightly upstream and keep pushing them and paddling them that way to get them across. If they could get to the other side the four infantrymen would get out and the boat would come back with the engineer in it. Bringing it back when it was empty we still had problems getting back to the same spot. These infantrymen were loaded with ammunition, food, shells, rifles; they were really heavily loaded, but that's the way they had to go across and take care of themselves.

The time came that General Mark Clark ordered another attack to cross and try to take Monte Cassino and push the Germans back. There was a

Texas division and I think another one that was from down south that were to make the attack. We had the Texas division part of it. The one that I had, my platoon was to go down in a gully, go to the bottom, and wait until they put down a smoke screen in front of us. Then go out and check for mines out to the river, get the infantry and bring them out, put them in the boats, and take them across.

In another area they were using a footbridge that they were going to run across the stream. In another area they found a bridge running across a stream that they were going to attack. They were going to attack in the afternoon, almost evening.

We got ready for it. I took my platoon down towards the river and they came off the upper flat, down into this gully, and we got to the mouth of it. We were down on the level of the river all right, but it was about seventy-five to a hundred feet away from us.

It was cold. The Germans had cut down all the trees along the river, and they'd left stumps sticking up one to two feet, even three feet, which would make it hard to load boats to cross. The Germans had a good field of fire for the men that did get across.

I was waiting for the smoke to come in and hide us so that they couldn't see what we were doing. There wasn't enough smoke. I could see clear across to the far side of the mountain. Hardly enough smoke at all in our area. Then came the general down the ravine with his infantrymen following him. He caught up with me and says, "Why aren't you out there digging for mines?" And I said, "General, we were told that we would be covered with a smoke screen. You look out there and there's hardly anything."

He said it was time to go get my men and go. So I said, "Yes, sir." We went out and got started. I lined my men up in a line about twenty feet from one to the other side of the area we were going to search for mines. I had them shoulder to shoulder on their knees. They'd take their bayonets out, poke right by their left knee, poke about right in front of them in the middle, and then in front of their right knee about six inches ahead. We cleared a path approximately twenty feet wide out to the river. We laid some yellow ribbon along the outside so that they could know the path was cleared of mines, and by the way, we didn't find any mines. But anyhow, we got to the river, then went back, and showed the general and they came out there in their boats to cross that river. Some of them fell in because they got far out and those infantrymen sank like rocks. They were so loaded with ammunition, bayonets, rifles, and whatever they had that those that tipped over sank, and that was it.

The river was about eight to ten feet deep and flowing quite fast and cold. Then there were these tree stumps there sticking up that made it hard to load them. The boats finally got across. Some of them floated down quite a ways. They couldn't keep them up to go straight across. When they got across, the infantrymen would get out and take off. The boats came back; some of them were downstream quite a little bit to where we had not cleared the mines.

The ones that got back to where we were loading, we loaded them again and went across.

Boats kept floating downstream. With only one man in it he couldn't make it come back straight across there and then there were boats in the road and you had to wait for them to go across before you could row back. We got all of the infantrymen across, but I decided that wasn't the way to do it. We were wasting our time. We'd lost eleven of the twelve boats either from being hit or drifting downstream. So I went over and cut a telephone wire that the infantrymen had laid across so that they had communications back. I could have been shot for that, I guess. Anyhow, I cut enough wire off the telephone wire to tie to the front of each boat so it would reach back to our side; then tied it on the back of the boat to reach across to the other side. The sergeant and I went across and got on the enemy side and we had two men stay back on our side. Usually any of them that came back were wounded men. It was dark and we couldn't see anything. When somebody would come back we would put them in the boat and the men on the far side would pull the boat across and we'd kind of hold on there and keep a little bit of tension to keep it going straight. And so we were using that and getting things done. It was dark and we couldn't see. Guns were flashing, flares were going, and everything was black. About 3 A.M. some of my men cane down to relieve us. By then I had been lying on my side and a shell had hit in front of us in the water and the shrapnel hit me in the back. I didn't know how serious it was, but I had an overcoat on and other coats to try and keep warm, so it didn't feel bad. I couldn't feel a warm flow of blood or anything, so I just stayed there until that time. In fact, when I was relieved, I went back and went to my tent rather than to First Aid and just went to sleep. When they relieved me, in all that time we hadn't taken very many men back across, and all that we did were wounded. When I got relieved I came back across the river and started up this little gully. These Nebelwaefers, the rockets that they were shooting, started up. They made a hell of a noise. One right after another. Zoom, zoom, zoom, coming over, it sounded like. The "screaming ninnys," we called them.

I was in the dark, just starting up the gully, and I landed right smack on someone lying on the ground. He started cursing at me; he was injured. I felt like two cents, but I got off and begged his pardon and took off up the hill. Meanwhile, that night two other officers and a platoon sergeant of our company were walking along the top and stepped on an S-mine and it killed all three of them. So that left our company in the morning with only two officers who were not hurt. The two others who had been with us all that time had died.

The infantry had been whipped. So many of them were taken prisoner and were taken up and paraded through the streets. We had never fired at Monte Cassino on top there because of the nuns that were in there, but we claimed that the Germans were using that as an overlook to see what we were doing. They were protected by that and we finally decided that we would bomb it.

After all that time, after two attacks, and we were finally going to bomb it. The bombers came over that day. The first ones hit the building and smoke went up in the sky and the rubble went down the hillside a little bit. Another raid of bombers came in and then the next raid of bombers came in and passed by the Cassino. We didn't see them so they were quite a ways out. They bombed the town that had Frenchmen, our allies, in it. They bombed the French there; there were some mad Frenchmen and some dead Frenchmen. That smoke and everything else going up in the sky, you could see it from over twenty miles away. I went down and got the shrapnel taken out of me.

They had a commander left, and myself, and one executive officer; two were gone who had been with us all the way from the States. We had to bundle up their stuff and all their belongings to send home. We went back and found a rest area and started training again, which we kind of hated in a way because we'd been through a lot of training. We were back there, and it was a little better than building roads, but there still was a problem.

While we were back there a Japanese battalion came in, I think it was the 404. They were the most decorated battalion in the army. In fighting they were deadly. While they were on that hill fighting the Germans more of them got frozen feet, frozen hands, and were put out of action that way than were actually killed, but they were a trained battalion. We had soldiers from Australia, we had six soldiers from India who were with the English; so were the Australians. It was a mixed-up party.

When the invasion came across the channel they started taking men from our army and shipping them back to England for the invasion. Several men went and we were very understaffed for being a fighting army, so we weren't doing much, just putting our time in.

I had wound up with enough points, you could get up to, I think, fifty points, to send me home if I wanted to go. I had about double that amount of points, so I was about the first one to go out of our regiment.

They told me they'd make me captain of the company I was with if I stayed there. They'd make me captain within two months. I said, "No, sir. I'm going home."

I went home all right. It took me thirty days on that ship. I could have walked faster than it was going, zigzagging back and forth. We were in a convoy eating C rations, and looking in and the sailors were having steaks and ice cream. Our officers, who were in the army, were going home and eating C rations.

I got back home for a little rest time. It was about ten days and after about eight days I got married to my sweetheart and we took off by train and went to Camp White, Medford, Oregon.

I got off the train and my wife wanted to know what we were doing and I said that I had to report in. "Go get yourself a hotel, and I might not see you, I can't tell you when I'll see you. It will probably be a long time, but I'll be back sometime. Today, tomorrow, I'll be back."

I went out to the camp and found out that all I had to do was report in each day to find out if I was on the list to be shipped out to some place. So I went back to my wife and we went out on the town. The people up there would open their houses up to us and we had a great time. Swimming pools, playing badminton, and such. It was great. For about eight or nine days we were up there having a wonderful time.

They asked me where I wanted to go and I said that I'd like to go back to Fort Belvoir on the engineering side and teach classes in engineering. They said, "We'd like you to go down to Santa Barbara and take over a hotel down there that we are bringing overseas returnees back to. You would take care of them until they are sent somewhere else, like we're doing here at this camp." I said, "No, I want to go back to Fort Belvoir and teach." They said okay, so they sent us back by train to Belvoir.

We went back and I went in and reported to the general. He said, "What are you going to do?" and I said, "I'd like to teach. That's what they told me I could do when I left back there." And he said, "Oh, that's back there. That's not here. You are going to train soldiers so that they can go over and fight and take care of themselves. You will see that they are equipped and trained to do it." Well, I said, "But…" and he said, "No buts at all. That's it." So I went up as company commander, and it took me another year to make my captaincy, but that was beside the point. I stayed there and had West Virginia troops and Pennsylvania troops and others come in from back east. We trained those boys. Some of them could not read but they sure could shoot.

Then a little while later on, they got down to where there weren't so many men coming in to be trained. They took the ZI boys and gave them to me. Now the ZI were soldiers that had come in and gone AWOL and done something bad enough to put them in jail. They had been in jail and they finally got out, and had come back to be trained. Some of them had been sergeants, some of them had been something else, but all had come back to be trained; there was a platoon of them.

There were two platoons of recruits, one of ZI and one of overseas returnees, who were like myself. When we told them to file out, the recruits would bang the doors open and out they'd file in formation. The ZIs would come out smoking in ranks, dragging their rifles, and just packing them any old way. The guys from overseas, they would wander out. A lot of them were sergeants, staff sergeants, full sergeants, and corporals and that, and they'd been through it but we'd finally get them out in line. That was getting tough, to train them that way.

Then in the morning we had sick call. They'd come out and get in formation, and the ranking noncom in that formation would have to march them over and past the battalion headquarters, past our headquarters, and to the infirmary. Well, every morning when they put one of the noncoms in charge, it would be an overseas returnee because they had all the ranking. He was supposed to be in charge of getting them in formation and marching them over. They would come over past the battalion headquarters talking in ranks, out of step, and then my phone would start smoking. I could tell every morning just when it was going to happen because we could see the men march past our headquarters and past the battalion headquarters. There wasn't much I could do about it. I could chew on them a little bit there, but those overseas returnees, I knew exactly how they felt. They came back and then we were taking them out on dry runs and rifle marksmanship and they would practice, practice, practice dry running and such, and they were about to blow a fuse. I finally got it down to where when they came in, we'd take them out on the range and see what they could do, firing live rounds. If they were good, they didn't have to go through any of that rifle marksmanship and that calmed them down a little bit.

One of my corporals came back from overseas. He came in and saluted me, reported, and looked at me and about fell over. So did I. He was the corporal that we had had over there, and a very good one in my platoon. Later on they called for a man from overseas to go to Chicago to march in parades whenever they had them. His sweetheart was not far from Chicago. I called him in and said, "I'm sending you to Chicago. They want you to go to Chicago."

"Nope, I'm not going. I won't volunteer."

And I said, "You're going to Chicago."

"No I'm not. I won't volunteer. I'm staying here."

I said, "You're going or you'll be tied up and put in the jail." He said all right. Well, he went to Chicago, married his sweetheart, and had a heck of a good time. But he wouldn't volunteer.

I finally got my captain's award, but before I got that they had these OCS classes who were graduating all the time. They had one coming up and I got a letter from my commanding officer asking me to address their young men who were about to be officers and were getting their diplomas. So I did. About two or three months later I got another letter from him asking me to address the ones who were graduating. I think we were up to about the eighty-second class that was graduating, so I addressed them. I found out I was the only officer below the rank of colonel that had addressed these graduating lieutenants and I was the only one who had done it twice.

I had my captaincy and well into December of 1945 they released me. We got in the car, my wife and I and one little one, and headed out for Utah.

I'd been in the army almost four years, one month and one day, and when it started out I was going to stay in for one year, get $21 a month; they tried to get us to come in for three years at $30 a month, and I said, "No, I'm only going to be here a year." A month later war was declared.

That was quite a time in my life, but there's one thing I'd like to tell you. I knew that I could tell my mother that I was okay and all right and she would know it. I just knew that feeling, that would be it, and it was proved when I got home. I asked my mother about it, and she said, "Yes, I knew it. And when you were behind enemy lines I knew something was wrong. I didn't know what it was, but I knew something was wrong and that you were okay." Well, that proved it to me.

I had one brother in the Air Force, one brother in tank destroyers, one brother in the paratroopers, and one brother in the engineers (which was me), and one brother was too young. My brother who was in the paratroops in the Far East got a broken leg and that was the extent of our injuries. But war is hell. It's not worth fighting with the weapons we have now. It isn't worth having just a pile of rubble. If we ever get armies fighting in the States again as we had when we had the Civil War, with the things that we've got now for destruction, there won't be much left.

I'd like to tell one, or two, or three stories about my work in Fort Belvoir with the men that I had in my company.

We were known as Hooper's Troopers, Colonel Hooper's troopers, and he was quite a stickler for things being just so. The word came down to me that the men could not go on a weekend leave unless the grass and weeds were cut around our complete company area. So I sent some men over to the headquarters company to get some mowers so they could do it. They came back and reported that they couldn't get any. There weren't any available. The men really wanted to go on leave, and I wanted them to go too, so I came up with an idea. I said, "Get hold of your mess-kit knives and your bayonets and come out and mow the weeds and the lawn," which they did. They went on their leave for the weekend. As usual, someone had an uncle or friend or someone there in the legislature or the Congress (we were close enough to Washington, about eighteen miles) and they'd tell them what we'd done.

The order came back from a congressman to Colonel Hooper, that he was wasting people's money there cutting lawns with mess-kit knives and bayonets. So he got on to the headquarters company and they came down to us and gave us some lawnmowers. "Here's some lawnmowers. Can't we give you some lawnmowers?" Well, that caused quite a stir but that was happening all the time there with anything that went wrong with the company. It would work when it was taken to the congressmen.

Another story is that Franklin D. Roosevelt died while I was there training the men. So we were told to go in to town, to take our people in. There was a battalion of them, which would be about a thousand. We were to take them in to line the streets when the hearse (it wasn't a hearse, it was a horse-drawn carriage), came down the street from the congressional area to the White House with his body in it. When we were almost there, they stopped the whole convoy on the road and told them there was a relief period there. They could get off the trucks and relieve themselves, and it was right on the main highway. That was something new to me. I hadn't ever seen anything like it before. Then we went on in, and started off, lining our men up on each side of the street from the White House; every ten feet on each side of the street we put a man. They were lined up out through there. The carriage came down with the body in it, and a horse with a saddle on it, but no rider.

I had a company, as mentioned before; a company of two platoons of raw recruits, one of ZI people and one of overseas people. Colonel Hooper had a rule that if you had three of your men AWOL you were restricted to the company area. I myself, the company commander, would be restricted. So I had two AWOL and another man was over in the stockade that the MPs were guarding. Well, the MPs gave this man a mule and told him to go out and do some work. He went out and did some work all right, but then he took off in a hurry and was gone. The word came back to me, "You've got three men AWOL. You've got to be restricted to area." I was mad, and went to our major who was over the battalion and us. I told him that I thought it was a really raw deal being kept in the company area there. I couldn't go home to my wife, just had to stay there. He said, "Well, that's gotta be."

And I said, "I want to go higher. I want to go to the regimental commander, Colonel Hooper, who had made this statement that we were to be contained in the company area."

He said, "We can't let you go."

And I said, "I want to go."

And he said, "You'll wind up in the stockade too if you go over there and see him." So that's the way that things went.

One time, Colonel Hooper came down to inspect the barracks. Now, the floor of the barracks was about three feet off the ground. He came around the outside, stooped over to look at them, and to feel underneath them. He happened to look around, and there I was and two other men that were with him kind of grinning at him stooped over. He said, "When I stoop, you all stoop." That's the kind of colonel commander we had there, but it was interesting to have details like that.

THE UNITED STATES OF AMERICA

TO ALL WHO SHALL SEE THESE PRESENTS, GREETING:

THIS IS TO CERTIFY THAT

THE PRESIDENT OF THE UNITED STATES OF AMERICA
AUTHORIZED BY ACT OF CONGRESS, JULY 9, 1918, HAS

AWARDED

A SILVER STAR

TO

First Lieutenant Jesse T. Davis, 01 108 070, Corps of Engineers

FOR

GALLANTRY IN ACTION

near Mignano, Italy, 18 - 24 November 1943

GIVEN UNDER MY HAND IN THE CITY OF WASHINGTON

THIS   19th   DAY OF   July   1949

[signature]
MAJOR GENERAL
THE ADJUTANT GENERAL

[signature]
SECRETARY OF WAR THE ARMY

THE UNITED STATES OF AMERICA

TO ALL WHO SHALL SEE THESE PRESENTS, GREETING:

THIS IS TO CERTIFY THAT

THE PRESIDENT OF THE UNITED STATES OF AMERICA
AUTHORIZED BY ACT OF CONGRESS, JULY 9, 1918, HAS

AWARDED

THE DISTINGUISHED SERVICE CROSS

TO

First Lieutenant Jesse L. Davis, O1 108 070, Corps of Engineers

FOR EXTRAORDINARY HEROISM
IN CONNECTION WITH MILITARY OPERATIONS
AGAINST AN ARMED ENEMY

near San Angelo, Italy, 21 January 1944

GIVEN UNDER MY HAND IN THE CITY OF WASHINGTON

THIS 19th DAY OF July 19 49

SECRETARY OF THE ARMY

MAJOR GENERAL
THE ADJUTANT GENERAL

RECORDED IN THE OFFICE OF
THE ADJUTANT GENERAL

Under the provisions of Army Regulations 600-45, as amended, the following named individuals of the Engineer Regiment (C) are awarded the Silver Star:

Jesse L. Davis—0-110070, First Lieutenant, Riverside, Utah
Ernest J. Lohnes—36045561, Technician, 5th grade, Pekin, Illinois
Raymond Ross—6957450, Private, 1st class, Vian, Oklahoma
Troy O. Wallace—6956370, Technician, 5th grade, Bluff Dale, Texas
Johannes D. Thomsen—39002204, Private, Eureka, California

For gallantry in action in November, 1943, in the vicinity of _____, Italy. When four M-10 Tank Destroyers and four M-4 Tanks became immobilized in a ravine due to high banks, the soft terrain, and a minefield, this officer and four men were detailed to the task of extricating these highly essential vehicles. The enemy was located on a ridge less than five hundred yards away and the vehicles were under constant enemy observation and artillery fire. In addition, the job was immeasurably complicated by the continued rain which turned the ground into a quagmire, causing the angle dozers, which the men were using to construct the fill across the ravine, to bog down repeatedly. Despite the shelling, the constant threat of small arms fire, and the technical difficulties, the crew persevered until noon of ____ November, when the vehicles were freed, only to be stopped a mile farther on by another ravine. Again they went to the rescue, working two days more, still under shell-fire, and once, strafing by enemy aircraft, until the vehicles reached safety. The courage and perseverance of this group, under constant danger and conditions of utmost hardship, reflect credit upon themselves, the Corps of Engineers, and the entire military service.

THE UNITED STATES OF AMERICA

TO ALL WHO SHALL SEE THESE PRESENTS, GREETING:

THIS IS TO CERTIFY THAT

THE PRESIDENT OF THE UNITED STATES OF AMERICA

AUTHORIZED BY ORDER OF

GENERAL GEORGE WASHINGTON, AUGUST 7, 1782

HAS AWARDED

THE PURPLE HEART

TO

First Lieutenant Jesse E. Davis, 01 100 070, Corps of Engineers

FOR

WOUNDS RECEIVED IN ACTION

near San Angelo, Italy, 21 January 1944

GIVEN UNDER MY HAND IN THE CITY OF WASHINGTON

THIS   19th   DAY OF   July   19 49

MAJOR GENERAL
THE ADJUTANT GENERAL

SECRETARY OF THE ARMY

3-20-06

Jesse Lawrence Davis

Jesse Lawrence Davis, long-time resident of Provo, died March 14, 2006, after devoted service to his family, church, and country. He was born December 10, 1917, in Riverside, Utah, to Jesse and Vesta Bigler Davis, the first of eight children. He graduated from Utah State University with a degree in Civil Engineering and many honors in cross country track.

During World War II, Larry served as an officer in the Combat Engineering Corps in the invasions of Africa, Sicily, and Italy. He was awarded the Purple Heart, Silver Star, Distinguished Service Cross, and the Italian Military Valor Cross. He also served as a Commanding Officer over an Engineering Corps at Fort Belvoir, Washington.

He was an engineer with the Bureau of Reclamation, Thorn's Construction in Provo, and Bingham Engineering in SLC. In his service to the LDS Church, Larry was Branch President in Paonia, CO, Scout Master for many years, Boy Scout Committee Chairman for nearly 10 years, second counselor in the Provo Oak Hills II Ward and High Counselor in a BYU Stake. He served in the Mazatlan, Mexico mission with his second wife, Jan Cummins Sondrup, and worked in the Provo Temple for 13 years.

Larry married Rae Buckley Davis on June 10, 1944. She died of a stroke in 1984. Their children include James Lawrence Davis, of Potomac, MD; Cheryl DiVito, of Brewster, MA; Marilyn Heiner, of Clifton, VA; and Kent Buckley Davis, of Orem, UT. Larry married Jan Sondrup on May 10, 1985. His step-children include Eric Sondrup, of Glendale, AZ; Kathy Jensen, of Berkley, CA; Suzanne Ron, of Houston, TX; and Christian Sondrup, of Lindon, UT. They shared 37 grandchildren and 20 great-grandchildren.

Services will be held at 1 p.m., Monday, March 20, at the Oak Hills II Ward Chapel, 925 E. North Temple, Provo. Viewings will be Sunday evening from 6-8 p.m. at Berg Mortuary, 185 E. Center St., Provo; and, Monday morning at the church, one hour before the funeral. In lieu of flowers, contributions may be made to the Boy Scouts of America, 748 N. 1340 W. Orem, UT 84057.

In Loving Memory of

Jesse Lawrence Davis

Born December 10, 1917 – Riverside, Utah
Died March 14, 2006 – Houston, Texas

In Loving Memory of

Jesse Lawrence Davis

Pallbearers

James L. Davis	Bradford W. Jensen
Kent B. Davis	Eric Sondrup
Michael DiVito	Christian Sondrup
Ronald A. Heiner	Avishai Ron

Funeral Services
Monday, March 20, 2006 – 1:00 p.m.
Oak Hills 2ⁿᵈ Ward Chapel
925 East North Temple Drive, Provo, Utah

Officiating....................................Bishop Randy Reneer
Family Prayer.............................. Christian Sondrup
~~~

Invocation ....Bradford W. Jensen
Life Sketch .... Cheryl Davis DiVito
Speaker..Kent Buckley Davis

Speaker..Kathleen Jensen
Piano Solo .... Jared D. Jensen
Speaker.......................................Marilyn Heiner

Speaker..Suzanne Ron
Speaker....................................James Lawrence Davis
Flute Solo........................Arienne Davis LeCheminant

"Sweet Hour of Prayer"
Accompanied by Jan LeCheminant
Remarks......................................Bishop Randy Reneer
Benediction................................Eric Sondrup
~~~

Dedication of Grave ....Adam Lawrence Davis
Military Honors ....BYU - R.O.T.C.
Interment .... East Lawn Memorial Hills
4800 North 650 East, Provo, Utah

In a beautiful blue lagoon on a clear day,
a fine sailing–ship
spreads its brilliant white canvas
in a fresh morning breeze
and sails out to the open sea.
We watch her glide away magnificently
through the deep blue and gradually see her
grow smaller and smaller
as she nears the horizon.
Finally, where the sea and sky meet,
she slips silently from sight;
and someone near me says,
"There, she is gone!"
Gone where?
Gone from sight – that is all.
She is still as large in mast
and Hull and sail,
still just as able to bear her load.
And we can be sure that,
just as we say,
"There, she is gone!"
another says, "There, she comes!"

EDWARD L. HART

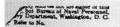

Pers 328- pr   BUREAU OF NAVAL PERSONNEL
. 290170   WASHINGTON 25, D.C.

                                    5 April 1946

To : Lieutenant (jg) Edward L. Hart, U.S.N.R.,
       U.S. Naval Supplementary Radio Unit, Pacific,
       Navy No. 128,
       c/o Fleet Post Office,
       San Francisco, California.
Via : Officer in Charge.

Subj: Navy Unit Commendation, Award of.

1. The United States Naval Communication Intelligence Organization
has been awarded the Navy Unit Commendation for service during the
period 7 December 1941 to 2 September 1945. By virtue of your service in this unit during this period, you are hereby authorized to
wear the Navy Unit Commendation Ribbon transmitted herewith.

2. This authorization has been made a part of your official record
in the Bureau of Naval Personnel. It is directed that, because of
the nature of the services performed by this unit, no publicity be
given to your receipt of this award.

By direction of the Chief of Naval Personnel.

                                    A V Ellrodt
                                    A. V. ELLRODT,
                                    Lieut., USNR,
                                    Medals and Awards.

Encl.

WORLD WAR II SERVICE OF EDWARD L. HART

At the time of the bombing of Pearl Harbor, 7 December, 1941, I was a graduate student at the University of Michigan at Ann Arbor, Michigan. The attack was a tremendous shock to everybody. I had a low draft number and had not yet been called up. Knowing I would have to serve my country, and while thinking about how best I might do so, I heard of an intensive course in Japanese that would be starting at the University of Michigan the next semester, soon to begin. I discovered that quite a few of my fellow students were thinking along the same line, and I and many more enrolled in the class. It was a full-time course; we took nothing else.

It was a tough course: sheer memorization to begin with. The first day's assignment was to learn the *hiragana*, the Japanese syllabary, similar to an alphabet. The second day we had to learn the *katakana*, a second syllabary, used frequently for foreign words in a way similar to the way English uses italics. The course began hard and became increasingly harder, as we learned both the written and the spoken language. Near the end of the semester recruiters came from both the army and the navy; most of us chose the navy.

In July of 1942 we went from Ann Arbor to the U. S. Navy Japanese Language School in Boulder, Colorado. It had formerly been in California, but had to move because most of the instructors were Japanese, and the Japanese had been relocated out of California. I began as a civilian with the title "Naval Agent," but when draft boards threatened to take some of us away, the navy quickly inducted us as enlisted men, Y2C(V4)USNR, Yeoman Second Class. We remained in that rating until completion of the year-long course, when we each received a commission as Ensign, I-V (S), USNR (Line officer, Intelligence) USNR. Except, of course, those who chose to go into the marines. The classes in the Navy Japanese Language School were small, only seven or eight in a class, and the learning was very intensive.

From Boulder, in July of 1943, our group of graduates, who came from all the universities in the country then offering courses in Japanese—mostly, besides Michigan, Harvard, Yale, Columbia, and the University of Washington—were dispersed around the world, one of us on most of the main ships of the navy and at least one as far away as Chunking. One of my good friends, a member of my small class that stayed together for the whole year, lost an eye aboard a ship in the Pacific. A large contingent of our graduating group was sent to a place called the Communication Annex, whose mission was to break Japanese naval codes and translate the messages into English. Another large contingent was sent to Hawaii to a place called FRU-PAC (Fleet Radio Unit, Pacific), which served the same function as the Communication Annex in Washington.

By sheer chance and with no say in the matter, I received orders to report to the Chief of Naval Operations in Washington, D.C., and was assigned to the Communication Annex. We were kept out of the main operation there until FBI and ONI (Office of Naval Intelligence) checks were completed, and then we were introduced to the workings of one of the most secret places of the war. Practically everything we touched was stamped "TOP-SECRET—ULTRA," Ultra being the British equivalent of our Top Secret, since there were British liaison officers working along with us. Our workplace was surrounded by a fifteen-foot-high chain-link fence topped with three or four strands of barbed wire and patrolled twenty-four hours a day by armed marines. The secrecy was effective; the Japanese never learned we had broken their codes.

Secrecy demanded, of course, that we never discussed our work outside the compound. Even inside the unit, the various divisions of work were separated. People assigned to a piece of work knew only what they needed to know to do their job. Since the work of translation was the final step in the process, we who translated had to know a good deal about how the codes worked in order to clear garbles—and there were at least one or two in almost every message. We were expected to read each day's intelligence summary that went to the president and the chiefs of staff. In the upper right-hand drawer of the desk we worked at was a loaded Smith and Wesson .45. Even the wastebaskets were emptied into sealed bags and escorted by armed escort to an incinerator.

It happened before I arrived in Washington, but the unit I was assigned to had been mainly responsible for the Battle of Midway being a turning point of the war. By knowing in advance what was coming and when, everything that could float or fly was assembled at Midway waiting for the Japanese, who, if they had not been turned back, were on their way to occupy Hawaii.

This has all been written about before now in books and articles, so I am giving nothing away. I will not go into detail about the codes, except to say that we had radio intercept stations on the Pacific Coast with direct lines to Washington; hence we were decoding and translating messages in Washington at the same time the people they were intended for were decoding and reading them. On at least one occasion we had broken out and read a message while the intended recipient was asking for a retransmission because of poor reception.

The work was demanding and fascinating. Our desk had to be covered twenty-four hours a day; that meant that two or three times each week we changed from a regular day of 0800 to 1400, to an evening's work from 1400 to 2400, and then to another schedule of 2400 to 0800. The changes were so frequent that getting accustomed to sleeping at the times provided was never easy. It was interesting to know what was going on a day or two ahead of the general public, but it was also sometimes wrenching. I knew, for instance, when the invasion for retaking Guam began; I also knew that the Third Marines were involved and that my brother was an officer with that division. I was kept on tenterhooks for some time before I learned by letters from my family that he had been wounded during the landings but that he had been taken to a hospital ship and seemed to be doing all right. He still carries some shrapnel fragments.

I think I was the first person in the continental United States to know when the invasion for retaking the Philippines began. I was the watch officer at the desk when a message came through from a frantic Japanese airman. He was so caught off guard by what he saw that he sent his message in plain text, not bothering to encode it—describing the fleet and air units he saw approaching during his reconnaissance patrol. When I took the translated message in to the captain he didn't believe it at first; but soon the airwaves were flooded with radio traffic, and by evening the news was in the local papers.

I was in Washington from July 1943 to July 1945, at which time I was given orders transferring me to Pearl Harbor to our complementary unit, FRUPAC, which operated under the direction of the Joint Intelligence Center, Pacific Ocean Areas, or JICPOA. I boarded the navy transport USS *George F. Elliott* at San Francisco, and as a line officer was assigned duties during the voyage. We traveled zigzag and darkened ship, arriving at Pearl Harbor on 2 September 1945, about the time the official peace with Japan was signed aboard the USS *Missouri*.

Shortly after my arrival at Pearl Harbor, volunteers were sought to join as Japanese translators and interpreters with the United States Strategic Bombing Survey, just then arriving in Japan after having completed its mission in Germany of assessing the effectiveness of bombing in the overall conduct of the war. I volunteered and was given a Class III Air Priority for travel to Japan by way of NATS, Naval Air Transport Service. On the way we made refueling stops at Midway, Guam, and Iwo Jima. At Guam, I was there long enough to locate my marine brother, who had rejoined his unit, and at Iwo Jima I was able to take a jeep ride to the top of Mt. Suribachi, site of the famous flag-raising photograph.

My assignment with USBS was as a Japanese language interpreter and translator with the Electrical Equipment Branch of the Capital Goods and Construction Division. I accompanied the army major who headed that group on his visits to the various sites he went to to evaluate the effectiveness of our bombing in slowing down or halting production at that plant. We frequently found that unless there had been a direct hit on a vital piece of equipment the damage was usually rapidly repaired and the plant soon back in operation. I helped also in writing the final report, and the conclusion was that conventional bombing by itself could not have won the war. My personal conclusion was that without the atomic bombs Japan would not have surrendered and that an invasion of the main islands would have been necessary, with the loss of untold numbers of lives on both sides. Contrary to some revisionist thinking, I firmly believe that President Truman had no other choice than to use the atomic bomb. I used an afternoon when I wasn't needed to look up another brother, this one in the air force and stationed at Yokota Air Base.

After the completion of the work of the U.S. Strategic Bombing Survey, I was released from my assignment to it and flown by air to San Francisco. From there I went by train to Salt Lake City, where I was able to be with my wife for the arrival of our first child. From Salt Lake my orders took me once more to 'Washington, D.C., and translation work, until released from active duty on 2 February 1946 and separated from the service on 1 March 1946. I remained in the Naval Reserve until 15 October 1954. On 5 April 1946 I received from the Navy Bureau of Personnel a Navy Unit Commendation Ribbon for being an officer in the United States Naval Communication Intelligence Organization, during the period of service for which the Unit Commendation was given.

P15-1(2)/00

**U. S. NAVAL
SUPPLEMENTARY RADIO UNIT, PACIFIC**
PEARL HARBOR, T. H.
NAVY 128, c/o FLEET POST OFFICE
SAN FRANCISCO, CALIFORINA

End-1

From: Officer in Charge.
To :   Lieutenant (jg) Edward L. Hart, U. S. N. R.
Via :   Officer in Charge, U. S. Strategic Bombing Survey,
          Washington, D. C.

Subject: Navy Unit Commendation, Award of.

1.   Forwarded with congratulations and appreciation of services
performed while attached to this Unit.

                              J. S. HOLTWICK, Jr.,
                              Captain, U. S. Navy.

- -

End-2
P15-1(2)/00   U. S. Strategic Bombing Survey
                                   Room 2013   A.A.F. Annex #1
                                   Gravelly Point, Virginia

                                        19 June 1946

From: Senior Navy Member.
To: Lieutenant (jg) Edward L. Hart, S(I), U.S.N.R.

1.   Delivered.

                              R. A. OFSTIE

                              R. L. WELLS,
                              By direction

C.R. (NEAL) PETERSON

C.R. (NEAL) PETERSON

Each boy at Allen Hall paid $27.00 per month for room and board. Each was required to work one day a month in the kitchen. I worked on Sundays. On this particular Sunday, December 7, 1941, over the radio came the shocking news that the Japanese had bombed Pearl Harbor. In the days following, gasoline was rationed and tires could be sold only under certain conditions. This affected my business at the service station. I was single and could see the "writing on the wall" so I started to see if I could enlist in some branch of service rather than be drafted. I decided to try and get into the navy, as navy personnel seemed to always have a dry bed and good food, and would either get killed outright or return home safe. I contacted the Navy recruiting office in Salt Lake City. I didn't know what I was qualified for but I could use a typewriter so I thought I would request duty as a yeoman, an enlisted man doing secretarial work.

The officer at the recruiting office suggested that since I was a college graduate I should try to get assigned as an officer. He said he had no openings at the time but would keep me in mind. One day he called and said he had an opening in the ordnance division as a gunnery officer. I didn't realize what this entailed, so I said I would be happy to be considered for it. He sent me the papers to complete, which I did and returned them to him.

When I received my orders I was an ensign assigned as a deck officer instead of a gunnery officer. I received them in April with instructions to report to Northwestern University in Chicago on May 12, 1942. They also instructed me as to how I was to proceed and to what I was required to purchase for my uniforms. There were many things I needed to do to get ready to leave.

I left the Salt Lake Union Pacific Depot by train in my dress-blue uniform with a white cap cover. Many of my family and relatives were at the station to see me off to the navy.

Jack Ollinger of Salt Lake City was also going to the same place for the same reasons. He wasn't wearing his uniform. Our instructions were to report for duty in our uniforms, so I was doing what I thought I should.

We arrived at Grand Central Station in Chicago. My first time in my uniform I didn't really know whom I should salute. As we passed a doorman at a hotel, all dressed up in his bright colorful uniform, Jack said jokingly, "You better salute him."

We reported at Tower Hall, a dormitory of Northwestern University, and were assigned rooms on the thirteenth floor. Here we slept, ate our meals, studied, etc. A swimming pool was available for our use. We would line up in formation and march across Michigan Avenue past the old Water Tower, which, we were told, was where Mrs. O'Leary's cow kicked over a lantern and started the great Chicago fire. We would find our places in the classroom and sit down. Someone would call, "Attention!" We would rise sharply from our seats to attention. The teacher would come in and get settled behind the rostrum and someone would shout, "Seats!" and we would all drop to our seats. This sort of activity was entirely new to me.

We studied seamanship, signaling, flags and their meaning, rules of the road, navigation, parts of the ship, safety, communications, first aid, navy etiquette, etc., etc.

Being a "dry-landlubber" I wasn't sure of the difference between the bow and the stern. Many officers from the East Coast owned their own boats, had used navigation, and knew many rules of the road. It was a new world to me. We were given large assignments to study. Each Friday we would have written tests on what we had studied. If we failed our test, our name would appear on "The Tree." If your name appeared more than three times you were dismissed and sent home, so it was a constant fear and important to stay off "The Tree."

We completed our course in ninety days and were known as "The Ninety-Day Wonders." We were told by our teachers that we had covered in ninety days, briefly, what it took those at Annapolis four years to cover.

Upon graduation each officer was interviewed by one of the administration and given an assignment along with orders. I was assigned to amphibious warfare and to the USS *Henry T. Allen*, an amphibious transport which was a luxury liner, one of the President Luxury Liners, which was being converted. At that time amphibious warfare was new to the navy and we hadn't heard about it. The officer who interviewed me said to keep my assignment to myself. That night Ollinger and I happened to be in top bunks across from each other. Ollie whispered to me and asked where I was assigned. I told him to an amphibious transport. He said, "Me too."

We left Chicago by train with orders to report to the USS *Henry T. Allen* in San Francisco with a few days leave en route. I spent this time in Ephraim with my folks. I met Ollinger in Salt Lake City and we went by train to San

Francisco, to find out that our ship had gone to San Diego. Our orders were changed so we went by train to San Diego where we boarded the ship we were to live on. It was a large ship with one thousand two hundred crew and had the capacity to carry two thousand troops. It had thirty-six landing barges on its decks. At that time I had no idea what I was getting into. We were each assigned to a stateroom and were introduced to the officer to whom we were to report. From here on I was in the real navy.

At first I wondered how much sea life was under the surface in case we were torpedoed. Later I realized that when the sea was calm, it was just like riding down the street in a car, but much larger, forgetting that there might be sea life under the surface. The USS *Henry T. Allen* was just like a city. You would go from one deck to the other for different services, e.g., laundry, ship's store, barbershop, "ge-dunks" (soft ice cream in a cup) at 1600 (4:00 P.M.). I was told that in the navy you were not to wear rings which might get caught in handling equipment, etc., and cause you to lose a finger.

After a few days of training and making trial landings in Monterey Bay we received orders to sail. We were steaming west. I thought we might be going to Hawaii. When our orders were opened the next day we headed for the Panama Canal. The captain doesn't always know where the ship is going until he opens his orders after one day at sea. From here it was all an adventure for me.

In school I had read about the Panama Canal and now I was having the opportunity to see and sail through it. Our ship was so large that as we were going through the locks there were only a couple of feet clearance on each side. The "mules," small tractors on each side, guided us through. We steamed through the Caribbean on our way to Norfolk, Virginia. We were in convoy with other ships. German submarines had been known to be in the Caribbean.

My first excitement aboard ship was when General Quarters was sounded. This meant for everyone to report to his battle station. The first signal was a rapid ringing of the bell. Then a pause. One single ring indicates fire forward, two rings, amidships, and three rings meant fire aft. This fire signal indicated there was a fire forward and it was announced that it was in the forward magazine. The magazine is where explosives are stored. As I could type I was assigned to work part-time in Communications in the decoding shack, which happened to be my battle station. My main assignment was as a deck officer and I also spent time in the pilot house directing the ship's course.

At General Quarters one puts on his life jacket, metal helmet, and web belt carrying his 45 pistol. The decoding machines are top secret. The communications officer was putting secret documents and codes in canvas bags with holes and weighted with lead so they would sink if thrown overboard. I was given an axe, which hung outside the door of the shack and stood ready to destroy the decoding machines by knocking them to pieces if necessary. Our ship lagged behind the other ships. A destroyer stayed with us to protect us. The signal to leave our battle stations was sounded, indicating that the fire was under control. We caught up with the other ships and proceeded on our course to Norfolk.

As we approached Norfolk the blades of our port turbine were stripped, which required extensive repair at the Norfolk shipyards. It would take some time to repair this turbine so the crew and the officers were assigned to certain training schools on the base.

Not long after that our ship received troops and orders to leave Norfolk at a certain date and time. After we had been at sea for one day the captain opened the orders and was instructed to steam to a certain rendezvous point. As we approached the designated area we saw many types of ships steaming from every direction. Each ship had its specified positions in a huge convoy. The ships ranged from battleships to tugs. We had loaded army personnel at Norfolk. We were told we were on our way to North Africa to make the first amphibious landing of the war. Our course was in zigzag patterns, shifting at different intervals to confuse any submarines which might see or follow us. En route I stood watches in the pilot house as a deck officer, calling out turns according to the zigzag pattern of the day so that the engine room would know what we were doing. The helmsman would turn when told the degree, as I would direct him on my watch. All the ships in the convoy would turn the same degree and at the same time together. It was a great sight to watch them.

One day the telemotor on our ship went out, meaning that we had no control of the rudder from the pilot house to guide the ship. It was necessary for us to leave to leave our formation and stay behind with a destroyer to protect us until the repair was made. I was on duty in the pilot house. The chief engineer came up to repair the telemotor. Up until now I thought I was a good sailor and hadn't been seasick. The sea was rough and the engineer lit up a cigar and I headed for the rail. I was doing my best to keep from "tossing my cookies" but the smell of the cigar triggered my fast move to the rail.

We were to make our landing at daybreak on November 8, 1942. The troops as well as the crew were given instructions while under way. This date had been chosen so the surf for our landing should be the most calm. Surveys had been studied for forty years, as the surf was usually high on these beaches on which we were to make the landing. On the afternoon of November seventh the sea was really rough. An alternative plan was considered to go through the Straits of Gibraltar and make a landing at French Morocco on the north coast of Africa or to continue on the west coast to have some ships land troops at Casablanca, some at Rabat, north of Casablanca, and some at Port Leyoty, north of Rabat. Toward evening it was decided to continue with the original plan. Our ship was to land at Port Leyoty. After dark we were steaming with our ships "blacked out." We were going south and we saw an excursion ship all lighted up approaching us from the south. Men from our convoy boarded the excursion ship and took over their communications so that they could not radio ahead to alert the French about our landing. At the exact time we were to make the landing President Roosevelt was to make the announcement over the radio that U.S. troops were making a landing in North Africa to fight the French.

Our ship prepared to land troops at the mouth of the Wady Sebu River. A French fort was located on a hill above the mouth of the river. I was the officer in charge of a boat crew of a personnel-landing boat. Our ship had thirty-six landing boats on its deck, had a crew of one thousand two hundred, and carried two thousand troops. The boats were lowered. We took our positions in the water at certain locations about the ship. A group of boats would circle in their designated spots until receiving a signal from the ship. We were called in alongside the ship to rope nets where the army troops would climb down from the ship into our boat. When all were in the boats we proceeded to a line of debarkation and at the appointed time we headed toward the beach in column and then abreast. Scouts had gone ashore earlier in rubber rafts and directed different colored lights seaward, marking the beach on which we were assigned to land.

The time came for us to take the troops ashore. Our battleship and cruiser began firing on the French fort. It took them by surprise. After awhile they returned our fire. Our course from the ship to the shore and return was between the firing of the ships and the fort. It was exciting and made us nervous to be in a boat carrying troops, equipment, or supplies under this path of artillery. The surf was much rougher than had been expected. When a personnel boat would hit the beach the coxswain would release the bow and the soldiers would run out onto the beach. He would then try to hurry and back off. Often before he was able to back off another large wave would hit the stern and push the boat farther up onto the beach.

The clouds were very low. We could hear their planes but could not see them. They could no doubt see us as they strafed our troops, which had been landed. They would also strafe the landing boats as they returned to the ship with the wounded or took supplies, jeeps, etc., ashore. When we couldn't see their strafing planes I had thoughts of what a good time I had had with Enid before leaving and really hoped I would get back okay. During the landing my boat crew and I were in the landing boat continuously for thirty-six hours. On occasion I would wake up, as my knees would buckle on my way to the deck from standing so long. The tugs were to pull the landing boats off the beach, which had been pushed up so far by large waves, but this was impossible. Therefore, the Navy had to leave fifty-six of the stranded boats on the beach.

Our ship was loaded with bombs, high-test airplane gasoline, ammunition, and metal airstrip matting. After the troops and equipment, etc., were landed we were to take gasoline up the Wady Sebu River to the airport we had captured.

Two amphibious transports at Rabat had been torpedoed and sunk by German submarines. We were ordered to Casablanca, passing Rabat on the way, to unload the rest of our cargo. The French had scuttled their ships in the Casablanca harbor so it was very difficult to get in there and unload. We were alongside the *Susan B. Anthony* hospital ship on our port side and had to unload bombs on her decks, which were carried away on the backs of Arabs. On the starboard side we unloaded ammunition onto lighters (flat barges). I was surprised when I saw the boxes of ammunition had come from the Ogden, Utah, arsenal.

We fought for three days. An armistice was signed between the French and the Americans on November 11, 1942. This was quite a coincidence. Now I could celebrate two armistices.

Another convoy of ships was due, bringing food and supplies, so we were ordered to leave Casablanca to make room for them and to return to the States before we could be completely unloaded. We carried three hundred tons of airstrip metal matting back with us. On the way back we ran into a very rough sea, which buckled some of the plates on the side of a battleship. The waves were so high the tugs had to go through them as they could not go over them.

We were glad to get back to the good old U. S. of A. We had had a rough time since leaving Norfolk and thought everyone back home would have known about our landing but very few did.

While we were making our landing in North Africa all of our mail, Christmas cards, letters, and packages, had accumulated and had been saved for us. The ship was loaded with combat troops, many of whom were convicts, and our orders were to proceed to the Panama Canal. We spent Christmas Eve there in Cristobal. Since we had combat troops aboard no one was allowed to go ashore except our communications officer, who took the secret codes for the Atlantic Ocean and turned them in for secret codes for the Pacific Ocean. Jack Ollinger and I hadn't opened our Christmas mail and packages in Norfolk but planned to open them Christmas Eve. I took all of mine to Jack's stateroom and we each opened our mail and packages together. I was amused when I opened a package and found a white woolen sweater. We were near the Equator. It was really hot.

Among my letters was a telegram from my good friend, Max Neff Smart, telling me that BYU had beaten the University of Utah in football for the first time in many, many years. Our friend, Floyd Millet, was the coach. After opening mail and being a bit nostalgic, Jack and I went up to the pilot house and turned on the public address system, and Jack said, "Now hear this, this is Santa Claus, Merry Christmas!" We quickly went back to his stateroom before anyone found out who Santa was. The next morning when we were out on the deck we saw a nest of our submarines docked alongside each other. On the top of each one there were many stocks (bunches) of green bananas.

It was a big day when we crossed the equator for the first time about five days after leaving Panama. Many of the crew had crossed it before. Those of us who hadn't were at the mercy of those who had. They remembered how they had been initiated and made sure to make it tough for us who hadn't. A shellback is one who has crossed the equator and has been duly initiated. The initiation consisted of the following activities conducted by shellbacks:

A wind scoop of white canvas with diameter of about three feet and about thirty feet long, sewed as a tube, open at each end with a wide piece of canvas at one end was used to direct fresh cooler air when under way to the enlisted men's or troop's headquarters. It hung from topside and lowered to serve the men below. We were to crawl on our hands and knees through this canvas tube. To keep us moving they could hit us on the rump with sandbags. I was about halfway through when those in front of me stopped and those in back of me kept coming. It was hard to breathe and I was getting claustrophobia. Those beating us with the sand bags kept hitting. I later discovered that at the front of the tube someone had a fire hose squirting salt water into the face of each one as he was coming out. I felt relieved when I got out alive. One then took me to a bench and rubbed a salve of asafoetida, which had a horrible, putrid smell, on my body. I was then led to the barber chair where they were to cut my hair short, finger height. The barber put his hand flat on my head and instead of cutting above his fingers he cut below, leaving about a quarter of an inch of hair above my forehead, which necessitated getting a new haircut later. The barber chair was balanced on a metal rail and was wired electrically. My clothes were wet and they gave me an electric shock. On the deck below was a pool of water about three feet deep and ten feet square. Someone tripped the barber chair so I fell backward to the deck below, landing in the pool. Two or three shellbacks were in the water. One pushed my head under water and asked, "What do you say?" I didn't know what to say. No one had told me what to expect. They kept pushing my head under water and asking me what I should say. Finally I asked what I should say and one said, "Say shellback," which I did and they let me climb out of the pool. All this happened while I was blindfolded. Before I entered the wind scoop they had tied a blindfold over my eyes. This was a day to remember. I was now a full-fledged shellback. Later I received a two-and-a-half-inch by four-inch wallet-size card to carry in my wallet with the following wording to prove I was a shellback:

ANCIENT ORDER OF THE DEEP
This is to certify that
ENSIGN C. R. PETERSON

Has Been Gathered to Our Fold and Duly Initiated
A TRUSTY SHELLBACK
Having Crossed the Equator on Board the
U.S.S. HENRY T. ALLEN
Bound from Panama, C.Z. to Southwest
Pacific to help lick the Japs.
30 Dec., 1942, in Latitude 000"00" and Longitude 100W
DAVY JONES   NEPTUNUS REX
His Majesty's Scribe   Ruler of The Raging Main
Signed: P.A. Stevens

Our next stop was at Pago Pago, Samoa, to refuel. I went ashore with the communications officer to pick any mail for the ship. Later we disembarked the troops at Guadalcanal and picked up war-weary troops and took them to Wellington, New Zealand, for rest and recreation. We stayed there for a few days so we had some shore leave. The favorite soft drink there was sarsaparilla (root beer), which they called "lolly water." One day I was officer of the day when Carl Jones, a good friend of mine from BYU, came up the gangplank with "Officer Messenger Mail." We were both surprised to see each other in New Zealand. We went ashore one time.

Next we sailed to Australia, stopping at Melbourne, Sydney, and Brisbane. Two Australian amphibious ships joined the *Henry T. Allen*. Our assignment was to train the Australian troops in American warfare. This we did at Redcliff, about seventeen miles north of Brisbane where there was a good beach for practice landings. Each Monday we would take on new troops with their simulated supplies and gear. They received training to make a real landing later. Each Friday just before midnight we would prepare to make the landing at dawn on the beach. General Quarters was sounded. We would go to our battle stations. Personnel landing boats were lowered, each with a boat crew of three and one officer. I was always the officer in one of the boats. When a boat would hit the water it would go to a designated position near the ship and circle until called alongside the ship to the disembarking rope-net where the troops would climb down from the main deck into the boat. The boat would then return to its original circle. There were two circles near the bow, two amidships, and two near the stern, or three on the starboard (right) side and three on the port (left) side, making a total of six circles. A boat would be called to the net by a blinking flashlight. This routine was followed until all the troops were loaded into the landing boats. They would then proceed in column and then abreast toward the beach they had been assigned to land on, which was designated by a colored light shining seaward. The landings were made at dawn.

After the troops with all their equipment had been taken ashore the boats would return to the ship and were hoisted aboard. The ship was scrubbed down and prepared for the next troops to come aboard the following Monday. After the ship was clean, all of the crew in their dress uniforms were permitted to go ashore at 1600 until 0800 Monday morning, except those who stayed to stand their watches.

Whenever a large number of troops were trained we would transport them to New Guinea and land them on the beach at Oro Bay. The next group we landed at Finschhaven, another at Humbolt and Tanamara Bay, all on the east coast of New Guinea. These areas were in the jungle.

Because we were in a malaria-infested area we were all required to take atabrine pills. Atabrine is a drug used in the treatment of malaria; it does not cure the disease but suppresses the symptoms so that the malaria victim can keep active. Malaria is a severe disease which attacks man in tropical and subtropical countries, and also in temperate regions during the summer months. It causes more deaths than any other disease in the world. In India alone there are over one hundred million cases and more than one million deaths from malaria every year. The parasites which cause malaria in man are carried and spread by female *anopheles* mosquitoes. There is no way of knowing whether I had malaria since the symptoms were suppressed by taking atabrine. Anyone who has taken atabrine in the tropics is not eligible to give blood to be given to anyone else, so when the Red Cross drive comes along it doesn't include me. When ashore in Cairns, Australia, I would sleep on a cot with a frame to hold mosquito net over me.

Drinking water was a very important item on the ship. While at sea our evaporator water tanks were to be 100 percent full in case of emergency. We showered in salty seawater that required special soap to get any kind of lather. Sometimes we were restricted to use fresh water two times a day, fifteen minutes each. Two officers were assigned to a stateroom with double bunks. The one with the higher rank got the bottom bunk. Each had his own desk-type safe with a combination lock. Instead of doors to our stateroom we had non-inflammable material hanging from a rod.

For a while our ships went to Sydney and left some of us officers ashore at Cairns, which is located near the northeast corner of Australia. Our office was in a lumber home built on stilts as all homes were built in that area for ventilation because of high humidity. About five miles from our office, on the beach, was an air force rest hotel where pilots would come for a few days to rest. It was called "Yorkey's Knob." On the way we would just miss running over small kangaroos called wallabies. Sometimes we would see a python crawling across the road. The USO would send entertainers to the South Pacific to put on shows for the servicemen. We were at Yorkey's Knob one time when John Wayne and others were practicing their show. We would eat our meals at the same table with them. They stayed there for a few days. We would go there each afternoon after we completed our work in the office. John Wayne and I became friends.

We went swimming at night in the Coral Sea just off the beach and inside the shark nets, which were metal nets suspended by floating metal drums which were supposed to keep the sharks out for the safety of swimmers. We wondered what would happen if a shark happened to get inside the net and couldn't get out. As we swam at night the water would light up with fluorescence. It was strange but interesting.

During some of our training Australian troops in American warfare I was assigned to go aboard the *Westralia*, an Australian amphibious transport in our group, to decode messages on a decoding machine which I took with me from the *Henry T. Allen* so they would get the same messages that our ship received. It was an unusual experience. They received me all right. I required a separate room with a key that only I had as the machine and the codes I was responsible for were "top secret." I would decode messages and would spend time at the bar, something American ships do not have. We were served meals of many courses. When I thought the meal was over they would bring in many kinds of cheese and crackers. It was a good experience but I was glad to get back to the *Henry T. Allen* with my friends. Friends in Australia are called "cobbers" or "diggers." They called us "Yankees."

After two years of being in Australia our assignment of training Australian troops in American warfare and making landings in New Guinea was complete and the USS *Henry T. Allen*, nicknamed by our crew while fighting the Japs, *Hank T. Maru* (Japanese ships were named "Maru"), was ordered back to San Francisco, California, U.S. of A.! En route we stopped at Pearl Harbor.

At San Francisco we were ordered to load barrels of oil to deliver to the island of Kwajalain. It took several days to get there. While the ship was being unloaded some of us would go ashore and pick up interesting shells. Some of them were very unusual and pretty. The island was flat and small. It was an atoll. On the way back to San Francisco, as we were passing Hawaii, it was announced that we were nearly out of ship's fuel, but we took a chance and made it to the mainland. We were told we had used more fuel to take our cargo to Kwajalain than the barrels of oil we left there.

At San Francisco, after being on the USS *Henry T. Allen* for over two years in Australia, I was given a short leave with orders to return to San Diego. I spent a few days at home. When I reported to San Diego I was assigned to a different ship, the USS *Randall*, with Commodore Gluting as my captain and an entirely new crew. Here I made friends with the supply officer, Bruce McClellan. While on this ship we went to many islands: Eniwetok, New Caledonia, Ulithi (known as "The Enchanted Isle of the Pacific"), the Philippines, Iwo Jima, Espirito Santos, Bougainville, Okinawa, etc.

My brother, Knute, was commander of the LST 897 (landing ship tank). I hadn't seen him in several years but knew the vessel he was commander of. One day outside the Philippines I noticed a convoy of LSTs steaming toward us, which would pass about two hundred yards to our port. The lead

LST was number 897. I quickly asked the captain if I could have the signal-men send a message to my brother. We were steaming in opposite directions and passing quickly. The message was sent but Knute was not on the bridge at the time. By the time he got the message the distance between us was too great to return a message. Later we discovered that our ships were at the same island, Ulithi. I invited him over to the USS *Randall* for dinner. We were glad to see each other again and had a good visit bringing each other up to date on what had happened since we last met.

Iwo Jima was an island about a mile wide and five miles long, low at one end and steep to the other. It was a volcanic island with many caves that the Japs lived in during the day and would come out of at night. American troops had a very bloody battle before they conquered it. We arrived a few days after our troops had landed there. We saw many Jap bodies floating around the island. We also saw many sharks swimming just off the beach. This was an important island to have conquered. Huge B-52 bomber planes would fly from Guam on their way to bomb Japan. They needed fighter plane escorts so they picked them up at Iwo Jima. The fighters couldn't fly as far as the bombers without running out of fuel. We saw many bombers returning covered with oil and with some of their engines not working. The army password was LOLLAPALOOZA. If a sentry asked for the password and received RARRAPAROOZA the Jap was shot.

While we were anchored at Purple Beach at Naha Bay, Okinowa, a typhoon was forecast. As our skipper was SOP (Senior Officer Present), he was in charge of the twenty-seven ships in the bay. One morning about 0200 an officer came to my stateroom, woke me up, and asked how I would like to go to each of the twenty-seven ships in the bay with a boat crew and typhoon sailing instructions. I told him, "Not too well." He said the captain wanted me and a boat crew to deliver these instructions as soon as I could get dressed. At the time the rain was going horizontal because of the strong wind. I was given twenty-seven envelopes, one for each ship in the bay. I was to give these instructions to no one except the captain and was to get his signature. The boat crew of three and I, with ship's sailing orders in a rub-berized bag, got into a small lifeboat. The sea was very rough with waves about thirty feet high. Lowering the boat was very treacherous as we were to be detached from the davit, which held the boat, at the exact same time as we were hanging from a chain on the bow and a chain on the stern. If one chain were to be detached sooner than the other the boat would dive into the water. The boat was to be detached as the wave reached its crest. Luckily we got in the water okay and we proceeded to the first ship.

All of the gangways were up and a rope "Jacob's Ladder" was lowered amidships of each ship. Our boat would come alongside the ship. I would wait until the boat was on the crest of the wave, then hurry and grab the rope ladder and climb as fast as I could before the boat came up on the next wave, which might have crushed me. It was raining and water from the deck would come from the scupper down into my face as I looked up while climbing the ladder. I would ask the officer of the deck to let me see the captain. I would give him the envelope containing instructions, get his signature, climb down the ladder and get in rhythm with the boat and when it was on top of the wave I would jump into the boat. This was all done in the dark and with a flashlight.

After reaching seventeen of the ships it was raining and blowing so hard it was difficult to see. There were large coral rocks just below the surface of the water we needed to avoid so the crew and I decided to go ashore and contact the other ships when the storm subsided. We radioed a message to our ship that we had delivered seventeen sailing instructions but had gone ashore as it was difficult for us to see and that we would contact the rest of the ships when the storm quieted down. The ship radioed back saying they had already gone to sea and for us to stay ashore till they returned. We stayed there for three days living on C rations we found in the boat. We found shelter in an abandoned box-type truck body. Our shoes and clothes were wet and we didn't take them off until we returned to the ship. The typhoon blew most of the tents and barracks on the island over. It was a frightening experience! We were glad to get back on the ship after three days ashore during the storm.

We were at Okinawa when the treaty was signed and the war was over! For several nights after the treaty was signed the ships in the harbor were covered with a cloud of smoke at dusk. General Quarters was sounded and we remained there for half an hour, as Japanese kamikazes didn't seem to know the war was over and they would dive towards our ships. One hit a battleship two days after the treaty was signed. The smoke screen was to cover the ships so they could not be spotted by the kamikazes.

Our ship received orders to proceed to Hong Kong, China, to transport Chinese Nationalist troops from Hong Kong to Manchuria. We docked at Kowloon, just across the bay from Hong Kong. En route to Hong Kong I heard that cigarettes were valuable for trading purposes in China. However, since I didn't smoke I wasn't aware there had been a rush on the ship's store for cigarettes. When I tried to buy some cartons for trading purposes I was told that there had been such a run on them they had stopped selling them. Smokers had already filled their safes with them. Ship's liberty was at 1600. As we would leave the ship small children, who looked like orphans, would line up and ask the sailors, " No mama, no papa, no chow chow," and hold out their hands for money. At night we would see them lying in a doorway with a brick for a pillow and a gunnysack for a cover.

It was interesting to see the Chinese troops come aboard carrying rice in a canvas tube-like sack about six feet long and three inches in diameter around their necks. Some brought aboard a live chicken in a cage. On our way north on the Yellow Sea it was interesting at lunch time to see men bring large baskets of cooked rice on their backs which they would set on the deck. Soldiers would come and fill their bowls, then sit in a circle around a pot of "stew" and with their chopsticks reach in and pick out some meat, a vegetable, etc., and would eat with their rice. One night one of their soldiers died. Many would chant weird tunes all during the night.

As we approached Manchuria we were told they would not let the admiral or any of the troops in, so we disembarked them at Chinwangtau, where the Great Wall of China goes down into the sea. It was a great sight! We returned to Kowloon, stopping at Tsingtau for a couple of days en route. Here it was interesting to see single merchants sitting on the sidewalks selling their wares from large, square pieces of material. This seemed to be illegal as when they saw or heard of a policeman coming they would grab the four corners of the material, throw it over their backs and run. Not long after the policeman left they would return, rearrange their goods on the material and continue their sales as if nothing had happened. As we approached Kowloon it was interesting to see Junk Bay, where the poorer class of people lived on "junks." Their sails were made of scraps of different materials sewn together. They would make fires on their small boats on which to cook. They would do their washing, etc., and just survive. There were hundreds of junks in the bay.

Many officers and enlisted men on our ship had enough points to be discharged from the Navy to civilian life. We received orders to return to the United States. We took the northern route home, passing Hawaii, and landed in Tacoma, Washington. It was in December 1945. I had been wondering what I would do when I was discharged as it was winter and I had no job, as my job of Alumni General Secretary had been filled by someone else. I called Mom and Dad to let them know I would be home for Christmas and then called Kiefer B. Sauls, Treasurer and Purchasing Agent of Brigham Young University, to see if there might be an opening in his office for me. He said he had nothing at that time but might have later. Captain Gluting had asked if I would remain with him and help process discharge papers for the crew. When we arrived at Tacoma there was a letter in the mail, which happened to be my discharge papers. I told Captain Gluting that I would be happy to remain with him if he could make arrangements for my discharge to be delayed. He was successful. My orders then were to report to the Motor Torpedo Base at San Diego, where I had previously reported before I went aboard the USS *Randall*, with a few days' leave en route. I was home for Christmas and really enjoyed being there. I was to report at San Diego on January 2, 1946. I left home on December 31, 1945, and was at the publicized corner of Hollywood and Vine Streets in Los Angeles on New Year's Eve. It was pandemonium with people in the streets with horns and kissing each other if they knew them or not. If a car tried to drive down the street people would bang on it with their hands. I met a naval officer there who was also planning to go to the Rose Parade in Pasadena and to the Rose Bowl football game so we had a cab take us to Pasadena, where Colorado Street was lined on both sides, several deep, by people who had come to the Rose Parade. It was hard to believe how the beautiful floats were made of flowers.

I had heard so much about the Rose Bowl football game on New Year's Day and I was lucky enough to obtain tickets for it. It was a beautiful sight. Since I had been up all night I caught myself dozing during the game. After the game I caught a bus for San Diego and reported on time the next morning.

NAVY TRAVELS, WORLD WAR II:

Panama:	Canal Zone—Colon, Panama City, Balboa
North Africa:	French Morocco—Port Leyoty, Waude Sebu River, Rabat, Casablanca
United States:	San Francisco, Norfolk, San Diego
Samoa:	Pago Pago, Tutuila
New Caledonia	
New Zealand:	Wellington
Bora Bora:	Eniwetok
Efate	
Ulithi:	Mog Mog—"The Enchanted Isle of the Pacific"
Bougainvillea:	Torakina Point, Empress Augusta Bay
Australia:	Melbourne, Sydney, Brisbane, Toowoomba, Townsville, Cairns, Yorkey's Knob
New Guinea:	Milne Bay, Cape Sudest, Finschaven, Hollandia, Humboldt Bay, Tana Merah Bay, Aitape—combat
Goodenough Island:	Beli Beli, Cola Cola
Hawaiian Islands:	Oahu, Maui
Kwajelain	
Iwo Jima:	combat—amphibious
Guam	
Philippines:	Manila
Okinawa:	Naha (Purple Beach), Buckner Bay—combat—amphibious
China:	Hong Kong, Kowloon, Taku Bar, Chinwangtao, The Great Wall, Yellow Sea, Tsingtao
Hawaiian Islands:	Hawaii: Hilo, Punaluu Black Sand Beach, Kona Maui: Kahului, Lahaina (Whaling Center and original capital of Hawaii), The Needle Kauai: Lihue, Kapaau, Hanalei Oahu: Honolulu, Kailua, Laie, Waimea, Waialua, Kaneohe, Pearl City, Wahiawa, countryside
Mediterranean Cruise:	Greece: Athens, Piraeus, Corinth, countryside Crete: Herakleon Egypt: Alexandria, Memphis, along the Nile River, Cairo, Pyramids, Sphinx, countryside Israel: Haifa, Nazareth, Capernaum, Sea of Galilee, River Jordan, Tiberius, Jericho, Kidron Valley, Mount of Olives, Jerusalem, Bethlehem, Masada, Dead Sea, Dead Sea Scroll area, Caesarea, Nablus, Megiddo, countryside, Mormon's Shepard's Field, Ashdod

Cyrus
Patmos
Mykonos
Turkey: Ephesus
Delos

EUROPEAN TRAVELS England
Denmark
Sweden
Finland
Russia
Poland
East Germany (communist)
Germany
France
Holland
Switzerland
Italy
Spain

SOUTH SEAS Tahiti
New Zealand (north and south)
Australia
Bali
Thailand
Hong Kong
China
Japan
Taiwan

Combat Experience
Kamikaze plane hit ship and badly damaged it.

Neal commanded a landing craft and forty men ashore; returned with wounded in Okinawa combat.

Bronze Star of Honor—qualified for.

Typhoon—warned other ships.

North Africa—delivered troops ashore; loaded with wounded to be delivered to hospital ship, etc.; couldn't find it. Neal's ship left Mediterranean and went into Atlantic because of enemy submarines in Mediterranean; alone on amphibian boat three days before ship returned.

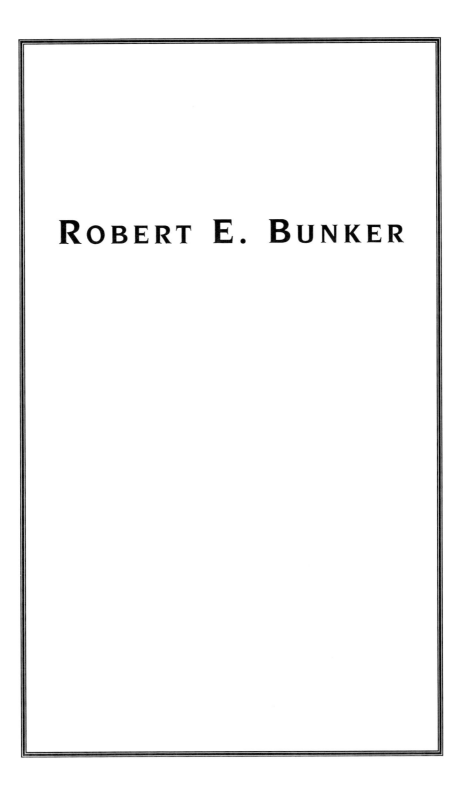

ROBERT E. BUNKER

Lt. Colonel Robert E. Bunker

Robert F. Barker with wife, Helen, and son, Robert F. Barker

MEET ROBERT E. BUNKER

He was born August 20, 1914, in Delta, Utah, into a family of eleven children and is now eighty-seven years old.

He played basketball and football in high school and college, graduating from Utah State University in Logan, Utah, with a degree in physical education, completed the Army Reserve Officer Training Corps, and was in the Army Reserve when the U.S.A. entered World War II. His reserve unit was then activated. He married Helen Palmer August 9, 1940. They had four children, two sons and two daughters. When he received his overseas orders and was leaving the U.S.A., his firstborn and then the only child, Robert, age three, promised his father he would "take care of [his] mother while his father was gone." He kept this promise.

The overseas assignment was as the commander of a 160-man anti-aircraft battery, one of five batteries in a 750-man anti-aircraft battalion This battalion was very mobile and flexible. All or part of the battalion could be assigned to armies in combat whenever the need arose to protect the combat troops and supplies from enemy aircraft. Bob's Dog Battery was assigned periodically to three different armies in combat: the Third Army, under the command of General George S. Patton, the Fifth Army, and the Seventh Army. Bob earned and received four Bronze Star medals.

Please note the letter from General George S. Patton which describes the accomplishments of the Third Army and what he expected from his troops; note his pride in his men and his humility for the honors his men created for him, the on-going responsibility he expected his men to fulfill, all for the destiny of the U.S.A. Lieutenant Colonel Bunker was a part of these remarkable achievements; as well as his achievements in the other two armies he was attached to. Note the respect and admiration Bob's commanding officers had for him while in the inactive reserves after the war.

Gruesome details have been intentionally omitted by Bob. He has only generally described a minimal amount of his combat experiences.

He remained in the Army Reserves after the war and served twenty-eight years, rising to the rank of Lieutenant Colonel, and commanded the Dale Rex Armory Hall Battalion located in Provo, Utah.

He was a coach and physical education instructor at BYU, retiring in 1979, after thirty years of service.

Bob is the first to acknowledge that he was protected and preserved by divine intervention combined with his faith in God all through World War II and much of his life. Being a very faithful and spiritual man, he recognizes his protected survival has enabled him to achieve his personal destiny and extend the destiny of the U.S.A. which he loves and serves.

We salute Lt. Colonel Robert E. Bunker.

At the request of Brother Tom Taylor and the unsolicited suggestion of my daughter Mary Ann, I shall try and relate some of the less gruesome involvements while serving in the military of the United States Army.

It all began in 1933 when I entered as a freshman at the Utah State Agricultural College. At that time, all able-bodied male students were required to take two years of military training—it being a land-grant institution, and if so interested and they could qualify could enroll in the advanced course. Upon completion and graduation they would receive the grade of second lieutenant in the Army Reserve of the United States Army. This became my lot.

In the late 1930s when Germany began its invasion of the European countries, and later Great Britain, the United States became concerned about becoming involved and began calling up reserve components of the military to serve for one year's active duty. September 1, 1940, I was called up to serve a year in the military service as a second lieutenant and then as the year escalated the one year of military service was extended to the end of World War II. When I was terminated from active duty, and placed back on reserve, at that time I had served five and a half years in the active army.

I think that becoming a patriot of this great country began in my junior year at Utah State while at a military summer camp training at Fort Warden, Washington. One evening at the conclusion of the day's activities and standing at parade rest and in ranks at the retreat formation, I observed a battleship steaming down the strait of Puget Sound with its stars and stripes fluttering in the breeze as it moved toward Seattle. I felt a tingling impulse running up and down my spine that has been with me until this day.

In 1940 as a lieutenant I began my active military training as a Professor of Military Science and Tactics at Utah State Agricultural College in Logan, Utah. After two years there, I was relieved of my assignment by limited service personnel and sent to regular troop duty at the Harbor Defense of the Columbia River at Fort Stevens, Oregon.

After spending several months there, they disbanded the term "coast artillery," dividing it into field artillery or anti-aircraft artillery, and giving the officer personnel their choice as to which they would like to enter. At this time I had advanced to the rank of captain as a Battery Commander of a battery in the 567th Anti-Aircraft Battalion. After our units had trained for several months in Riverside, California, and the Mojave Desert, we then trained for maneuvers in Louisiana; from there to Savannah, Georgia, for more training; then to a port of entry at Camp Kilmore, New Jersey, ready to be shipped to Europe.

Upon reaching Camp Kilmore, all the battalion personnel were to receive a three-day pass before embarking for overseas duty. At this point, with certain situations that will come up at a later date, I should try to explain what an anti-aircraft battalion is. The personnel of the battalion is composed of 750 enlisted men and officers, of which headquarters battery had 110 personnel. The four fire batteries, A, B, C, and D, using the phonetic alphabet for transmitting purposes, are called Able, Baker, Charlie, and Dog. I was in command of Dog Battery.

Getting back to our issue of the three-day passes at Camp Kilmore, I was in the process of making out the passes for Dog Battery when I received word that Colonel Lamburton, the battalion commander, wanted to see me. When I arrived at headquarters, I was informed not to issue the passes for we had just received word that a ship was leaving the next day. They had room enough for our one battery and D Battery had been selected. The challenge was how to explain that kind of a situation to 160 GIs who had been deprived of their three-day pass in New York City.

Leaving the harbor and the Statue of Liberty that day I wondered if it would ever be my first and last look at it, making quite a mark on my mind. Our ship put to sea the next day—an armada of approximately twenty to twenty-four ships.

For the first four days at sea our ship was approximately in the center of the armada. On the morning of the fifth day when I awoke, I thought it strange it was such smooth sailing. I arose and looked out of the porthole and the only ship in sight was a U.S. destroyer circling our ship. We had had a rudder malfunction, according to one of the ship's crew, and it was a very eerie feeling. When the repair was completed and we again got under way, this destroyer left us and it wasn't until sometime during that night we caught up with the rest of the fleet. The rest of the voyage was rather uneventful except that the sick bay was usually full of land-loving GI Joes.

Our ship docked at Newport, Wales, and from there we were transported by train and truck to our bivouac area near the town of Leeds, England, waiting for the arrival of the other units of the battalion. The second day at the bivouac area I became more familiar with the often-quoted statement, "There is opposition in all things," or in other words, learning to take the bitter with the sweet. On that day I received a Red Cross telegram that my mother had died ten days earlier. A week later I received a letter from my wife Helen that we had a new addition to our family. Our second son had been born into this troubled world.

While waiting for the other units to arrive, I had the opportunity to visit London and there witness the destruction of buildings and hear the buzz bombs come over and explode in the city from across the channel on the other side.

The remainder of the battalion arrived ten days later. After acquiring our vehicles, armament, and supplies, we were convoyed to Southampton, England. We crossed the English Channel on a converted luxury liner, the SS *Longford*, arriving on European soil in La Havre, France. Being a mobile unit, we were assigned duties with different organizations, being attached to units of the 7th Army, the 5th Army, and finally the 3rd Army under General Patton where we remained until the end of the war. As such, the 567th AA Automatic Weapon Battalion was in four different battles or campaigns: the Rhineland, Central Europe, Northern France, and the Ardennes, which included the Battle of the Bulge.

For clarification there were two different size guns in the anti-aircraft artillery: the 90-mm gun and the 40-mm gun with 50-caliber machine gun. The 90-mm weapons were for high-flying enemy aircraft. The 40-mm were for the strafing or low-flying attack planes. The 567 Battalion employed the 40-mm weapons.

As we began our trek across the war-torn countries of Europe, we touched the borders of Holland, went through Belgium, and returned through parts of France and then on into Germany. Each day it seemed it was a new challenge, not knowing what would develop. On one particular occasion, we were to defend a bridge crossing of a river and I had my headquarters located in an abandoned house near the bridge. The windows of the house were mostly broken out with just wooden shutters in place and held out some of the cold.

My executive officer and I had unfolded our cots in one of the rooms. He was under a window and I was in a corner of the room with a nail hanging directly over my head on which I hung my valpack. During the night a large enemy artillery gun began shelling the area. One of the shells hit the frozen ground, exploding a short distance from the house, and a piece of the shrapnel came through the window, breaking many of the wooden shutters, and broke the strap holding my valpack which was directly above my head. It came down on top of me. My executive officer and I were soon out of our sleeping bags and down in the basement of that home, waiting till the shelling was over. I thought I might qualify for a Purple Heart, but you know I couldn't find a scratch on me.

Another interesting incident occurred while we were deployed around Third Army Headquarters in Luxembourg. This particular day I heard a groan of an airplane that soon appeared at about twenty thousand feet overhead. Soon one of the 90-mm gun stations nearby began firing at it. Soon a black stream of smoke appeared and the plane began to descend in a spiraling fashion. Soon two white parachutes could be seen floating down carrying their occupants. I could see one of them was trying to land in an open area near where I was located. I said to my jeep driver, "Come on, let's go capture us an enemy pilot." We reached his point of landing just as he was gathering up his parachute. I noticed from his uniform that he wasn't an enemy at all, but a British pilot. He climbed aboard my jeep and we took off toward the battalion headquarters. On the way he wanted to know who it was that had shot him down. I told him that it was one of our own United States units and that he had entered an I.A.Z. zone which meant that he was in a restricted area and must be required to give identification and unless identified he was an enemy. He told me that he was just returning from his bombing run and that he had lost his communication through enemy fire. That is why he couldn't identify himself as he passed over this restricted area. I never forgot his comments. On the way he said to me, "That was blooming good shooting, boys, that was blooming good shooting!" After leaving him in the hands of the personnel of the battalion, I have often wondered how and when he ever got back to England.

During Christmas, an event occurred which was very memorable for me. At this time the battalion had received orders for a new location some hundred kilometers distant, which required an advanced party to locate a position for the battalion. The advanced party consisted of the battalion commander and the four battery commanders. It was late in the day when we left. Darkness overtook us before we reached our required destination. We were in a small town when Colonel Lamburton decided we should stop for the night and to rendezvous the next morning at a set time. With my jeep driver and another enlisted man, we started to look for a suitable place to spend the night. After driving around for a short time we could smell smoke coming from somewhere, and after closer observation we detected the smoke coming out of a chimney. We decided that this was for us. After banging on the door of this house for some length of time, a small opening appeared. We abruptly pushed it wide open and moved into the room, discovering an old man and woman, a younger woman who had opened the door, and two small children, I would judge between the ages of six and four years old. I don't think I had ever seen anyone so frightened or frustrated. As those five individuals huddled in a group on one side of the room, I guess they had cause with those three men standing there with guns cocked and ready for action.

After assurance there was no one else in the house, we tried to communicate by hand signal and they didn't understand English or we understand German, except for a word or two. We had not eaten for quite some time during the day and we decided it was time for us to have some of our "C" rations. A "C" ration was something with different items such as Spam, hash, crackers, candy bars, etc., which was put into a box. We took the liberty of heating some of the rations on their stove, in which we had seen the smoke, and I kept glimpsing at our "host" out of the corner of my eye. The expression on their face was something else for me to behold. I had never seen anybody look so desperately hungry as these individuals were in this home.

I sent one of the enlisted men to go out to the jeep to bring in another box of rations. We opened up the box and placed it on the floor in front of them. A great change took place, a smile appeared on their faces. The elderly woman then got up, went to a cupboard, and brought out a small loaf of black bread. The only German I could remember was "Danke Schoen."

After our meal we indicated we wanted to sleep. They pointed to a room which we entered. We rolled out our sleeping bags, had a good night's rest, and met our rendezvous the next morning, bidding our German family goodbye with a smile on their face.

As I said before, there is opposition in all things. Approximately a week or ten days later, we were advancing through Germany. We ran across one of the concentration camps which had been liberated quite awhile before. All that was left were the buildings with a fence surrounding it, and you could not forget the odor remaining in that area. As you looked into the gas chambers, the stench in the building was something awful. I believe this was very opposite from what we had witnessed a short time before with our German family.

In Bastogne, Belgium, a terrific battle was taking place. The Germans had launched a new offensive drive. Before the Battle of the Bulge ended, there were approximately eighty-one thousand Americans killed. That ordeal was one for Patton's liberating forces. This time Dog Battery was sent into the Bulge for anti-aircraft protection for a supply depot. Going down the road into the Bulge, one could witness many tanks on both Allied and German units still burning after being hit by the opponent. It wasn't until late December that General Patton's Third Army lifted the siege around Bastogne.

I guess the two most dreadful means of destruction that often went through my mind was going through areas where mines had been planted. You never knew when your vehicle would blow up one of those mines, probably from the mine detail missing one or two in their search for them.

Another dreaded feeling I often had was the artillery fire we would encounter after we had emplaced our guns around a certain object we were to defend. It was something different to hear those shells come whizzing through the air and finally exploding. You hoped to be some distance from where they exploded.

I can now move to a more pleasant trend of thought that would be called mail call. I think this was one of the best morale-builders that a soldier looked forward to as he moved across the battlefields of Europe. Often the letters were two or three weeks old, but any written material that a soldier received was like manna from heaven. Another responsibility of the battery commander was to read all outgoing letters to make sure that information was not included that indicated the location of the troops in the war zone; morale matters were eliminated if they were derogatory, and many of these situations had to be cut out of the letter as it was sent forward. I, of course, was unable to read all of these letters that the men were forwarding, and relied on the executive officers to help me with this duty.

Speaking of letters, I think the most difficult task I ever encountered as an officer in the Army of the United States was to write home to the family of a deceased soldier under my command. Trying to put into words the loss that you could never express.

As the Allied army units drew near to Berlin they turned the Third Army south into Austria to alleviate trouble with the Russians who were advancing from the East. This was where we were when the war ended. We were located on the Danube River where we pitched our tents. As we bivouacked for a time, we were given the assignment to disarm the area in which we were located to make sure that no armament was left in the hands of any of the German people.

As the war ended, I often thought how fortunate I was to be among the living and I attribute much of that to my own prayers and the prayers of many of my family members and friends who I often felt were given in my behalf. After spending two weeks checking the surrounding area, we convoyed back to France while large camps of thousands of soldiers were being deployed back to the States. All the officers of the battalion were located in a large building in Epernay, France, and the enlisted men were detailed as mail personnel in these large staging areas. I had my first and only chance of attending an LDS sacrament meeting while I was in Europe. It was when I went on a pass to Paris on one weekend, and I happened to notice on a bulletin board where church services for the LDS people were meeting. This was held on a Sunday morning in a hall that had been a beer hall the night before, which shouldn't make any difference to the fifteen or so LDS people who were gathered there for sacrament meeting that day.

Because of my length of service, I was permitted to bid my good friends and Dog Battery goodbye, leaving Lieutenant Stoddard in charge. My jeep driver took me to Brussels, Belgium, where I boarded a troop ship to the U.S.A. It was a wonderful feeling and reunion when I arrived home to meet my wife and two young boys, one of them a year old and whom I had never laid eyes on before.

At that time I reverted back to the standing reserve. Four years later when I moved to Provo, I joined up with the regular reserve, finally retiring from military service as a lieutenant colonel after twenty-eight years of active and reserve service.

Brother Taylor, there were many other difficult and unpleasant events that took place during this year's time I spent in Europe during the war, but possibly this will give you a slight viewpoint of what took place for a particular soldier of the U.S. Army.

—Bob Bunker

SUPREME HEADQUARTERS
ALLIED EXPEDITIONARY FORCE

TO ALL MEMBERS OF THE ALLIED EXPEDITIONARY FORCE:

The task which we set ourselves is finished, and the time
has come for me to relinquish Combined Command.

In the name of the United States and the British Common-
wealth, from whom my authority is derived, I should like to
convey to you the gratitude and admiration of our two
nations for the manner in which you have responded to
every demand that has been made upon you. At times,
conditions have been hard and the tasks to be performed
arduous. No praise is too high for the manner in which
you have surmounted every obstacle.

I should like, also, to add my own personal word of thanks
to each one of you for the part you have played, and the
contribution you have made to our joint victory.

Now that you are about to pass to other spheres of activity,
I say Good-bye to you and wish you Good Luck and
God-Speed.

Dwight Eisenhower

GENERAL ORDERS

NUMBER   98

9 May 1945

SOLDIERS OF THE THIRD ARMY, PAST AND PRESENT

During the 281 days of incessant and victorious combat, your penetrations have advanced farther in less time than any other army in history. You have fought your way across 24 major rivers and innumerable smaller streams. You have liberated or conquered more than 82,000 square miles of territory, including 1500 cities and towns, and some 12,000 inhabited places. Prior to the termination of hostilities, you had captured in battle 956,000 enemy soldiers and killed or wounded at least 500,000 others. France, Belgium, Luxembourg, Germany, Austria, and Czechoslovakia bear witness to your exploits.

All men and women of the six corps and thirty-nine divisions that have at different times been members of this Army have done their duty. Each deserves credit. The enduring valor of the combat troops has been paralleled and made possible by the often unpublicized activities of the supply, administrative, and medical services of this Army and of the Communications Zone troops supporting it. Nor should we forget our comrades of the other armies and of the Air Force, particularly of the XIX Tactical Command, by whose side or under whose wings we have had the honor to fight.

In proudly contemplating our achievements, let us never forget our heroic dead whose graves mark the course of our victorious advances, nor our wounded whose sacrifices aided so much to our success.

I should be both ungrateful and wanting in candor if I failed to acknowledge the debt we owe to our Chiefs of Staff, Generals Gaffey and Gay, and to the officers and men of the General and Special Staff Sections of Army Headquarters. Without their loyalty, intelligence, and unremitting labors, success would have been impossible.

The termination of fighting in Europe does not remove the opportunities for other outstanding and equally difficult achievements in the days which are to come. In some ways the immediate future will demand of you more fortitude than has the past because, without the inspiration of combat, you must maintain ---by your dress, deportment and efficiency--- not only the prestige of the Third Army but also the honor of the United States. I have complete confidence that you will not fail.

During the course of this war I have received promotions and decorations far above and beyond my individual merit. You won them; I as your representative wear them. The one honor which is mine and mine alone is that of having commanded such an incomparable group of Americans, the record of whose fortitude, audacity, and valor will endure as long as history lasts.

s/ G. S. Patton, Jr.
t/ G. S. PATTON, JR.,
General

Reproduced by Hq 567th AAA AW Bn (Mbl)   17 May 1945

RÉPUBLIQUE FRANÇAISE

MINISTÈRE DE LA DÉFENSE
SECRÉTARIAT D'ÉTAT À LA DÉFENSE CHARGÉ DES ANCIENS COMBATTANTS

COMITÉ RÉGIONAL DE BASSE-NORMANDIE

DIPLÔME

En reconnaissance de la France envers les soldats des armées alliées engagés dans les combats du débarquement en Normandie et de la Libération 1944-1945

à M. **Robert E. Bunker**

CERTIFICATE IN RECOGNITION OF THE ALLIED SOLDIERS

WHO TOOK PART IN THE NORMANDY LANDING AND

CONTRIBUTED IN THE LIBERATION OF FRANCE

1944

1945

Le *30 Mai 2001*

Le Président du Comité Régional de Basse-Normandie

Le Secrétaire d'État à la Défense chargé des Anciens Combattants

Long Timers Award

This is to certify that

LIEUTENANT COLONEL ROBERT E. BUNKER, USAR

has been a loyal and dedicated member of this association for 40 years and is entitled to the respect and honor due to one whose loyalty and support have materially contributed to the achievement of ROA's missions and programs.

J. Milnor Roberts, Executive Director
Major General, USAR (Ret.)

1 OCTOBER 1979

Reserve Officers Association of the United States

29 November 1945

Captain Robert E. Bunker
278 East First South
Preston, Idaho

Dear Captain Bunker:

Your return to civilian life will bring forth your just pride in the contribution you have made to make our Nation again victorious. Without you and the others who, like you, left their normal lives to defend our country's principles, our cherished civilization would certainly have perished.

Your experiences and the friendships you have made will be a source of great pleasure to you for the rest of your life.

Your service as an officer has no doubt brought the responsibilities of citizenship forcibly to your attention and I am sure that you will assume these responsibilities with the same loyalty, devotion, and leadership which you have displayed in a military sense.

To the everlasting gratitude of our Nation, the Army and the Army Ground Forces, I add my personal sincere appreciation.

Sincerely,

JACOB L. DEVERS
General, USA
Commanding

WORLD WAR II ENDS
VISIT TO WENGEN, SWITZERLAND
5 AUGUST 1945

THE STONEWALL.
THE BATTERY ROLLING.
QUALIFICAMPSTEAD BREAK.
SAVANNAH, GA.
BEFORE PHOTOGRAPHER.

BOB ROAD JEEP WITH MOUNTED 30 CALIBRE
MACHINE GUN. TWO JEEPS PER BATTERY

Family tied to BYU football

By DICK HARMON
The Daily Herald

OREM — My goodness, have times changed for BYU football and the Crowton family.

Almost 50 years ago, Dave Crowton recruited Lincoln High star LaVell Edwards and lost him to Utah State. Now, the stadium bears Edwards' name.

When newly crowned BYU football coach Gary Crowton coaches his first football game in LaVell Edwards Stadium next fall, his 90-year-old grandfather will likely be a special guest in one of the luxury press box loges which are stocked with food, nice chairs, a Mitsubishi TV for replays, piped-in radio commentary, carpet and nice soft chairs.

Perched in that lofty setting, Dave Crowton will reflect back 50 years, before his grandson was born, a day he was a member of BYU's four-man coaching staff. He might as well have been on another planet.

Half a decade ago, Dave coached BYU football when every year the Cougars prayed for four- or five-win seasons. Today, it's considered a terrible year if BYU doesn't win at least six games and make a bowl appearance.

Dave, who lives in Orem's Seville apartments with his dog, Sherman IV, may be the ultimate authority on just how far

Courtesy photo

Seeing it all: The 1950 football coaching staff at BYU includes: Dave Crowton, left; head coach Chick Atkinson, center; Reed Neilson, right; and Bob Bunker, top. Almost 50 years later, Crowton, 90, sits with his family as he awaits the announcement of his grandson, Gary Crowton, as the new head football coach at BYU.

"When it came time to get my reimbursement check, I went to the bookkeeper and I was told the board of trustees hadn't approved for me to be paid to go around recruiting in my car."

Back in those days, BYU's coaches were P.E. teachers, who taught a whole slate of classes and then coached anywhere from one to four sports.

"It took me 20 years to make $5,000 a year.

"When I finally left BYU to take a job as head professional at the old Timpanogos golf course, President Ernest L. Wilkinson offered me $2,200 to stay."

Today, people pay $3,500 just for the right to buy tickets in the floor-level pit in the Marriott Center.

"The Y gave me more than I ever gave the Y," Dave said. "I still think BYU is one of the best

THOMAS S. TAYLOR

MY GUARDIAN ANGEL

by Thomas S. Taylor

As a World War II veteran in the U.S. Navy, I had numerous experiences that convinced me and gave me testimony that I had been preserved and protected from serious harm and death at a time when many of my buddies and friends were killed. A veteran who survives a war almost always asks himself why he was spared and survived but many of his companions were not. The gospel has taught me that all of us have an individual destiny within the Plan of Salvation and which includes our personal actions and conduct.

By further introspection, I have come to the conclusion that I have had and do have a "guardian angel" that has been very active in my entire life and has intervened to protect me on many occasions. My research and writing of my understandings of the Prophet Enoch over the last several years, together with the compilation of this Book of Faith, have taught and strengthened my conviction of the existence of my guardian angel. It is my belief that all of us have a guardian angel.

In the scriptures a guardian angel is defined as a "ministering angel." Heaven has intervened in the affairs of men since the beginning of this mortal earth. Particularly is this true in the creation of the United States of America and its preservation. Surely, "ministering angels" are a part of heavenly intervention.

President John Taylor has written an article entitled "Origin and Destiny of Women." I discovered this article while doing research on the Prophet Enoch and obtained a copy of it from the archives of the Brigham Young University. On page four of this article, President Taylor is describing the fact that in heaven the pre-mortal spirits were having a discussion and that "THEY BADE FATHER AND MOTHER FAREWELL, AND ALONG WITH THY

GUARDIAN ANGEL, THOU CAME TO THIS CELESTIAL GLOBE....AND THY GUARDIAN ANGEL MINISTERS UNTO THEE AND WATCHES OVER THEE."

My guardian angel is still ministering over me and I believe will accompany me from my mortal existence.

In Chapter 7 of Moroni it states as follows:

7:25 "Wherefore, BY THE MINISTERING OF ANGELS, and by every word which proceeded forth out of the mouth of God, men began to exercise faith in Christ; and thus by faith, did lay hold upon every good thing; and thus it was until the coming of Christ."

7:29 "And because he hath done this, my beloved brethren, have miracles ceased? Behold I say unto you, nay; NEITHER HAVE ANGELS CEASED TO MINISTER UNTO THE CHILDREN OF MEN."

7:37 "Behold I say unto you, nay; FOR IT IS BY FAITH THAT MIRACLES ARE WROUGHT; AND IT IS BY FAITH THAT ANGELS APPEAR AND MINISTER UNTO MEN; wherefore, if these things have ceased, wo be unto the children of men, for it is because of unbelief, and all is vain."

D&C 67:13 "Ye are not able to abide the presence of God now, NEITHER THE MINISTERING OF ANGELS; wherefore, continue in patience until ye are perfected."

D&C 76:88 "AND ALSO THE TELESTIAL RECEIVE IT OF THE ADMINISTERING OF ANGELS WHO ARE APPOINTED TO MINISTER FOR THEM, OR WHO ARE APPOINTED TO BE MINISTERING SPIRITS FOR THEM; for they shall be heirs of salvation."

D&C 130:5 "I answer, Yes. BUT THERE ARE NO ANGELS WHO MINISTER TO THIS EARTH BUT THOSE WHO DO BELONG OR HAVE BELONGED TO IT."

D&C 132:16 "Therefore, when they are out of the world, they neither marry nor are given in marriage; BUT ARE APPOINTED ANGELS IN HEAVEN, WHICH ANGELS ARE MINISTERING SERVANTS, TO MINISTER TO THOSE WHO ARE WORTHY OF A FAR MORE, AND AN EXCEEDING, AND ETERNAL WEIGHT OF GLORY."

With the above background on guardian and ministering angels, I wish to recite a series of events in my life that I believe are examples of the activity that my guardian angel participated in. It starts before my birth.

After her temple marriage to my father, my mother experienced several miscarriages. It was apparent that she had difficulty carrying children to full term. She gave birth to three children; Vesta, my oldest sister; approximately four years later my sister Nellie Jane; and approximately four years later, me. She was unable to have more children after me. She worked very hard to bring me into this world.

My first memory of being protected and preserved was when I was about five years old. I accompanied my sister Jane and some of her friends to the North Park in Provo, Utah, about two blocks from our house. The older children were climbing the twelve-foot ladder of the "chute-the-chute" to the top, sliding out on the metal horizontal pole to the vertical support, and then sliding down to the ground instead of sliding down the chute. I watched them and then decided to do the same thing the older ones were doing. When I arrived at the vertical metal pole, I slipped and fell head first to the ground. My head struck the concrete footing of the vertical metal pole. I still feel that blow in my mind when I think about it. It left a lasting impression. I believe I lost consciousness. My mother was very concerned when my older sister brought me home. As I look back on it, it was a miracle that I was not killed or left with a serious permanent injury.

While our family was living in San Francisco, California, I came home from delivering my newspapers one afternoon with a bad pain in my stomach. I was in junior high school at the time and was ten years old. My oldest sister Vesta, eighteen years old, had been shot accidentally and died in the Stanford University Hospital in Palo Alto, California. This created in me a fear of hospitals because that is where my sister had died. I remember that someone at home suggested I should have some milk of magnesia to relieve the extreme pain I was having; but my mother vetoed the suggestion. I learned later from a doctor that if I had received the milk of magnesia it would have been fatal for me. A doctor was called; he was not there. His nurse recognized the medical symptoms, recognized the emergency, and told my parents to get me to a hospital immediately. Just before leaving home, my father and an uncle of mine who happened to be there gave me a priesthood blessing. Immediately after the blessing, the pain left me and the fear of hospitals vanished. I felt calm and relaxed. When I arrived at the hospital, they prepared me for surgery and took me into the surgery room. The doctor was not there. I remember watching a large clock on the wall and listening to it click. It was approximately one hour before the doctor came into surgery. He had been to a party, was drunk, and had to be sobered up before he could operate on me. After I regained consciousness, the medical people were talking about the surgery and said that my appendix was over double its normal size, was completely full of infection, and would have burst inside me within ten minutes of its removal; that the spread of the infection would have been fatal for me. There were no antibiotics, sulfa drugs, or other medications that could have cleared up the infection at that time. I am sure that I would have panicked during the above events and made the above events perhaps impossible for me to survive without that beautiful, life-saving priesthood blessing. The surgical scar that I still carry is quite broad and irregular; it is evidence of a nervous surgeon's work. My guardian angel was there to protect me.

In San Francisco I entered the newspaper business very young. In the fifth grade I was selling newspapers on a street corner after school. Earning ten cents a night was a successful night on the papers. I also delivered groceries for the grocery store on that corner. Remember, this was during the Depression. While in junior high school I graduated to an afternoon delivery route, then to selling newspapers out in the middle of very busy streets with cars speeding past me on both sides of the street. I sold newspapers on troop ships before they left port for the Orient. One troop ship "gangway" rolled up on my foot and it felt like the weight of that large ship was on my foot. It should have destroyed my foot, but didn't; no permanent harm was done. I graduated to early morning newspaper routes all during high school; two hundred fifty newspapers every morning at 4:30 A.M., seven days a week, on a bicycle. I was competing with the cars while on the bike and when I look back, it was a miracle I survived. My guardian angel protected me all during my newspaper career. I successfully resisted many temptations.

My most dramatic preservation experiences occurred during World War II while I was in the U.S. Navy. Many of us were placed in "harm's way." The training for "harm's way" is a definite part of the harm and can be fatal on many occasions. Natural causes, storms, create serious harm. Accidents and mistakes take their toll with fatalities, both in and out of combat.

While serving aboard a destroyer, I was asleep below decks when the collision alarm sounded at sea. I did not hear the alarm. The last man below decks, other than me, shook me awake as he was going topside. By the time I arrived on deck, I could see the wakes of our ship and another ship boil together off the stern. If the collision had occurred, I would have been drowned. On several occasions I was nearly washed overboard at night in storms while I was going on and off duty. If I were washed overboard under those conditions, no one would have known and very little could have been done to save me.

The submarine chaser ship I served on was a small ship, only 110 feet long and 110 tonnage. We searched for and chased submarines. If a submarine ever surfaced in our presence it was faster and more heavily armed than we were and could have destroyed us easily. We were in heavy storms on several occasions where the waves at sea raised up much higher than the mast of our ship and broke upon our ship. We could have been swamped on many occasions and destroyed at sea.

My last navy assignment was to a beach battalion; an amphibious group consisting of navy personnel for transportation and ship-to-shore communication, marine personnel to man the guns and protect the amphibious operation, and Seabees personnel to operate the heavy construction equipment to build airplane runways, roads, bulwarks, and whatever was needed. These units are the first wave of troops to go ashore in an amphibious operation. We were being trained for the invasion of Japan. We had completed our training and had been assigned to a Personal Attack ship, which was to be a flag ship in the invasion.

The atomic bomb was dropped on Hiroshima and a second one on Nagasaki. Japan surrendered. We were one very boisterous happy unit. We were at Okinawa when a huge typhoon (storm) struck. It was necessary for us to remain at sea, away from the island when the storm hit. The wind caused the sea to appear as snow, the wave swells rose way above the mast of our large ship, some of the waves breaking upon the deck of our ship. Our large ship could have been swamped. That storm caused the destruction of many ships in the area.

We were then assigned to go inspect Hiroshima and then on to Tokyo, Japan. Before the two atomic bombs were dropped, the estimate of the top brass was that there would be U.S.A. casualties of approximately one million men during the invasion of Japan. Their entire population, men, women, and even children were trained and armed to resist the invasion, all in the name of religion. This was proven by the experiences of their kamikaze suicide pilots who dove their airplanes into ships during the war, and the suicide fighting in many of the Pacific islands. Our beach battalion would have been the first wave ashore. We went up the inside sea of Japan on the way to Hiroshima. There were very few sandy beaches on the islands; they had natural steep and rocky shores, natural fortification. If the atomic bomb had not been dropped, Japan would not have surrendered. Their military leaders would not have permitted it. Those bombs saved my life along with those of many other U.S. servicemen. I thank heaven for having them to drop and end the bloodshed.

We were the first ship and personnel to go ashore at Hiroshima after the atomic bombs were dropped. I went ashore with others. I walked around what was left of the city and around the area of the University of Hiroshima. The only thing still standing was a part of a few reinforced concrete pillars. As I look back, I could have been easily shot by those that remained. There was complete devastation there. Since my discharge from the service, I have talked to several scientists that have told me there had to be substantial atomic radiation at the time I was there. Some health problems I have had since then have convinced me that I did receive atomic radiation. This has been confirmed by some experts. It is obvious that my radiation has not been fatal. My guardian angel has preserved me from that event that I had no control over. I received no warnings of that potential danger.

From there we went to Yokohama, the seaport for Tokyo, Japan. The trip from Yokohama to Tokyo allowed us to see the devastation from the bombing that had taken place. I have recently learned from my neighbor, Edward L. Hart, that while serving in naval intelligence, he was assigned to Japan for the purpose of assessing the effect of our air force bombing of the Tokyo area. The area was devastated. His analysis and report back to his superiors was that the bombing alone, without ground troops invading after the bombing, would not have won the war with Japan and that they would not have surrendered, and that our casualties from the invasion would have been very heavy. It was the dropping of the two atomic bombs that caused Japan to surrender. I believe that there was divine intervention that enabled the bombs to be created, and dropped to end the war, which enabled the U.S.A. to be a determining factor in saving the world from governments of oppression, force, and terror; who did not tolerate individual free agency, a basic principle in the Plan of Salvation. This victory in war has enabled the U. S.A. to fulfil another part of its destiny in the Plan of Salvation. Our collective guardian angels appear to have been active in this eternal plan. My life was preserved as a result of the above.

Since September 11, 2001, we have been and will be active in a new war—against terrorism. Some of the chapters in this Book of Faith describe specific experiences of the authors relating to terrorism. Again, the U.S.A.is at the forefront of this new active war against evil. As a nation we must exercise our faith in God and His plan of salvation. By doing this, our destinies and the destiny of our country will be fulfilled to preserve this country. Our guardian angels will be very busy strengthening us for our allotted assignments in this present age-old conflict. Let us so live to warrant our guardian angels. Exercise our faith in God and we have nothing to fear. This war enlists all citizens, not just armed forces. God bless America.

Some of my described experiences are mundane and not dramatic, but they all add up over my lifetime into one great whole. My life has been full of the basic eternal truth that there needs to be opposition in all things. My daily experiences contain this principle. I have learned to follow rules of health as opposed to not following them; to follow the rules and laws of society as opposed to not following them; to keep the covenants I have made with the Lord and His Commandments the best I can; all opposed to a decision of not doing so. I want to follow the Plan of Salvation as opposed to not doing so. My guardian angel has strengthened me to follow this pattern to the best of my ability. With his help, I will improve. My guardian angel has preserved me from death or serious harm in events that I had no control over. He has taught me faith in God. He has directed my earthly timetable along my trail of destiny. I suggest we all should acknowledge and honor our guardian angels. I LOVE MY GUARDIAN ANGEL.

DEAN FUHRIMAN

DEAN FUHRIMAN

SECOND YEAR ON THE FACULTY AT UTAH STATE—1941–42

At the beginning of the school year in the fall of 1942 all military reservists had been called to active duty. This included the major part of my graduating class who were in the officers' training program (ROTC) during their junior and senior years. Quotas for the military draft were increasing monthly as the country mobilized for the war effort. A large number of the faculty were recruited to form work parties to unload military supplies at the Ogden Supply Depot on Saturdays each week. I volunteered to help and was able to earn a small amount of pay to supplement our income. We traveled from Logan to Ogden on special railroad cars (on the electric inter-urban railway). Many faculty members were involved in this project. Most all of my friends were on active duty in the armed services, and I often felt as if I should be doing more. A number of recruiting teams came to the college on a regular basis, offering commissions into some branch of the service for persons with specialized training—especially in the engineering field.

Alta and I discussed these programs and came to the conclusion that it might be worth while for me to consider going into the service in some way in which my education and experience would be worth while in the country's war effort. At the same time, I could gain experience, hopefully to improve my own education. Of course, there was also the possibility that my draft situation would change in the future. The war was having an unsettling effect on the lives of many people, with many married couples facing the probability of separation from each other as the war went on. We finally made the joint decision that I would look into the possibilities of a direct commission into the service. Maybe it would be more accurate to say that Alta supported me in whatever I should think was the best thing to do.

Sometime in the fall of 1942, I met with a U.S. Navy officers' recruiting team that came to the college in Logan, and submitted an application for possible service in the navy. I was ordered to take a physical examination, and was told that my eyes might disqualify me. We heard that carrots could have a beneficial effect in strengthening the eyes, so we ate carrots in many different forms for quite a while. The papers which I had submitted were shuffled from one Navy bureau to another—Bureau of Ships, and Seabees were the ones we heard from first—then without any warning, on about March 3, I received a letter in the mail from the California Institute of Technology at Pasadena, California, that I had been enrolled by the Navy in a twelve-week post-graduate course in Aeronautical Engineering which would begin on March 13, 1943.

We called the 12th Naval District office in San Francisco to find out what was going on and they told me that they were typing orders at that moment. I received them on March 9, ordering me to take another physical, obtain uniforms, and report for duty on March 13 in Pasadena. I had my physical exam at the Naval Reserve Training Station in Salt Lake City on March 10, and also bought uniforms at that time. At the time of my physical exam they said, "Oh, your eyes do not pass, but since they are corrected by glasses, it will be okay." We rented our home to Ruby and Tone, sold our car (because of gas and tire rationing, we thought it would not be feasible to own one—a bad mistake). We said our goodbyes, and on March 11 Alta and I boarded a Greyhound bus headed to Pasadena.

NAVY TRAINING AT CALIFORNIA INSTITUTE OF TECHNOLOGY

Upon arrival in Pasadena, we rented a room in a Cal Tech professor's home—I "reported in" and was sworn in as an ensign in the U.S. Naval Reserve, serial number 253722. I learned that there were about eighty of us in the course—all with degrees in some branch of engineering, and all of us with the rank of ensign. All were there for our first duty in the Navy—fresh out of civilian life.

Although my schedule at Cal Tech was a very busy one, it was nice having Alta to come home to each day. Our classes started at 7:00 A.M. and we had five hour-long aeronautical engineering classes each morning, then lunch, and a one-hour class in Navy orientation. At two o'clock we went out on the field for an hour of marching/drill, followed by calisthenics and then sports—usually basketball for physical exercise. In the evening we had homework assignments in our five morning classes, so I'm afraid I wasn't very good company. I'm sure there were many days when Alta felt mighty neglected, but from my standpoint, it was wonderful having her there.

One aspect of our daily lives that was new and somewhat frightening to us, having lived in relative safety far from the ocean, was the fact that all of the neighborhoods in the sprawling part of the country known as the Greater Los Angeles Metropolitan area had blackout regulations every night. Of course, all of the coastal areas of the U.S. had similar regulations, but it was new to us. Civilian block captains patrolled the neighborhood in which we lived to enforce the blackout.

Alta and I were free to do some things together on the weekends and attend church on Sunday. To me, the twelve weeks passed rapidly, but we hadn't been there very long before we realized that we had to have a car, so we bought a much-used Chevrolet coupe and that helped us to do quite a bit of sightseeing around the greater Los Angeles area. We were able to visit my brother Jay and his family, my sister Guen and her family, and my uncle David Fuhriman and his family. We also visited some tourist spots—Huntington Library and Art Gallery in Pasadena, Forest Lawn Cemetery, and the zoo (we were too far away from the ocean to attempt a trip to the beach). We learned to get around on the rail and bus transportation systems, and we were in awe of our first car ride on the first freeway we had ever heard of—the Pasadena-Los Angeles Freeway.

New Ensign Dean Fuhriman on drill field at California Institute of Technology, Pasadena. May 1943

All of us taking the training at Cal Tech knew that at the conclusion of our twelve-week course, we would be assigned somewhere where we would be supervising repair of combat aircraft somewhere throughout the world. We were not to know where it would be until we had completed the course at Cal Tech. Alta and I, therefore, felt that we were somewhat living on borrowed time, so to speak—not knowing what would lie ahead—but nevertheless knowing that it was important for all of us as citizens to be firmly committed to doing what was necessary to save our nation, and to preserve freedom, not only for America, but for the entire world.

During the last week of classes, a list was posted on the bulletin board showing where we were all being ordered to go for our next duty station. I was assigned to the Naval Air Station at Sand Point in Seattle, Washington.

After a formal graduation ceremony on June 9, 1943, I was detached from duty at Cal Tech, and ordered to report for duty in Seattle after a delay of about ten days for travel en route and a short visit home to Utah. We packed our belongings into our little Chevrolet, and headed for several days of visiting in Utah before traveling to Seattle. Luckily, our car worked fine for both parts of the trip. We had a wonderful ten days together. We arrived in Seattle in the later part of June 1943.

DUTY AT NAVAL AIR STATION, SEATTLE, WASHINGTON

Housing in Seattle was a problem. We lived in a motel for a short while. While there Alta had severe abdominal pains, which ended up as a miscarriage, and she spent about a week in the hospital. We felt so bad—we had been wanting a baby for a long time. The baby was not fully formed, and we could not tell whether it was a boy or a girl. I also felt bad that we didn't have a better place for housing. We learned that one of my classmates from our Cal Tech class had been able to rent a house in the University district, and asked us to move in with them and share the rent expense. It was very awkward, especially because they had a small dog which they fed off of the same dishes that we used. We only stayed there a short time and then found a very small apartment built into a garden shed at a landscape garden in north Seattle. It was very minimal, but we were glad to be able to be by ourselves. The summer weather in Seattle was delightful and we learned that summer was about the only part of the year that it was not cold and rainy.

My duty at the Naval Air Station was a training program involving observation of the workings of the different repair functions in the Assembly and Repair Shops (called A&R shops). About fifteen of us who had attended the Cal Tech course were assigned for the training at Seattle. We were divided into groups of three, rotating between the various shops in the huge aircraft hangers, spending several days in each area—engine overhaul, accessories, pattern making, machine shop, parachute shop, etc. We all knew that it would only be a short time until we would be reassigned, likely to an overseas station.

Thinking through the possibilities for the future, it was plain to us that we would soon be separated. I could see that our training schedule was nearing completion, since I had been through almost all of the different shops where we were scheduled to receive orientation.

This training was completed on 27 September, and I was granted a few days of leave while awaiting further orders. We knew that the next duty station would likely be somewhere overseas where Alta would not be able to go with me. Lloyd, the husband of Alta's sister, Metta, had been drafted into the Army, and Metta had a small apartment in Logan because it was not possible for her with two children to go with him when he had to enter the

Army. She suggested that Alta might wish to live with her when I went over-seas. We were quite dissatisfied with our housing in Seattle, so we decided to drive to Logan, so Alta could get settled with Metta. We left our apartment and made the trip back to Utah. Luckily again, our car functioned very well.

After the weekend getting Alta moved, I took a bus back to Seattle, and within just a few days received my orders to report for duty to the Commander, Alaskan Sector, northwest Sea Frontier at Adak Alaska, for further assignment. I was detached from duty at Seattle on October 22, 1943, and after a quick trip back to Utah, I was ordered to report aboard a troop ship, the SS *Henry Failing* in the Seattle harbor on 5 November, 1943.

Subconsciously, I wondered if the name of the ship had anything to do with its seaworthiness.

The trip back home ended all too quickly, and then I found myself on the train for the lonely ride back to Seattle. It was hard to think of leaving Alta, as we had not been apart any time before joining the Navy. I prayed that all would be well with us during the time we would be parted.

On the train, I thought about many things—about the purpose of life, about my life up to that point, and about the Church and its teachings. I realized that there were many things about church doctrines and teachings that I had taken for granted up to this point. I had a strong desire to know more about these important things. I realized that, although I had been very active in the church most of my life, I wondered if I really had a testimony. Had I gone along with all of these things only because I had seen my parents and grandparents as they went on with their lives, active in the church? What did I really know for myself? I had the scriptures with me and the little pocket-size book of "Principles of the Gospel," prepared especially for men and women in the armed services. I decided to read the Book of Mormon all the way through, which I had never done before. I knew that I would have a lot of time for reading as I traveled toward my next duty station.

EN ROUTE TO DUTY IN THE ALEUTIAN ISLANDS OF ALASKA

It was about midnight on the rainy evening of November fifth when I arrived at the Seattle dock to board the SS *Failing*. We were scheduled to weigh anchor at about 0800 the next morning. It wasn't long before we had moved out of Puget Sound and into the stormy north Pacific Ocean, headed straight toward the island of Kodiak. I learned that the ship we were on was one of the famous "Liberty" cargo ships constructed in the Kaiser shipyards in the San Francisco Bay area. Ours was to be the last voyage before the ship was scheduled to be officially converted to a troop-carrying vessel. The conversion would involve pouring many tons of concrete into the bottom of the ship's hold to serve as ballast; such ballast is not needed in cargo ships, because the cargo itself serves as ballast.

Soon after leaving the harbor we found out what this lack of ballast did to our ship, because we bobbed around on the ocean surface like a cork. The ship rolled a great deal from side to side. My bunk was oriented crosswise on the ship, so each time it would roll from side to side my head would be down and my feet up, and then when it rolled back the other way, my feet would be down and my head would be up. Almost everyone on board, including the crew, became deathly seasick from this continual rolling motion. Almost everyone—except me. I felt fine, and I just went on with my reading of the Book of Mormon. I even had trouble finding anything to eat, because the cooks were all sick and there was virtually no one who had even the slightest desire to eat anything. I have since felt that I was spared the seasickness because it was important for me to keep the commitment I had made with myself to do this important studying.

The ship was about two weeks traveling from Seattle to the island of Adak, stopping briefly at Kodiak on the way. As I read the last chapter of the book written by Moroni, the last of the Nephites as far as Moroni knew (this was about the year 421 a.d.). I read:

> "And when ye shall receive these things, I would exhort you
> that ye would ask God, the Eternal Father, in the name of
> Christ, if these things are not true. And if ye shall ask with
> a sincere heart, with real intent, having faith in Christ, he
> will manifest the truth of it unto you by the power of the
> Holy Ghost."

I did ask, my heart was certainly sincere, and I did have faith. All alone, in my quiet little corner deep inside of that violently rolling ship, I prayed to know. As I finished the prayer, a most marvelous thing happened. I felt a warm tingling sensation beginning in the center of my body and spreading slowly to the top of my head and to the soles of my feet. There was no doubt in my mind that this was the answer to my prayer. All of the questions in my mind melted away. I knew that this book was true, and that the Prophet Joseph Smith translated it by the gift and power of God. Now I also knew that Joseph had seen God, our Heavenly Father, and His Son, Jesus Christ, and talked with them face to face. I also knew that the Lord guided Joseph step by step in the ten following years, to restore the Priesthood to the earth and re-establish His true church once again on the earth.

This wonderful experience brought into my life a knowledge that has been a guide to me in everything I have done in my life from that point on. It has helped me to understand why my father, and grandfathers Gottfried Fuhriman and Joseph Campbell would give up several years of their lives to serve on missions; why my great-grandfather Benoni Campbell and his wife, Mary Leonard Campbell, would give up their property and comfortable living in Pennsylvania and Illinois to suffer the hardships of life, and both die of cholera somewhere in Nebraska while on their way westward; why my great-grandfather Milton D. Hammond would leave his comfortable home in Utah to establish the Limhi mission to the Indians in Idaho—and why the Prophet Joseph Smith and many other church leaders and members gave their lives—because they were following the Lord's instructions to build His Kingdom here on the earth.

The ship on which we were traveling stopped at Kodiak Island and we were permitted to go ashore. The weather was wet and the streets were muddy, so we didn't have much of a chance to see anything. Going on westward, we arrived at Adak harbor, found that there were quite a number of ships awaiting the opportunity to get to the docks for unloading. This condition was apparently the result of the heavy storm which they had experienced in the days just past. We finally were able to go ashore on November eighteenth, and I reported as ordered. I learned that I was assigned to the Naval Air Station on the island of Attu. I would fly on a naval transport plane as soon as the weather cleared enough for the flight. It was snowing hard when we arrived in Adak, and continued for several days. I learned of LDS Church services to be held on Sunday, and I attended. Lieutenant Milton Hess, an LDS chaplain, conducted the meeting, said he was planning a trip to Attu in the next few weeks for the purpose of organizing a branch of the Church, and asked me to help locating LDS servicemen who might be interested in attending.

When our flight finally left for Attu, November twenty-second, I found that I was one of two passengers on a cargo flight to Attu. Our plane was an amphibious PBY (known as the "flying goose"). As we arrived in the area of Attu, the pilot found that the airport was fogged in, so we flew to the nearby island of Amchitka, landed there, and stayed overnight, flying to Attu the following day. Leaving Amchitka, we were very much aware of the fact that the Japanese had occupied the island of Kiska, just a few miles east of Amchitka, and were still there as far as anyone knew. As we landed at the Attu Naval Air Station, I noticed quite a bit of snow piled high on the edge of the runway and the wind was blowing very hard, but the air was clear and we had good visibility to land. It was November 23, the day before Thanksgiving.

NAVY DUTY ON ATTU ISLAND

Upon arrival at Attu, I reported in to the Commandant of the base and was assigned to Assembly and Repair (known as the "A & R" Department). The department head was Lieutenant Leonard Perkins, who had come up through the ranks, had fought in the South Pacific, and had received a battlefield promotion while serving on Guadalcanal. Other officers assigned to our department were Ensign Fred Fendell, from Staten Island, New York;

Lieutenant (j.g.) Bert Keeney, from Pittsburg, Kansas; Ensign Russell Kuchel, from Iowa; Ensign William Bruyere, from Austin, Texas; Ensign Harvey Gates; and Chief Warrant Officers Leonard Handy and Royce Adams. I developed a really close friendship with Fendell, Keeney, Kuchel, and Bruyere, since we bunked together and also worked together. Our department head, Lieutenant Perkins, was kind of a braggart, but we got along reasonably well. A large part of his bragging was about his many sexual conquests involving students and women faculty members at high school in his home town of Doerun, Georgia.

Our department was housed in a large aircraft hangar, to which damaged planes were brought for repair. We had about 120 enlisted men in our department. The planes from our base were assigned to make aerial maps of all of the northern Japanese islands. A couple of times there was sadness on our base when one of the planes would fail to return from their photographic flights. Occasionally the planes would be shot at and receive a few bullet holes that would need to be repaired, but most of the damaged planes we had to repair were the result of problems in landing or takeoff or from wind damage. We worked mainly on Navy PV-2 and PBY planes.

Soon after arriving on Attu, I posted notices on the bulletin boards on the base to learn of any LDS members who might be interested in having LDS church services, and we started meeting informally before Lieutenant Hess came. When he came, he organized an official Attu servicemen's branch and I was appointed the branch president. As word got around, we eventually had a branch of about twenty-five members, including a navy lieutenant, Dale Holbrook, from Layton, who was assigned to the Communications Department on our base. Also included were two army officers, Major Joseph Lacy and Captain Dean Rogers, who were with an army artillery unit. Both had been in the ROTC at Utah State and had been involved in the battle to recapture Attu from the Japanese, which had taken place several months before I arrived there. We held sacrament meetings each Sunday evening.

A & R Dept. officers and enlisted men in front of repair hangar
Notice the steel matting surface on the ground - 1944

The (Flying Goose) airplane, the "work horse" of the Alaskan Military Command. It is an amphibious plane, with retractable wheels. It can land on land or water. Official Navy Photograph

Leonard Perkins, A & R Dept. Head
and Dean in front of hangar - 1944

My bunk-mates
on Attu - 1944
(l to r)
Harvey Gates,
Bill Bruyere,
Bert Keeney,
Russ Kuchel
& Fred Fendell

Some of the A & R officers
in front of the hangar
(l to r) Jim Grogan,
Lt. Perkins, Dean,
CWO Leonard Handy
(with adopted puppy)
unidentified man, and
Bert Keeney

Hanging out
in our hut
Harvey Gates,
Leonard Perkins,
Russ Kuchel,
and Dean - 1944

PV-2 Airplane - the primary plane used by the Navy in the Aleutian Islands. It was used as a bomber and aerial mapping plane to photograph all of Northern Japan.

Official Navy Photograph

Attu LDS Branch members at organization meeting. Front Row: Bro. Craig, David Wilde, Dean Fuhriman, Dale Holbrook, Rex Reynolds, Chaplin M.J. Hess. - December 1943

Dean by Christmas tree - Attu 1943

The island of Attu is mostly mountainous, with steep, rugged mountains, and practically no flat lands except near the mouths of the streams draining into the sea. There are no trees on the island, but the deltas formed by the mountain streams are covered with grass and wild flowers in the summer months. In the spring of the year these streams were filled with salmon swimming very crowdedly upstream to spawn. There was no native population, as the few native Aleut Indians had all been killed by the Japanese forces or evacuated. Japanese armed forces had occupied the island and established a base sometime in about the year of 1942. Our naval installation was located on Massacre Bay, which name was given because of the massacre of all of the Aleut natives by the Russians many years in the past—before Alaska was acquired by the United States. The recapture of Attu from the Japanese by our Armed Forces had taken place in the summer months of 1943, and there were no Japanese left there when I arrived, except for a lone starving Japanese soldier who came to the army base and showed up in the chow line during the winter months to get some food, and thus was captured. I heard about it shortly after I arrived there. Everyone wondered how he could have survived all of that time. The war operation to recapture the island in the summer of 1943 was quite a bloody operation, with over four hundred American casualties. The mountain near our base was known as Bloody Ridge, where most of the casualties were suffered.

The navy officers' clubhouse, where we had our meals and other recreation, also included a bar where liquor was available. It was common practice for officers receiving a promotion in rank to invite their friends and associates to come to the bar where they were treated to alcoholic drinks. One officer, whose name I cannot recall, made a special point of inviting me to his promotion party. When I arrived he took me to the bar and asked what I would like. I said I would have tomato juice. He was already somewhat drunk, and he bristled, and loudly stated, "Nobody at my party is going to drink plain tomato juice!" I told him I did not mean to insult him, but I didn't care for any other drink. He still made quite a scene, but I excused myself and started to leave. I didn't realize that one of the chief warrant officers of our department, Officer Handy (who himself had quite a reputation as a drinker), had watched the whole thing. He came over to my side, put his arm around me, and said "Don't let that get to you, Dean, you have something that the rest of us don't have."

During the winter the weather was quite stormy, but the temperature never did get down to zero. I think the lowest temperature ever experienced during my stay was eighteen degrees above zero Fahrenheit, but the winter weather was miserable. We had lots of wind, rain, sleet, and snow. The nights were long, but not nearly as long as I had always heard about in northern Alaska. Our latitude was about fifty-two degrees north of the equator. and some distance south of the Arctic Circle, which is about sixty-seven degrees north latitude. Stormy winter weather often limited the good flying days for the mapping project our planes were assigned to accomplish, so it was rather boring duty most of the winter time.

There was a Ship Service Store (like an Army Post Exchange or "PX") on our base. Since there was virtually nothing for the servicemen to buy with their money, they would buy most any kind of new gadget that showed up at the Ship's Store. Soon after I arrived, the store received a large shipment of cheap slide rules. Most of the personnel bought one although they didn't know how to use it. Quite a few of our department servicemen bought one. They heard that I was an engineer and came into the office to see if I could help them.

Dean beside a wind-blown snowdrift
that blocked the entrance to the
Quonset Hut - my home on
Attu - 1944

Dean on board walk at Quonset Hut at Attu

Dean
Fuhriman
Lt. (jg) at Attu
Alaska - 1944

I got the carpenter shop to make a slide rule about eight feet long, on which I laid out the markings and had it all painted white with the numbers and markings on and we held an evening class in a corner of the hanger, where I was able to demonstrate for them how to make calculations with a slide rule.

Most all of the buildings on our base were Quonset hut construction made of corrugated iron sheets bent in the shape of a half-circle. These sheets formed the walls and ceilings, with vertical walls to provide the end-walls and partitions inside the building. The officer's housing area consisted of a number of these buildings clustered near a similar building with showers and toilets. The hut I was assigned to had a small section at one end of the building furnished with lounge-type chairs, some straight chairs, and a table. The larger section at the other end was the sleeping quarters and contained six single beds, each with a small bedside table, a small chest of drawers, and a wardrobe closet. The officers "club" was a rather large building containing a dining room and kitchen, a recreation room (pool table, table tennis table), a lounge area, and a barroom. Here we would go for all of our meals, or whatever else we might wish to do when not on duty. My hut-mates were the officers with whom I worked in the A&R Department and we became very good friends. They called me "Deke" (for Deacon) because of my church activity.

One day I noticed an announcement on the bulletin board that a class to learn Russian language was about to begin. I signed up for the class, which was so large that they didn't have nearly enough textbooks. I decided not to continue because I didn't want to be in the position of being an officer depriving some enlisted person of the text materials.

On our base, we had a gymnasium (a large Quonset hut) where we could play basketball and work out to keep in good physical condition. The gym also served as a theater, where movies were shown once or twice a week. As we got into the spring and summer months, we had some softball games. The junior officers (ensigns and junior grade lieutenants) played against the senior officers. Our executive officer (the second in command to the base commander) was a small-built feisty lieutenant commander whom nobody liked very well. He was the pitcher for the senior team, and on one of my times at bat I got lucky and hit the ball clear over a shed in center field. I almost always struck out, and was certainly a mediocre player, but that one hit really made me feel good.

One of the members of our LDS Branch, Rex Reynolds, was stationed on a small ship which patrolled the area around Attu. He arranged an invitation for me to go on my off-duty time on a trip to patrol the ocean all the way around the island of Attu (which is about fifty miles long and twenty miles wide). It was interesting to see the island from all sides, but it didn't look much different than it did near our base—steep rocky slopes leading down to the ocean from the rugged mountains that covered the whole island. I met Rex many years later in Provo, where he worked as the manager of a home mortgage company.

On another day off, myself and two other officers checked out a small boat and some fishing gear and went out into the mouth of Massacre Bay to fish for flounder. The flounder is a very good-eating fish with a flat body and both eyes on one side of the body. We caught about fifty of them and turned them over to the mess hall cooks. Another day off was spent with a couple of other officers going to the remains of a Japanese army camp on the north side of the island. On still another day off, I went with Major Lacy on a snowshoe trip to set up a target, which his Army Artillery Unit would use for gunnery practice.

During my time with the A&R Department, on several occasions I was assigned some extra duties censoring the mail of the personnel on our base to make sure that no sensitive military information was sent home. Any such information was blacked-out before the letters left our base. Another duty that I had on a couple of occasions was to serve on an auditing committee to review the financial records of all of the departments on our base which had to handle money—the officers' club, the ship store, the theater, the laundry, etc. In May of 1944, I was promoted to the rank of lieutenant (junior grade) in the U.S. Naval Reserve.

In April of 1944, I received word that my stepfather, Charles Vogel, had died at home in Providence, Utah. I worried for mother about getting things settled at home and applied, through the Red Cross Representative, for an emergency leave to go home and be of assistance to her, but my request for leave was denied. My mother sold her home in Providence and, along with Carol, Helen, and Anna, moved to San Jose, California. They lived with my sister, Rowena, for a short time and then mother bought a small home there.

CHANGE IN DUTIES ON ATTU

As the war with Japan proceeded into late 1943 and early 1944, the U.S. successes in the central Pacific ocean made our northern bases much less important, and people stationed on the northern bases such as ours had less and less activity. The commander of our base decided that this provided an opportunity for the junior officers to be rotated around to different departments on the base to broaden our experience. Accordingly, on June 12, 1944, I was given a temporary duty assignment to the Intelligence Department, where I served as duty officer in the Communications Department operating encoding and decoding machines used to send and receive communications for the Naval Air Station. This was quite an interesting assignment. I was returned to the A&R Department on October 17, 1944. On January 11, 1945 I received a letter of commendation from the A&R Officer, citing "exceptional ability and fine cooperation" in my service in the A&R Department.

On January 7, 1945, I was given another temporary duty assignment as Navy Liaison Officer at the U.S. Fleet Air Wing Four Radar Surveillance Center at Alexai Point station about five miles from the Naval Air Station. At this center the radar screens would show incoming aircraft so that the various bases (Army and Navy) could be notified of any approaching enemy aircraft anywhere to the west of us in the vicinity of the northern Japanese islands. About the only enemy planes we tracked while I was on duty were patrol planes operating in the area of the Japanese islands and not headed in our direction. The navy officers on this duty were housed and fed by the Army. The food and housing were vastly inferior to that at the Naval Air Station, but we did have a jeep assigned to us so we could go back and forth to the navy base to get some snack foods and an occasional meal at the officers' club there. I continued in this duty until April 27, 1945, and returned to the A&R Department, but had already received my orders to go to Pensacola, Florida.

TRAVEL TO NEW DUTY STATION IN FLORIDA

On May 1, 1945, I was detached from NAS Attu and left by Naval Air transport plane, arriving at Adak, Alaska, at 3:45 P.M. Our plane was delayed in Adak two days because of bad weather conditions. We left at 4:30 P.M. on May third, and had a brief stopover at Anchorage. As we approached the airfield at Anchorage it was wonderful to see the beautiful pine trees bordering the airport, as I had not seen a tree in the past eighteen months. My plane proceeded on to Seattle, arriving at 11:10 A.M. on May fourth. I arranged a train ticket, left Seattle at 11 P.M. and arrived at Cache Junction, just west of Logan, on the morning of May sixth. What a wonderful reunion with Alta after eighteen long months of separation. I did not need to report for duty in Pensacola until June ninth, so we had some happy times visiting relatives and enjoying being together again. Just a day after arriving home, the news of Germany's surrender was announced. So the war in Europe was over! Happy day!

My buddy,
Major Clyde Gessel
was released from
active duty and
visited us in
Pensacola, Florida
in 1945

EARL H. PEIRCE

WORLD WAR II
MILITARY SERVICE
1942-1046

Copied from my autobiography

Earl H. Peirce
1633 North Oak Lane
Provo, Utah

FOREWORD

The following story is written about my life in the military from 1942 to 1946. In retrospect, I had realized things concerning events in my life that only came to my full understanding years after the War.

On page ___ following, some detail is given concerning a typhoon on Okinawa that pounded us for twenty-four hours. I found myself helping our men and Japanese prisoners of war holding down a hospital tent in the typhoon wind so that an operation might be completed. It was a hospital that we were building as an Engineer Battalion and it was only partly completed. It took about twenty-five of us to hold the tent down as the eye of the storm was passing over and the wind velocity was increasing.

The adjacent Quonset buildings we had partially completed were coming apart in the wind. Large pieces of their sheet metal were tearing off and flying through the air like sheets of paper. We were able to hang on till the operation was over, then headed back to battalion headquarters in a weapons carrier truck. It was several miles and we had to drive about five miles an hour in the storm along a road close to the beach. It seemed to be raining sand and water in a horizontal direction. Debris was coming along and across the road but none struck us.

Finally arriving at camp we crawled, as walking was not possible, to our previously reinforced nine-foot by nine-foot tents. We had heard we were in the typhoon season and lined the tents with a lumber frame, following which we anchored them with cable and pieces of the Okinawan Railway. The tent expanded and collapsed against the restraints like a balloon. As it collapsed it would spray rain right through the canvas so we sat on our cots in our rain gear till the storm passed.

Years later when I was reflecting on why none of us in our little country LDS Ward, when I was at home, ever had Patriarchal Blessings. I determined to get my Blessing. I was a relative of the then Patriarch to the Church, Eldred G. Smith. He agreed to give the Blessing. In it he said "...Many physical dangers and difficulties have passed by thee, giving unto thee blessings in disguise. The Lord shall continue to reward thee..."

Now the realization came over me that this had been true, the maximum example being perhaps that typhoon on Okinawa. I remembered all that debris blowing through the air at a speed that could maim or kill. As a matter of fact ten servicemen lost their lives that night on the island. It came to me that my life had been protected and spared that night just as the Blessing indicated. There had been other times in my life that I then recognized where the same had happened.

There had to be a reason. There are personal events in my life that prove that I would not relate more here than this military story. Of course I thank the Lord for these remarkable blessings. They have been a testimony to me.

Earl H. Peirce
Provo, Utah
7 June 2001

154

I was working at the Arms Plant shortly after we were married. It was at 21st South and Redwood Road. A concrete inspector at the concrete batch plant—a rather dismal job. If I ordered the right amount of water for the cement, which was coming into the batch plant red hot from the cement plant, then the concrete would set up before the trucks could get it to the job site. Then they would chew me out. If they caught me putting enough water in the concrete so the truck could get to the pour site and empty they would chew me out. This was a good practical problem for a new engineering graduate. They never mentioned things like that in school.

A lucky break came when they needed a hydraulic engineer at the U.S. Geological Survey in Salt Lake. I became a hydrographer for the next year. That is a person who stands in rivers or rides in cable cars, equipped with a current meter, to measure the depth and velocity of a river, thereby determining the daily flow of the river by reference to the measurements and a stream flow stage recorder next to the measuring section. This was followed by periods in the office making the flow calculations. It was rather enjoyable going around the state making these measurements. In the winter when the streams froze over the flow had to be estimated. In the long term our records were used for irrigation distribution, dam construction, and water rights assignments.

Our apartment at 969 East South Temple was pleasant. Ten dollars filled the Ford with groceries and the only unpleasant thoughts concerned the draft looming in the background.

Ida is a born schoolteacher. She has always been an excellent teacher. She used her experience at Grantsville to get a job teaching in Holliday. Here she encountered something new, children of a polygamous family. She always felt sorry for these children, who in many ways were shunned by other families.

We spent enjoyable times at Willard visiting with Dad and Mother Stauffer. One such time was 7 December 1941. Listening to the radio after dinner there was a news flash—the Japanese had bombed Pearl Harbor. We knew for sure now what we had expected all along—we were at war. The next day President Roosevelt addressed the Congress and there was the official war declaration. The local Japanese were immediately suspected of being traitors or saboteurs. My friend Doctor Hashimoto, as American as anyone, tried to face the problem with a little humor. "Don't look at me that way," he said. "I'm just an Irishman."

I had gone to Brigham City for the draft board physical exam and passed. Passing, we joked, was looking in one ear and not being able to see through the head and out through the other ear. I read somewhere concerning qualifications for becoming an aircraft maintenance engineer. The basic qualification was being a graduate engineer or having a degree in physics. So I procured the necessary papers and later in 1942 submitted them to the Army Air Force. They accepted the application and scheduled me for a physical exam. The same day that I took the physical I also went to the Navy and passed their physical for a direct commission as an ensign. The Air Force required a six-month school as a cadet before receiving a commission. I chose the Air Force, thinking airplanes would be of more interest to me than ships. Later on when I crossed the Pacific to Okinawa I realized I could have really enjoyed life on the ocean.

The then Army Air Force said to report to Fort Douglas for another physical exam to be appointed as an aviation cadet. So I went through that somewhat humiliating experience of being in a line of naked persons waiting to be poked and probed. I passed and soon after my orders came. In November there was that sad farewell to Ida as I boarded the train at the Union Pacific depot in Salt Lake. Ida cried and I know I suppressed the tears. Who could know when next we would see each other. War is hell in a thousand ways.

I was to report at the Army Air Force Cadet training facilities near Wayne, Pennsylvania, at the Valley Forge Military Academy. Here we used the facilities of the academy, a boys' school, and lived in the huge old homes of the wealthy that were no longer occupied by these Philadelphia suburbanites. It was not formally announced but one purpose of a cadet school was to raise hell with the cadets to see if they could take it. Otherwise they were not considered worthy of a commission. In retrospect, I think we as graduate engineers having to go through that childish military nonsense was preposterous. All we needed was a minimum of military matters and a lot of technical training so we could get on with the job. If we didn't do every little thing required of us we would be washed out and relegated to being a buck private in the air force. So we had no choice but to perform like monkeys or asses, I don't know which of the two describes it better.

I lucked out and had a three-day pass at Christmas so some of us went to Philadelphia and stayed in a hotel there for two nights, visited the USO show, and went to some movies. It was a welcome relief from the nonsense.

I learned later that Valley Forge is adjacent to the very country settled by my Quaker ancestors. I had known that my ancestors were supposed to be Pennsylvania Dutch but that meant nothing in particular to me at the time. Many years later I was able to search this area in Chester and Delaware counties and learn a detailed history of my direct ancestors. Well, I made one contribution to Valley Forge. We were on a six-mile hike around the Campbell Soup estate (it was that huge and was surrounded by an iron picket fence). The army had given me shoes too small, they rubbed my heel till it bled, and at a rest stop I squeezed a bit of blood on the snow, just like George Washington's men did at Valley Forge in the Revolutionary War.

All at once orders came to move the Cadet School to Chanute Field in Illinois. Chanute was somewhat enjoyable compared to Valley Forge. There were better classroom facilities and a mess hall second to none. Because there were so many airmen on the field a wide variety of food could be served on the standard ration allowance. Here I was arrested, the only time in my life, by the MPs, for walking in the street on my way to the dentist. There was a blizzard, the sidewalks were covered, the streets were cleared so I walked there. The officer of the guard asked why and I gave that much appreciated remark by those in authority in the military: "No excuse, sir." He let me go with a threat that I would hear about it from my tac officer but I never did.

It was decided that there should be an aviation cadet school at Yale University in New Haven, Connecticut, for aircraft maintenance, armament, communications, and photographic officers. It sounded good to us. We all had to pass a physical before we left. They assembled us in the post theatre, stationed a doctor on the stage, and we all filed by as he peered into our throats with a flashlight. I suppose only the medical profession knew what he was looking for. We had Pullman accommodations to New Haven. Two cadets in a lower bunk and a single in the upper bunk for large persons like myself. It was a nice trip and the movie newsreel people were there to meet us as we arrived to "take over Yale."

I was assigned a room in Sterling Law residence halls with another cadet, Eric Moeller, from Brooklyn. We had our mess in a large hall normally used by the students. There were only a few students attending school at this time as most had gone into the military. In the grim business of being cadets we had the best of all worlds in our living facilities which we were to occupy till our class was commissioned in May. But the contractor for the mess hall said he couldn't feed us on the ration allowance. So they deducted a portion of our pay, $42 per month, to give to him. I was so strapped for a tiny bit of spending money that Ida, who was still teaching school, had to send money to me. Later on they made up to us for this really illegal action, if there is such in the military.

After a couple of months Ida quit her job as schoolteacher and came to New Haven on the train and we had a happy reunion. She arrived on a Sunday and I had to get a Church pass to meet her, we were restricted that tightly to the campus. I had a fine cadet friend from Oklahoma, Alvin Porter. His wife had an apartment near the campus and Ida moved in with her. Ida could come to the campus in the evenings to see me in the reception lounge and I had a day off once a week when we could be together. Ida and Mrs. Porter met an old army officer who had been on General Pershing's staff in World War I, living in the same house they were. The Colonel showed them around New Haven and they had a rather enjoyable time.

Of some historical consideration was the enjoyable lunch and dinners we had in the mess hall, a complete change from the grim realities of the rest of the day, when the Glen Miller Air Force Band played for us. He also played for our review parades on the green in next door, downtown New Haven in the evenings. He made "Roll out the Barrel" an official military march while we were there and somewhat revolutionized military music. Why the band was assigned to Yale we didn't know, rather just enjoyed it. Later it was assigned overseas where Glen Miller lost his life. Tony Martin, a popular radio big band vocalist, now a private in the air force, sang with the band. He had a hand-tailored GI uniform the likes of which no one before had ever seen.

The pressure in the school was intense. One person I knew became mentally unbalanced and everyone looked as if they had been drawn through a knothole. But I made it and in May I was commissioned a second-lieutenant. Saks Fifth Avenue had a store in New Haven where we procured our uniforms, on a uniform allowance no less. The quality of these uniforms was excellent. I could see why the military professionals could succumb to the siren song of the fancy military uniform.

Next came where would we be assigned? There were about twelve of us in our class. Four assignments in England were determined by drawing straws. After that, since my marks were second in the class, I had second choice of a number of bases that needed engineering officers in the United States. I chose Santa Ana, California. Ida and I, using our one allowable military moving allowance, purchased Pullman tickets. We could only get one upper berth to Los Angeles, California. We arrived there and transferred to a train to San Diego to visit Arlene and Clyde. Clyde was stationed at Camp Callan in La Jolla. We had a nice visit there and then returned to Santa Ana. At the base they informed me that if I had expected to be assigned at Santa Ana, I was misinformed. I would be going out in the desert to Hobbs Army Air Base in Hobbs, New Mexico. I had never heard of Hobbs.

Army of the United States

SEPARATION QUALIFICATION RECORD

SAVE THIS FORM. IT WILL NOT BE REPLACED IF LOST

This record of job assignments and special training received in the Army is furnished to the soldier when he leaves the service. In its preparation, information is taken from available Army records and supplemented by personal interview. The information about civilian education and work experience is based on the individual's own statements. The veteran may present this document to former employers, prospective employers, representatives of schools or colleges, or use it in any other way that may prove beneficial to him.

	MILITARY OCCUPATIONAL ASSIGNMENTS		
1. LAST NAME—FIRST NAME—MIDDLE INITIAL	10. MONTHS	11. GRADE	12. MILITARY OCCUPATIONAL SPECIALTY
PEIRCE, EARL H.	17	Capt.	Aircraft Maintenance Officer (4823)
2. ARMY SERIAL NO. O 862 429 **3. GRADE** Captain **4. SOCIAL SECURITY NO.** 529-09-7989	13	Capt.	Airport Engineer (7970)
5. PERMANENT MAILING ADDRESS (Street, City, County, State) RFD # 1 (Box Elder County) Brigham City, Utah	6	2nd Lt.	Weight and Balance Officer (0911)
6. DATE OF ENTRY INTO ACTIVE SERVICE 31 May 1943 **7. DATE OF SEPARATION** 21 July 1946 **8. DATE OF BIRTH** 11 Apr 1918			
9. PLACE OF SEPARATION Separation Center Fort Douglas, Utah			

SUMMARY OF MILITARY OCCUPATIONS

13. TITLE—DESCRIPTION—RELATED CIVILIAN OCCUPATION

AIRCRAFT MAINTENANCE OFFICER: Supervised maintenance and repair of aircraft in a squadron. Planned and layed-out work and assigned work crews. Supervised repair of aircraft and inspecting of work performed. Work included all repair on component parts of aircraft such as engines, wings, landing gear and etc. Supervised issue of tools and parts. Supervised preparation of reports and records.

AIRPORT ENGINEER: Supervised construction of basic permanent and temporary buildings. Maintained air strips, dispersal areas, roads, and hardstands. Insured compliance with construction specifications and regulations. Supervised preparation of reports and records.

WD AGO FORM 100

This form supersedes WD AGO Form 100, 15 July 1944, which will not be used.

MILITARY EDUCATION

NAME OF SCHOOL—COURSE OR CURRICULUM—DURATION—DESCRIPTION

AAF Technical School - 24 weeks. Studied all component parts of aircraft, and repair of same.

Wright Engine Course - 6 weeks. Complete study of aircraft engines and overhaul and maintenance.

Engineer Aviation Officer Course - 8 weeks. Airport and facilities construction.

Heavy Equipment Maintenance - 4 weeks. Care and maintenance of heavy equipment.

Chemical Warfare - 1 week. Techniques of gas protection.

CIVILIAN EDUCATION

HIGHEST GRADE COMPLETED	DEGREES OR DIPLOMAS	YEAR LEFT SCHOOL	OTHER TRAINING OR SCHOOLING	
			COURSE—NAME AND ADDRESS OF SCHOOL—DATE	DURATION
17	B.S.	1941		
NAME AND ADDRESS OF LAST SCHOOL ATTENDED				
University of Utah Salt Lake City, Utah				
MAJOR COURSES OF STUDY			None	
Civil Engineering				

CIVILIAN OCCUPATIONS

TITLE—NAME AND ADDRESS OF EMPLOYER—INCLUSIVE DATES—DESCRIPTION

JUNIOR HYDRAULIC ENGINEER: U.S. Geological Survey, Salt Lake City, from November 1941 to November 1942. Field office work relative to all surface water records for state of Utah and Nevada.

CIVIL ENGINEER: Gibbons and Reid, Salt Lake City, from June 1941 through August 1941. Worked as grade foreman and instrument man on construction of airport.

ADDITIONAL INFORMATION

REMARKS

Served as a member of Enlisted Reserve Corps from 4 June 1942 to 18 November 1942. Served overseas in Asiatic-Pacific Theater from 18 July 1945 to 14 May 1946. Authorized Unit Meritorious Service Award.

SIGNATURE OF PERSON BEING SEPARATED	SIGNATURE OF SEPARATION/CLASSIFICATION OFFICER	NAME OF OFFICER (Typed or Stamped)
Earl H Peirce	Charles E Sutcliffe	CHARLES E. SUTCLIFFE 1ST LT., AC

2nd Lieutenant Earl Harvey Peirce
1943
From Cadet 19073751 to Officer 0862429
MOS 4823 (Aircraft Maintenance Officer)

LIFE IN THE WARTIME MILITARY SERVICE

Hobbs, we found out, was a small oil boom town in the southeast part of New Mexico, so near to Texas that in the evening the dust and sand from Texas blew into Hobbs and during the daytime it blew back. Other than that it was an ideal place for a training field. There were almost 365 days flying time available per year (three hundred sixty-four because they did shut down on Christmas Day). There were no mountains, it being flat like a pool table, and there was space available.

We bought another railroad ticket and were off for the desert. There was a small hotel where we could stay; later we rented a house and then an apartment and finally a garage that had been converted to a small house. We were really happy in Hobbs even though we had these humble accommodations. It just goes to show that it is the quality of the people in the house not the quality of the house that makes for happiness. I was assigned as assistant engineering officer for one of the squadrons of B-17s on the field. As I remember there were about twenty-five planes each in the four training squadrons. Ida was soon teaching school and as usual reports of the excellence of her teaching ability were soon heard. We met some very fine people, the Whitsitts from Oklahoma, and went with them frequently. One time we saw an oil well that had broken loose and was gushing like Old Faithful geyser. Another time we went with them to El Paso and Juarez, ending up sleeping in the car as there were no hotels available in El Paso. We also went to Carlsbad Caverns and walked through that remarkable cave.

We were at Hobbs till about January 1945, that is a year and seven months till I was transferred. We developed many friends and became quite attached to the place. We were able to visit Clyde and Arlene. He had been transferred from Camp Callan in La Jolla to Fort Bliss in El Paso. They lived in a large house on the post with room for us to stay with them when we visited there. Mother Stauffer came to Hobbs to visit us. It was quite courageous on her part as the only practical way to travel from Utah was on the bus. I took Ida and Mother out to the base and gave them an inspection trip through a B-17. I think Mother enjoyed it. We put her on a bus at Amarillo, Texas, for the return trip. We had our fingers crossed for her safety; however, she made the trip with no problems.

I knew about weight and balance for aircraft following courses we had at Yale so they made me weight and balance officer for the field. I was assigned two enlisted men to help. We procured some scales from Wright Field in Dayton, Ohio, weighed all the planes, determined their center of gravity by technical considerations which gave them all a clearance to fly, taught a course for the flying officers, and then were given leave to go home for ten days.

Ida and I purchased bus tickets and returned to Utah. I visited with my sisters and my father and with Ida's folks. Wouldn't you know, Dad Stauffer said, "Your Ford is built too low to the ground," so I stored it out in the barn at the farm. He had bought it from us when I went in the service and Ida came to New Haven. Now he was giving it back to us. I took it to the garage and had some spacers put in the springs so it wouldn't ride so low and we drove it back to Hobbs. I have never seen people like Ida's parents who were forever doing kind things for other people. I always loved them for the kind of people they were. I am so happy that never, never, never was there a cross word with them.

9 - 1 - A

1944 — Hobbs New Mexico
I become 1st Lieutenant Earl H. Peirce

SECTION C FLIGHT A SHIFT I

At Hobbs Army Air Force Base. Shown here one of three shifts in the Squadron where I was Engineering Officer. I am on the extreme right. We had to have our planes ready 24 hours a day- 364 days a year to fill out the demand for pilots being trained at this field. I was quite proud of one of our B17-Fs, not the newer B17-G shown here, when it was in the air 11 hours a day for 30 days -- a record.

At Our Hobbs Apartment
1943

The picture quality is poor as I carried it in
my wallet to Okinawa little appreciating the fact
I would need the picture forty eight years later.

We drove the robin's-egg blue Ford to Hobbs on our return from leave. There were only a handful of cars in use at the base. Nowadays you would say we were living in Fat City. Because of my eagerness getting the planes weighed and balanced, in my absence during the leave, I had been made Engineering Officer for one of the squadrons. That meant a lot of problems and decisions but they seemed to work out.

It was interesting at times when we had an engine change on one of our planes to go with the test pilot to put some slow time on the engines and test them out. I went several times as (a somewhat clumsy) copilot with a Major Ashworth, who had been in the Eagle Squadron in the Battle of Britain earlier in the war. He could fly a B-17 like a fighter plane; he never had a tug pull a plane into a hangar, rather he taxied it in even with the small wing-tip clearance those hangars had. One time when I was officer of the day for the flight line, two of our planes had an accident landing on a training mission at Santa Ana. They assigned me as investigating officer and flew me to Santa Ana as part of a high-altitude training mission. There we were at 32,000 feet, 60 below zero outside, flying into a headwind, totally dependent on oxygen masks. I thought we would never get there, as it took four hours. The B-17 was a remarkably safe, dependable plane. I can't remember one from my squadron having other than minor accidents while I was there. One did fly into the ground one day when there was pilot error in reading the wrong engine number when the oil pressure failed. Then they feathered the wrong prop, gave too much boost to the other engines, lost power, and flew it into the ground wheels up with no one hurt. All that was wrong in the beginning was a capillary tube for oil-pressure indication having failed. There was really nothing wrong with the plane. I recite this as an indication of the unexpected that characterized aircraft maintenance.

The invasion of Europe finally took place and as we listened to it we could see why we had been so hard-pressed to provide pilots for the bombing raids over Germany. They were cannon fodder and we could hardly meet the new demand for trained pilots, flying training missions twenty-four hours a day, 364 days a year.

In February 1945, as I remember, I had gone to a show in "downtown" Hobbs. The military police called me out of the theater and said, "Go out to the field and get ready to leave, you are going to have to catch a plane tomorrow morning." So I rushed out there, took the ever freely given physical examination, went to the squadron, checked out all my property, picked up my orders, and went back to town to tell Ida. Here she was to be stuck in New Mexico without any family around and to live alone. We had to say goodbye all over again. They had pumped me full of shots; I was half sick from the typhoid shot and felt miserable about what was going on. There was nothing that could be done except obey.

167

I had been transferred to the Corps of Engineers for training in an Engineer Aviation Battalion at Geiger Field in Spokane, Washington. This type of outfit, somewhat similar to the Seabees, constructed airports, highways, etc., as needed. Another officer from Hobbs was transferred with me. We were both graduate civil engineers. We were therefore hopeful that we would get to practice our own profession. We did.

At Geiger Field we were told to divest ourselves of the propeller insignia on our uniforms (butterflies they called them) and put on the engineer "Castles." We were told that we now would find out what military service was all about. So we went to heavy equipment, construction, and soil mechanics classes with a bit of military training thrown in, like finding your way through the forest in the night with a compass.

Ida, bless her, found a GI who would drive her back to Utah, so she drove the Ford to Willard, having to quit her school-teaching job in Hobbs. As soon as I could locate a place for her to stay, she and Glade drove to Spokane and Glade returned to Salt Lake on the bus. That was a long drive, under wartime conditions, with gas and tires scarce. Ida and Glade did a bang-up job. We were able to rent a small house in a public housing project. There was no refrigerator but the iceman came regularly to fill the icebox.

I was assigned to the 801st Aviation Engineer Battalion. This battalion had just returned from service in the Azores and was an experienced construction group. Well disciplined also, with a fiery colonel of Italian extraction in charge who drilled us at great lengths in the school of the soldier. How unnecessary that was when we should have been getting on with the job of winning the war.

Another sad day came in July. I had to leave Ida again. We are well versed in the sadness of farewells. Who knew where we were going as we left on the train for Fort Lawton in Seattle? It was secret, but the taxicab drivers in Spokane told us we were going to Okinawa and they were right. We never could figure out how they knew.

Ida started off again in the robin's-egg blue Ford for Salt Lake. She ended up living in a big old house, turned into apartments, on 1st South and about 6th East in Salt Lake. She was able to get a job teaching at the Ensign School and I was later told she was one of the best teachers they ever had.

We went by train to Seattle and I was assigned as loading officer for the ship that would carry our construction equipment. I said I knew nothing about loading a ship. I was told that this was a good time to learn. I did. However, when I saw all that equipment that had to be put on that L.S.T. (Landing Ship Tank), I knew that it would not all go on and if it did it would sink the ship. It didn't.

Before we left the port I was able to call Ida and was happy that she had driven back to Utah with no problems. We sailed in late July, out through the

Strait of Juan de Fuca at full cruising speed for an LST, that is six knots. Its flank speed was nine knots. Not that we were in a hurry, we were not cowards, but does one want to hurry to war? I really enjoyed the ship and the travel. I believe I could have been a mariner. I never was the least bit seasick as some were. Eleven days later we had gunnery practice outside Pearl Harbor and later that day entered the harbor where we were anchored for a week. We were able to go into Honolulu on the sugar cane railroad, no longer there now. Also Lieutenant Mahew, our executive officer, and I went on a bus trip around Oahu, saw the temple, and had an enjoyable trip.

Our stop after Pearl Harbor was Eniwetok Atoll. As in Hawaii there were ships anchored as far as we could see. What a military might the U.S. had in those days. It was unbelievable how many ships had been made. I had seen them in New York harbor, in Hawaii, and now again in Eniwetok. What a fantastic job had been done by our country, not only in equipment, but in loyalty and service. It seems to me that we were more united than we have ever been since. We went ashore on this beautiful island so narrow and loaded with military installations over that crystal-clear water into the small lagoon. Here our orders were to accompany another LST to Saipan and there join a convoy to Okinawa.

It was so beautiful to go topside at night, especially in the moonlight, and see the green fluorescence that followed in the ship's wake. It was an incredible experience, so peaceful out there in the blue Pacific. It was hard to realize there was a war on.

Then came the incredible news over the ship's radio. An atom bomb had been dropped on Hiroshima and then another on Nagasaki. We were halfway to Saipan when the news came. Many thought the ship would immediately turn around and take us home. We were pretty naive and unprepared for what was necessary following a war. Just as we are today as we have troubles in the Middle East: What will we do if we win?

Japan surrendered, the captain broke out the grog, the helmsman got too much of it, and in the night we almost ran into the LST ahead of us. That would have been an ironic fate, to go down in the Pacific because the war ended. We spent a week in Saipan till a convoy was organized. I wonder why? Perhaps because they didn't want somebody who hadn't heard of the war's end to put a torpedo in us.

Fifty-four days after we left Seattle we arrived at Okinawa. The LST was designed to run up on the beach, which it did, open its bow doors, which it did, and we drove our equipment out on to the beach—bulldozers, trucks, jeeps, cranes, compressors, shovels, etc.—and drove to our camp some twenty miles north just below Yontan Airfield. Captain Schroder, company commander, and I, first lieutenant and platoon officer, pitched our tent at the door of an Okinawan tomb that had been used as a bunker five short months ago during the invasion. The tomb still had bones of deceased persons stuffed in urns pickled in sweet potato juice, in the fetal position. It was their custom. It was a week before we could rig a shower. The weather was hot and humid. I can't describe the luxurious feeling when we were able to get that shower. It felt as if a quarter of an inch of grime and sweat had been removed from us.

Coast Guard LST 205 Ship's Officers
801st Engineer Aviation Battalion Officers

Coast Guard & Engineer Aviation Battalion Enlisted Personnel
15 August 1945 celebrating the Japanese Surrender
Somewhere between Hawaii & Eniwetok

At the joyful news the skipper broke out the grog. The Helsman had too
much and in the middle of the night we almost ran into the LST ahead of
us. We were saved by the Radarman in the nick of time. Note that every
square foot available was covered by our engineering equipment or a gun
tub. There were twelve 40mm gun tubs for future kamikaze attacks.

We set to work and made a camp of tents. We had heard about typhoons so we used lumber to frame the tents and steel cable over the top to hold them down in a wind. How wise we were because when the typhoons came only the mess tent and the commanding officer's 9x9 went down. Secretly no one was sorry for the CO; he was such an unreasonable person.

My first job was building Quonset huts for a hospital. The hospital had been established in tents. We moved them into the buildings as fast as possible. Later I was in charge of construction for a power station and headquarters war room for the 8th Air Force, which had been transferred to the Pacific after the war's end in Europe. We had a large crew of Japanese prisoners of war working for us. They were a hard-working group and as obedient to our authority as they had been to their own officers.

While building the hospital we experienced a mild typhoon and then a terrible one. We had gone to the hospital site on orders and against our better judgment. We ended up there with twenty-five pows holding down a tent while an operation was in progress. Those Quonset huts we had not finished and anchored were picked up by the wind and moved all over. The sheet metal was torn off and flew through the air like sheets of paper. We made our way in a truck at about five miles an hour back to the camp and prepared to sit in our tents for the duration. During the twenty-four hours of the storm as the eye passed near the wind changed direction 360 degrees. It seemed to rain sand and water horizontally. We heard the wind indicator the Navy had went out of order at 130 knots. Our tents flapped so hard that water sprayed over us inside the tent. We were very lucky to still be able to sit the night out and have the tents still standing. That storm certainly was an experience of a lifetime. The next day, after things had calmed down we drove along the beach at Buckner Bay. We saw at least a dozen large ships had been blown high and dry a good distance from the shore. Ten men were killed that night. Now that was irony, to survive a war and be killed by a storm before you could get a ship home.

I received a transfer to another battalion when the 801st was disbanded and was there near Kadena airport till I had enough points to start home in May. The call came to go to the replacement depot to be processed to go home. We were in the depot about a week till our ship, a PA Military Transport Ship, was ready to receive all five thousand of us. I had a bunk in officers' country so the trip was really pleasant even though a bit tedious. We officers sat on guard, four hours on and twenty-four hours off, to prevent any difficulties between black and white troops. Everyone was so glad to be going home that there was no trouble. I did see white and black soldiers throwing a white boy in the salt water shower because he wouldn't use it himself and he smelled so bad.

We were on the ship twenty-six days because it was to be decommissioned in New York and that's where the skipper wanted to take it. We stopped in Pearl Harbor for stores on a Sunday morning. The radio was playing over the ship's loudspeaker. The Mormon Tabernacle Choir program was on. That was the sweetest music I have ever heard in my life. The ship continued through the Panama Canal, an adventure in itself. I have always wanted to do that again sometime. We had a boat whistle reception coming into New York Harbor.

My sister Marie had gone to work in New York as a secretary and had come down to the harbor to meet me. I had to report at Camp Kilmer in New Jersey but I came back to see her in the evening. We went to the musical "Oklahoma." We had a wonderful visit. I had second thoughts about her being in New York. She came home soon after.

There followed a rather uneventful trip to Salt Lake on a troop train. Ida came to the station to meet me and we drove to a motel in the robin's-egg blue Ford. Was I ever glad to see her! Two days later I was back at Fort Douglas for the inevitable physical exam. They wanted to know if I had any physical complications in the military. I told them I had some serious bouts of sinusitis. So they made a superficial check of that and the results of the examination was, "a tendency toward weak feet." I let it go at that and now forty-five years later my feet are still working just fine.

That was the military service starting in November 1942 and ending in May 1946. I had it so easy compared to many who suffered and died in the service. As I walked through the cemeteries in Okinawa where thousands of servicemen had so recently been buried I hoped that in the eternities what they had done for their country would be made up to them by the Lord. We never could.

On 20 May 1946, I was discharged from active military service and appointed captain, Air Corps, Army of the United States in the reserve corps. This was the end of my military service.

On Okinawa as a Aviation Engineer Construction Battalion Officer I was assigned my own Jeep and here it is with a plywood body, built by myself to help keep out the wind and the rain. Of course it was named Ida Belle in honor of my wife Ida.

These Prisoners-of-War working for us had been Royal Japanese Marines. They had been in battle in Manchuria and claimed to have killed many Chinese. (Recorded here lest we forge t a cruel side of Japanese people, at least in War)

The Typhoon in 1945 had a devastating effect on ships caught in Buckner Bay, Okinawa. Most ships had left the harbor to ride out the storm . Either way, in or out of the Bay, was a momentous decision.

The Okinawan women here were hired to wash our clothes in our homemade laundry. These women, many of who must have been widows, represent the terrible loss in the battle of natives and those Okinawans forced into the Japanese army. Over 100, 000 of the Japanese army were killed. The US had 39,000 casualties. While we were there it was common to encounter women and children and men.

Lest we forget those who died for us. I took the photo only 4 months after the battle.
There were other US Military Cemeteries on Okinawa

This had been Naha, the Capitol of Okinawa. The only structure surviving from the battle was the shell of a Christian Church

On the Ways

PUBLISHED BY THE LAKE WASHINGTON SHIPYARDS • HOUGHTON, WASHINGTON

| Volume 4 | JULY 20, 1945 | Number 14 |

LST 205 Now Ready to Seek More Glory in Pacific

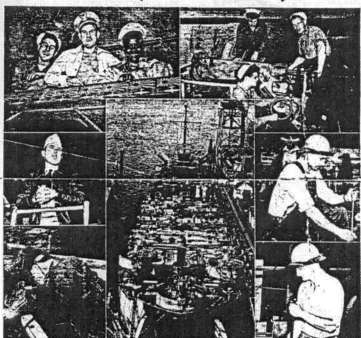

Top—David G. Maxwell, A. M. Elmore and Robert H. Banks point to the eight flags painted on the stack of LST 205, representing the Jap suicide planes brought down. Center—The new skipper. Left: Sims F. Sogaard. Lower—Chester Laurent, LWS welder, does his bit to put ship back in fighting trim.

With one and better guns the LST 205 will prove a more formidable foe to the Japs when it returns to the Pacific.

George Sturm, Jr., Donald Varboro and Leonard Adams are thrilled with the new twin-40 that will be menacing when they return to battle. Ernest Matter and Jim Perrone, LWS joiners, are shown by an working on the launching ways for the LCI.

Those Walking Sailors

Sailors aboard our big aircraft carriers walk so much they wear out more than 140 pairs of shoes each week. Reducing to keep these men on their feet are the ships' sweating cobblers, who have nothing but kind words for the stitching and finishing machines which make the sailors' shoes look like new and yet feel as comfortable as an old pair.

* * *

EIGHT SUICIDE PLANES DESTROYED

Lake Washington Shipyard workmen recently tallied up the U.S.S LST (Landing Ship, Tank) 205 as another victory in the "Battle of Repairs."

And as the repaired and refitted little ship made ready to rejoin her fighting sisters in the far Pacific, her heroic Coast Guard crew members were asked to tell their ship's story as they saw and lived it.

It's a simple story of heroism and straight shooting. The 205 took part in initial landings which led to recapture of the Philippines. She made "Suicide Gulch" shuttle runs to Mindoro through Sulu Sea areas flanked by Jap-held islands and airfields.

She shot down not one or two, but eight suicide planes, then fought

Plywood Radio Masts

Hurricane-proof radio masts made of molded plywood have been developed during the present war. The new molded plywood is so light that a single man, using boom and tackle, can erect a 55-foot mast, and two men can erect a 75-foot or even a 90-foot mast, yet it is so strong that when properly guyed it will withstand a gale of 120 miles per hour.

* * *

LST 205 REPAIRED AT LWS
(Continued from Page 1)

the ninth to a dead heat. The ninth Kamikaze managed to reach the 205 and crash the deck, but its load of explosives tore loose from the plane, slithered over the side and into the water before going up in a shattering concussion.

"The shooting was good, but our luck was good, too," crew members said.

To this Lieutenant Simo F. Negard of Marksville, La., the 205's new skipper, adds: "The ship has a proud record. The men who made that record are good men and brave men."

George C. Owens, Jr., GM3c, USCGR, of Camden, Ark., was standing about 20 feet from where the ninth and almost-successful Jap plane hit. Asked if that was close enough, he admitted that was "a little too close. I like 'em much better when they fall about a mile away."

Owens said the plane crashed and broke up on deck, then parts skidded overside, dragging the plane's bomb into the sea. "For which we were very grateful," the Coast Guard gunner's mate added.

Leonard D. Adams of Manning, Iowa, EM3c, USCGR, was at his battle station on a forward gun mount when the Kamikaze that "almost got us" came in.

"That doggone Jap went right over the top of our mount," Adams recalled. "Seemed like inches, but I guess he missed us by 25 or 30 feet. Then he crashed and broke up and went tumbling over the side. I'll never know how he stayed together long enough to reach us. He was breaking up in the air so badly that pieces of the plane were falling for some time after he hit. Most of the men who got hurt were injured by falling steel or shrapnel."

Even in the midst of a life-and-death battle with a vicious and desperate enemy the American fighting man usually finds his sense of humor still working.

On the 205 it was Robert H. Banks, StM 3c, of Washington, D. C., who provided the laughs. He had been at his battle station forward when Hirohito's suicide expert dived in and left part of his plane hanging on Bank's gun tub.

When the youthful steward was relieved at his station and went below, Chief Machinist A. M. Elmore, USCG, of 1119 Pine Avenue, Long Beach, Calif., noticed the Negro boy's long face. He said, "Come on, Banks, give us a little smile now." To which Banks promptly replied:

"Mr. Elmore, sir, what with my heart jumped right up on the roof of my mouth, I don't think I'll ever smile again."

According to DeSand'G Vernon, S1c, USCGR, of Butler, Ark., "The slant-eyed so-and-so came over our gun mount so close I had to reach up and feel to see if my helmet was still on. After the plane hit, we just gritted our teeth and waited for the explosion. But the bomb was in the water before it went. We were sure lucky."

The men below decks during a sustained enemy attack work under a terrific strain because they "don't know what's going on topside," said David O. Maxwell, MoMM2c, USCGR, of Detroit, Michigan. "We lost contact and communication with the bridge three times. We figured our luck had run out, then, because we thought the whole bridge had been blown off. But our luck held and our gunner's didn't miss, so I'm back to tell about it."

So today, readied for sea by the skill and sweat of American workmen the "unsinkable 205," her battle scars healed, is heading back with her sturdy bow doors pointed at Tokyo.

Fighting men—skilled workmen—tough ships by the hundreds and thousands—these are the things that Hirohito dreams about in his nightmares these days.

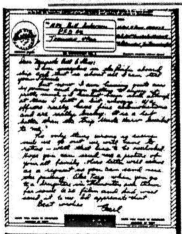

We were about 54 days on LST 205 from Seattle to Okinawa with stops in Hawaii, Eniwetok and Saipan. Below is a sample of the mail we sent home. It had to be censored. As an officer I censored my own mail. The trip on the ship was a bit tedious but I enjoyed it thoroughly.

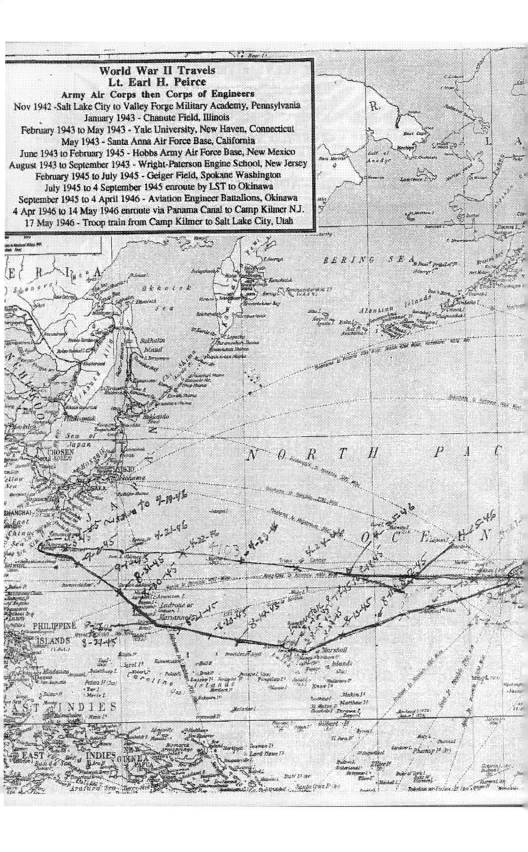

World War II Travels
Lt. Earl H. Peirce
Army Air Corps then Corps of Engineers
Nov 1942 -Salt Lake City to Valley Forge Military Academy, Pennsylvania
January 1943 - Chanute Field, Illinois
February 1943 to May 1943 - Yale University, New Haven, Connecticut
May 1943 - Santa Anna Air Force Base, California
June 1943 to February 1945 - Hobbs Army Air Force Base, New Mexico
August 1943 to September 1943 - Wright-Paterson Engine School, New Jersey
February 1945 to July 1945 - Geiger Field, Spokane Washington
July 1945 to 4 September 1945 enroute by LST to Okinawa
September 1945 to 4 April 1946 - Aviation Engineer Battalions, Okinawa
4 Apr 1946 to 14 May 1946 enroute via Panama Canal to Camp Kilmer N.J.
17 May 1946 - Troop train from Camp Kilmer to Salt Lake City, Utah

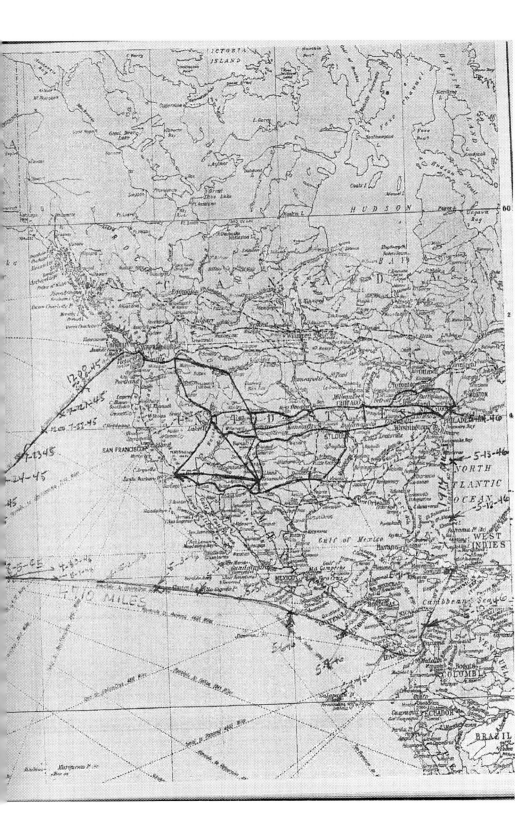

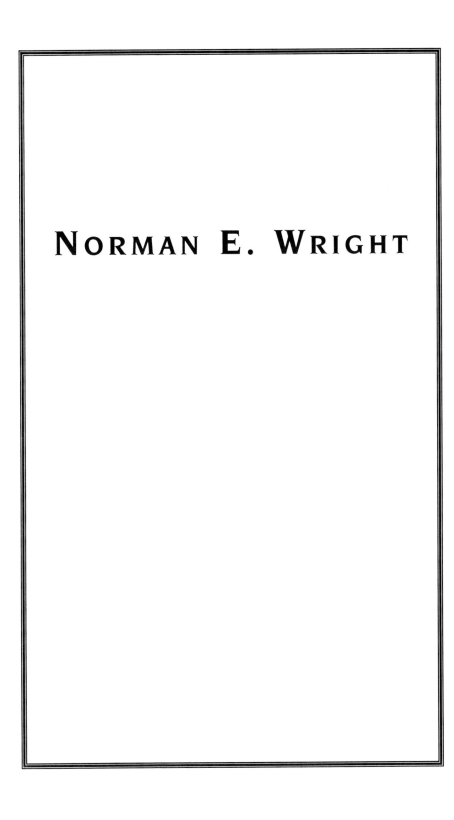

NORMAN E. WRIGHT

THE MILITARY AND I

Being an Account of the Experiences of Norman E. Wright in the United States Army, April 1944 to April 1946

When the Japanese commenced war at Pearl Harbor on December 7, 1941, I was in my junior year of high school. During the months that followed December eighth and our declaration of war, I followed in detail the fast moving events of the war. But through it all, I thought little of how this great train of events would affect me.

Not until the spring and summer of 1943 did I think seriously of entering into military service, for October seventeenth of that year (my eighteenth birthday) would make me eligible for the draft. Therefore, I began investigating the various programs of enlistment that were being offered to try and find something better than being a "buck private in the rear ranks." I found what I was looking for in the Enlisted Reserve Corps. What it offered was this: If a man enlisted in the army before his eighteenth birthday he would be put on an inactive status for six months after reaching eighteen, and then be called into active service. After completing basic training the enlistee was to go into the Army Specialized Training Program.

September 28, 1943, found me in Salt Lake City going through my first army physical examination. Finding me whole, I was sworn into the Army of the United States about three o'clock that afternoon.

A few days later, I registered as a freshman at Brigham Young University and commenced my college studies. The fall and winter quarters of school went quickly by and on April seventeenth, 1944, my orders arrived. I was to report to Fort Douglas in Salt Lake City on April twenty-fourth, 1944. Some of my friends at school who were on a similar status were to report on the same day. They were Frank Faux, Leo Vernon, and Robert Roberts.

April twenty-fourth was on a Monday. The evening before my brother Kenneth arrived home for a short leave. He was in U.S. Navy submarine training at San Diego. Having him home made it much easier for Mother to say goodbye to me, for which I was grateful. The next morning I kissed Mother goodbye and walked with bag in hand to the orderly room of the reception center at Fort Douglas. Thus began two years of schooling in the school of life. I wouldn't want to live them over again, but yet the lessons and experiences and blessings of those two years will help me the rest of my life.

The first week was one of processing physically and adjustment mentally. The former meant issue of clothing and equipment, records, tests, and assignment. The latter meant getting established in a new routine of life. The problem of applying to entirely new situations that which I had been taught and tried to live. It was a problem, too, for some of those with whom we had to live had little or no morals. It was difficult at that time to make changes. To move from one barracks to another seemed to throw me into a whirl of confusion. Then gradually everything was well again. Fortunately, at least we thought so, men who were in the E.R.C. were put in charge of barracks. That meant that Frank, Leo, Robert, and I were all given a barracks to watch over. We took charge of the cleaning details and then stood inspection. It was quite an experience for four rookies. Due to this responsibility we were exempt from KP. We were happy about the whole thing for KP here was reported to be "rough duty." The four of us did, however, get one detail. It was our first and consisted of KP in the officers' service club. We worked from about 6 P.M. to 11 P.M. one evening.

It was during these two weeks at the Reception Center that I formed an attachment to the library. Afternoon and evenings would find me there reading and writing. My brother Gordon came home on furlough during this time and got married. It was my honor to be best man at the wedding reception.

On Monday May 8, 1944, Frank and I learned that we were assigned to the Signal Corps and would leave for Camp Crowder, Missouri, that night. About 10 P.M. we boarded a Pullman and were off. We were on the D.R.G. & W. and as we moved south from Salt Lake Valley the great mountain Timpanogos came into view. It was set aglow by a beautiful full moon. To me it was a glorious farewell to pass by the "wonder-mountain." We fell asleep to the clickety-clack of the rails moving east to Missouri.

There were thirteen of us with the same travel orders. Newell Parker, an LDS fellow from Idaho, was among them. We moved east through Colorado and Kansas, then south from Kansas City. At Pittsburg, Kansas, the train made a ten-minute stop. There was free milk, cake, and cookies for the servicemen. This was my first experience with the generosity and kindness of the people of America. This was but one example of what I was to see.

Our train pulled into Camp Crowder at 1 A.M. Thursday. That night and the following week we were quartered in Co. C. 27 Battalion A.S.F.R.T.C.

(Army Service Forces Replacement Training Center). Activities during this time consisted of details of every description.

On Saturday, June twentieth, we moved to Co B. 27 Battalion and prepared to start basic training on the following Monday. For the next six weeks we were really busy training. I have learned since that it was an easy basic as compared to the seventeen weeks for the infantry. During this time I joined the 6 Regiment Chapel Choir. The chaplain was Gudmanson.

In nearby Joplin, I met for the first time in a branch of the church. Oh, how glorious it was to meet with the saints. This blessing of being always near the church was one that I enjoyed throughout all my army career.

Memories of basic are many. Little things like falling in and out "on the double," drill, the white and orange company flag, classes in the barracks, classes on the drill field in which a portable rostrum played an important role, Corporals True-Half and Rodrigius (NCOs of 4th Platoon), trying to keep awake, rifles, the all-important training films, the most important being the "Why we fight" series, shots, hikes over the Ozark hills with its firebugs at night almost lighting the way, and the water towers of camp telling us how much further, sweat-soaked clothes, the rain, the mellow moonlight, waiting in the black of night for someone to come through my guard post, marching with the band to the battle noises demonstrations. But above all I shall never forget retreat, nor taps, nor prayer.

When the whole battalion snapped to present arms, a glorious feeling would go surging through my every fiber; "I'm here for a purpose—to defend liberty and freedom. Men have died today for that freedom. I'm proud to be an American. Live worthy of the price that is being paid."

When taps was sounded at 2300 every night, the strains "All is well, safely rest, God is nigh" would linger in the air from loud speakers in distant parts of the camp. Thoughts would come stumbling over one another, thoughts of my mom, my mountains, campfires, stars, life, my testimony, gratitude to my Heavenly Father—and tears would well up in my eyes.

I felt that I could not open my heart in prayer in the barracks where such vile influences oft prevailed. So, in secret, I sought to commune with my Heavenly Father. One of the teachings of my mother and father was to seek God in prayer. I shall be eternally grateful that they so firmly established that principle in my life. At this time, it became a source, my only source of strength and hope and courage. Each night before retiring I went to a secluded spot and there poured out my heart to God. Joy flooded my soul with the realization that the Lord was with me, for my prayers were heard and answered.

With a week's firing on the rifle range, an overnight hike, the mock village attack, and the grueling crawl up the infiltration course, our basic training came to an end June 30, 1944. We then received our assignments to our specialty schools. I was to go to radio operators school. The next day

(Saturday, July 1), I moved to Company C 30 Bn, where I resided during the next eight weeks while attending radio school.

This work I really enjoyed. It was something new and entirely different. During these few weeks I learned some lessons that have always remained with me, namely this: ability is not the deciding factor in success. Persistence, practice, and a humble, prayerful attitude with faith in ultimate achievement are factors that will cause aptitude to bow low. My ability to take code was meager. It was hard for me to grasp. As the class members learned the letters and later the speed of any one classroom, they were moved to the next level. Some that I began with made rapid progress. In fact, I was about the last to leave the beginning classroom work. But I was determined to succeed. I put the above-mentioned principles on trial and at the completion of our school I found myself receiving speeds above that of any member of the class, twenty-two words per minute. That experience helped to convince me that in life a person could do about what he wanted if he were willing to pay the price of work. "Genius is ninety-eight percent hard work," said Thomas A. Edison and I believe it!

I must mention one fellow who bunked just two beds away. His name was Rabinowitz. Yes, he was Jewish and one of the first I was ever closely associated with. He was small in stature and smoked a little curled pipe. His small build was made up for by an elaborate air of what he had done and what he was going to do. Yet under all the outer crust of pride I found a man I learned to love. Something drew me to him. He was of the house of Israel. Experiences later brought us together.

August twenty-sixth found our whole company transferred to Co. B. of the 28 Bn where we made preparation to make a three-week trip into the field. Those three weeks beginning August twenty-eighth and ending September fourteenth were full of unforgettable experience: torrents of rain, the mellow, mellow Ozark moon, the radio shacks, sending and receiving messages, bivouac, Rabinowitz and I tented together, chow, the mock amphibious operation on a big pond, "Save the Pigeons," moving up at night, and the fifteen-mile march back to camp on the last day.

The first weekend after returning I got a pass and went down to Little Rock, Arkansas and Fort Robinson to see Stanley Weeks who was training as an infantryman. We had a very good but short visit.

The next phase of my training was at the O.S.C.S. (Central Signal Corps School) at Camp Crowder which began September twenty-fifth. I transferred to Co. E 804 Reg where I resided while attending school. We learned to copy code with a typewriter as well as how to operate the bigger radio sets.

By this time the army routine was becoming a way of life and I began to "enjoy" myself. Friends played a big part in that enjoyment. It was here that I met Donald Goslin of Clarion, Iowa, William Knudsen of Provo, Bruce Willett of Madison, Wisconsin, Earl Hansen of Idaho, and Lloyd Guest of

Salt Lake City. The branch of the church at Joplin and the good saints made life most pleasant on the weekends by their kindness to us. The Rayles and Croutches played the major roles in this.

Then came that glorious day of December fifteenth. The First Sergeant handed me my orders to go to Fort Jackson, South Carolina. This included a fifteen-day delay en route. That meant a trip home for my first furlough. I was gloriously happy as the train pulled out of the station in camp. But that did not approach the thrill of taking Mom into my arms on the train platform in Salt Lake. It was a wonderful furlough. I completely forgot the army. Old friendships at the Y were renewed, one in particular with a fine young lady (she has since married) who played an important role in my morale throughout all my army career. As intense as had been my happiness so was my sorrow when the train pulled out of the Salt Lake Station leaving Mom, Beverly, and Grandma Wadley standing there that January 1, 1945.

This trip was an interesting one. I went through Denver; Kansas City; St. Louis; Cincinnati, Ohio; Frankfort, Kentucky; Knoxville, Tennessee; Ashville, North Carolina; and finally Columbia, South Carolina, and Fort Jackson. I reported to the 3324 SIAM (Signal Information and Monitoring Company). In the company I was happy to find many Crowder friends—Don, Bruce, and Earl. The 4th Armored Platoon was my first home for the first months. After I received my promotion to T/5 I was transferred to the army headquarters platoon. Activities in the company included more code with emphasis on field training, P.T., and some night patrol work.

To me these night patrols were quite realistic affairs. One night, I remember we were patrolling a wooded area when we were signaled to hit the ground silently. This we did just as another group passed right by us without seeing us at all. I was on one side of a large old log. As the men of this "enemy" patrol passed by, I was questioning myself as to whether I would ever have to rise from some such a position in the field of combat to kill the man who passed by me. I'm grateful I was never called upon to do so. On that same patrol three of us accidentally became detached from the rest of the group and wandered back into camp a half hour or so late, much to our embarrassment.

About March 1, 1945, the company went onto the rifle range. It was there I received word that Steven, Marilyn's and Gordon's first child, was born while there Major Rogers, our C.O., told us, "Men, we're hot," meaning that we were due to ship overseas (Europe) sometime in June.

Following our tour on the rifle range, we made preparations and set out for a three-week field trip in which we were to operate under simulated battle conditions. This excursion was really "good training." While in the midst of this activity the news came through that Germany had surrendered. Even though we were in the field we loaded on our trucks and went back to camp for the mammoth dress parade to celebrate victory in Europe.

During that last week in the field I received word from home that President Grant had died. I remember my feelings when I read that letter. "One of the great prophets of God has been taken home—what does the future hold?"

At the end of May—in the meantime we completed our field trip—we learned that our company was to be deactivated. Before that took place however, I was given a seventeen-day furlough. It passed all too quickly. June twenty-third found me back at Fort Jackson and a member of the 596 J.A.S. Co. (Joint Assault Signal Company), for while I was gone the reorganization had taken place. Rumor was that we were to leave post-haste for California where we could receive training. This was no rumor, as we later found out.

But before leaving South Carolina, I must mention my church activities there. There was a fine branch in Columbia and all we LDS fellows spent Sundays there. Those meetings gave us the spiritual strength necessary to carry on each week. My morale sagged between Sundays. Each Sunday our "batteries" were recharged. The saints were good to us. We were taken into their homes and treated as sons. The Wallace McBride and Frank Graham families were particularly good to us. Brother Graham had a small swimming pool in his backyard. Our trips to their place were frequent. Just before we left we had a big watermelon bust there. Sandwiches and all the trimmings were enjoyed by about twenty-five servicemen.

There is one other event I must mention before going on, and that is the three-day pass I took to Charleston, South Carolina. It was a highlight of my stay in South Carolina. The city is literally filled with interesting places and things. (By the way, I thumbed down and back.) Old buildings were everywhere and behind each a fascinating story. The old slave market, the unique little shops, narrow streets, the old revolutionary cannon pointing out to sea, and the sword gate are some of the things that give the city such a characteristic air. I took a bus out to the Isle of Palms beach and there had my first look at the Atlantic. I was impressed by its gray countenance which fit well into its activity of angrily throwing itself at the beach. I was overpowered by it all and on that lonely expanse of beach I knelt and prayed.

I was in Charleston over Sunday and therefore was able to go to church there. It was district conference and President Meeks of the Southern States Mission presided. The spirit and power of that man deeply impressed me.

On July 27, 1945, our company boarded a troop train bound for Oceanside, California. It was an enjoyable trip. I remember the first night out, I pulled a guard detail in the mess car. It was a cloudless night and I remember how happy I was as I looked up at the stars through the mess car door. Our train traversed the following route—Atlanta, Birmingham, New Orleans, Shreveport, Fort Worth, Dallas, El Paso, Phoenix, Los Angeles, and Oceanside. I was happy to get to California. I had been there a number of times with my parents when a small boy and there was, therefore, a familiar atmosphere about the place. At Oceanside our training took on the Navy slant as each day we dropped over the sides of a large mock ship into small landing boats, then out three or four miles off the coast, up to the ready line, then the line of departure, and at last we would take off at high speed for the beach. As soon as we had landed we found appropriate spots and there dug our radios in and carried on communications for the afternoon. After three weeks of such intensive training we were nearing the ready stage to land on the island of Japan. The dropping of the atomic bomb on Hiroshima and Nagasaki made that unnecessary, however, for therewith the war came to a screaming halt. After the armistice was signed, September second, our training stopped and we immediately moved to Camp Callan just fourteen miles north of San Diego. While there I was very fortunate to receive a promotion to T/4.

Weekends were spent in San Diego. The Hillcrest Ward and the Servicemen's Dome were the center of church activities. Willis Brimhall from Pleasant Grove was stationed at the Naval Air Base there and we spent some fine times together. Among other spots we went out to the mission in San Diego where the Mormon Battalian stayed when it reached the coast.

While at Callan I received a five-day pass over Labor Day and was very fortunate to be able to spend it with Gordon in Los Angeles. Soon afterward he left for overseas duty in Japan..

On September 15, 1945, we entrained at Callan and made our way up the coast to Camp Cooke (twenty-three miles southwest of Santa Maria). We arrived there the next morning in a blanket of fog. The place was desolate. "A hole on a hill" we called it. Nevertheless, my stay at Camp Cook was the most enjoyable phase of my army life. We were in reality waiting for discharge and in the 262 Sig Co. to which we were assigned there was no training, no details (for me at least), no nuttin'! We would fall out for reveille in the morning and then be free for the day. This went on for about three weeks. It was during this time that I made an intense study of the Book of Mormon. The spirit of the Lord was indeed with me and bore record to my soul that that record was true.

Weekends were spent in Santa Maria and Lompoc. There were about twenty LDS fellows, among whom were Andy Wall, Don Peterson, and Eldridge Warnick, who actively took part in every phase of the work in the branch. We would return to camp from a Sunday or Tuesday MIA meeting full of the spirit of thanksgiving for the privilege of belonging to the church. Brother and sister Parley Maughan were particularly kind to us here. We spent many wonderful hours in their home.

The lady missionaries there were indeed an inspiration. Sister Deaun Moulton of Salt Lake and Sisters Vi Farnee and Violet Keller, both of Wyoming, were those we knew. Their wonderful spirit carried over into my life and indeed enriched it.

From October 1, 1945 to November 5, 1945, I was home on an extended furlough. February 10, 1946, found me on my way to the XII Corps headquarters at the Presidio of Monterey at Monterey, California. I was in a Special Service Section for a short time (four days) then immediately transferred to the 286 J.A.S. Co. at Ford Ord.

This was a notorious outfit due to its strict military commander, Major Edward Hayes ("JASCO Eddie"). "Now men, you know you shouldn't do that," he used to say in his high-pitched voice. Three weeks of my two months here was spent in the hospital getting rid of a case of the flu and taking care of a minor operation. During this time in the hospital I was visited by a very faithful friend, Ralph Jack. We had met at Pacific Grove Branch. From that day till the present we have been close friends. It would be difficult to find a more devoted friend than him. Needless to say, it was with him that my few months at Fort Ord were made much happier. Then came April, 1946. After rumor had seen my name on discharge orders some ten times or more, the official word finally came through. My heart jumped at the thought of again being a free man. On April 19, 1946, we boarded the train for Fort Douglas, Utah, and discharge.

I shall long remember one brief experience on the way home. As our train approached the Great Salt Lake from the west, a dark thundercloud passed over and dropped its load. We were traveling through a sea of sage brush and the fragrance of the wet sage filled the air. I felt then that it was a special treat for one who loved sage and who was homeward bound.

A fast two days of processing at Fort Douglas, and I was again Mr. Norman E. Wright. I was handed my discharge on April 22, 1946, and thenceforth returned home rejoicing.

J. ROBERT BULLOCK

Recollections of My Life

J. ROBERT BULLOCK
1916-1999
MILITARY SERVICE

1. Washington, D. C.

The Utah State Agricultural College was a land-grant college, which meant that because it was partially funded with federal monies, all male students were required to take at least two years of ROTC. While I did not consider myself an activist in opposition to the compulsory aspect of it, I neverthe-less did not like it and I remember attending a few meetings on the campus in student protest. As the military part of my life will attest, attitudes can and do change and my military experiences and memories are some of the most cherished and rewarding of my whole life. I did not necessarily choose the military career which I had, but neither did I let the war circumstances of the times entirely direct its course.

The Selective Training and Service Act, which provided for the first peace-time military draft in history, was passed by Congress on September 16, 1940, by a one-vote margin. At that time I was single, twenty-four years of age, and in very good health. I was employed as a file clerk at the Bureau of Internal Revenue. That job was simply filing tax returns in acres of filing cabinets, room after room. It had to be the work of the least importance to national security and the most boring in Washington. I was about to start my third year of a four-year law course at GW and the military draft was starting to blow in my direction. I decided the draft was probably inevitable, but since there wasn't any war yet, I might be able to postpone the inevitable long enough to finish law school if I could get a job at the Selective Service System, which was a new agency provided for under the draft law. This, I thought, would give me a basis for two or three years' military deferment and I could finish law school.

Fortunately, I was able to get a job as a personnel clerk and went to work the latter part of 1940 at the Selective Service System as a civilian. I liked the job very much as it gave me an opportunity to become acquainted with the military reserve officers who had been ordered to active duty to run and generally manage the system and who for the most part were neat guys. My military draft number was high enough that being drafted soon was not then that much of an immediate problem and I didn't think it would become a problem unless there was a war. Nevertheless, in about July 1941, I decided I probably would eventually be drafted when they got to my number sooner or later, so I had better consider trying to get a direct commission in the Reserves. That would defer me until such time as the Reserves were called up, which I thought would be much later than the draft.

I first made application for a direct commission in the Marine Corp and after being tentatively accepted, they told me later I was too old. I would reach twenty-five before completion of their school at Quantico, Virginia, which I didn't want to go to anyway because it would be out of Washington and it would therefore be difficult if not impossible to continue in law school because of time and distance problems. I went to the Navy Department and they offered me a commission as an ensign in the reserves, which I accepted. They didn't know when they might call me up, but I figured that if there wasn't a war I might have time to finish law school, but if there was a war, then all bets would be off anyway. About this time I was contacted by the office of Senator Alva B. Adams of Colorado, to whose office I had previously applied for a job and who had helped me get a job at the Public Works Administration. Senator Adams offered me a job in his office as a legislative assistant. I could hardly believe it because in my wildest dreams I did not think I could get a job on Capitol Hill in a democratic administration, which of all student jobs in Washington I most wanted. I told him I had not been active in politics myself, but that my parents had been lifelong Republicans. He said that didn't make any difference and all he would require of me was loyalty, ability, and ambition. I told him I didn't think I would have any trouble with those requirements and I knew I could do the work to his satisfaction if he would give me the chance. I hated to leave the Selective Service System, but this was the opportunity of a lifetime! The Senator knew I was going to law school and I figured if I did him a good job he eventually might offer me a place in his law firm of Adams and Gast in Pueblo, Colorado. He had hinted that he might do so.

After being in his office approximately six months and enjoying every day (I could go on the Senate floor to converse with him and sometimes just observe the great senators of the time, such as Connally in his tails and Alben Barkley, to name two). Colonel Shattuck, general counsel of the Selective Service System, called me and said he would try to get me ordered to active military duty at the Selective Service System if I wanted him to. Wow! What should I do now? I had a fantastic job on Capitol Hill, was going to law school, and here was another incredible opportunity—to be on active duty in the military service and go to law school at the same time. After thinking it over, I approached the Senator the latter part of November 1941 and told him about Colonel Shattuck's call and that I wanted his advice as to what I should do. He told me that he had a lot of information by reason of his chairmanship of the Armed Forces Appropriations Subcommittee and that in his opinion war would be avoided. He felt I would be better off for a future in the legal business to stay in his office and not go on military active duty, unless I had to, which was not then the case. I told him I would think it over and appreciated his advice and I would again be consulting him in a few days. Notwithstanding the Senator's advice, after thinking about it really less than a few days, I told Colonel Shattuck to see if he could make sure that if I were called up for active duty by the Reserves, I would be ordered to the Selective Service System, and if so, I would like him to start the process. But I did not tell the senator.

A few days later, on about December 1, 1941, Senator Adams had a heart attack and died. He never knew that his information on Japan's intentions to start a war was erroneous. Five days later, on December seventh, the Japanese bombed Pearl Harbor and war was declared by the U.S. against Japan and Germany the next day. I received orders to report for active duty at the Selective Service System eight days later on December 16, 1941, my birthday, and was assigned to the Selective Service System as a naval liaison officer. I was even more lucky because the job immediately given to me by the director, General Hershey, was in the legal division with office and secretary, and the first project was to research the question as to whether or not federal courts had the power to review draft board classifications. The case sparking the inquiry was *Greenberg vs.* U.S., wherein a U. S. District Court in New Jersey had ordered the discharge of a draftee after he had been inducted upon the grounds that his draft board erred in classifying him 1-A—available for service—instead of giving him a Class III, dependency deferment, on account of a claimed dependent. It was not difficult to see that if courts could review the millions of classifications made and to be made by thousands of civilian local boards the whole system would bog down and it would be incredibly difficult if not impossible to raise an army by draft.

It so happened that at this same time I was on the Board of Student Editors of the GW Law Review and I wanted to use my research for publication purposes in the Law Review. I was given permission to do so, and

General Hershey also approved. The reasons in the form of a law review article were published in the GW Law Review, thereafter cited by many federal
courts in draft cases which came before them. The general sent me a note
expressing positive feelings about the article.

Thereafter, my work in the legal department was the daily handling of
many emergencies involving aliens. The U.S. draft law specifically provided
that all male persons residing in the United States, whether citizens or not,
were liable for draft registration and for military service. As a result, non-res-
ident Britons, Canadians, Mexicans, Cubans, etc., in the then various diplo-
matic corps, foreign businessmen selling war materials to the U.S. government or to U.S. government contractors were often detained or arrested by
U.S. law enforcement officers because most of these people did not think
they could be liable for military service in the U.S., failed to register and,
therefore, didn't have a draft card showing compliance with the registration
requirement. Law enforcement officers in the U.S. nearly always, whenever
they had an occasion to examine anyone or anyone trying to come into the
United States, asked for a draft card showing that they had complied with
the military service law. Immigration officers, local police, FBI, and other law
enforcement agencies were constantly involved in the arrest of these people and, of course, the United States did not want an international incident
and looked to the Selective Service System in Washington, D.C., to straight-
en out the problems on an individual basis as they occurred. While most of
them were handled on the local level, many got to the National
Headquarters via the State Department, State Selective Service Directors,
foreign embassies, consulates, and others. My job was to take the corre-
spondence, telephone call, or other communication to National
Headquarters, ascertain the facts, and resolve the problems without any
unnecessary delay and without waiving any law or unduly upsetting the law
enforcement people involved. I probably wasn't the first Navy officer to get
an army commendation medal while in the navy, but I did get one for this
duty. And, I continued to go to law school where I graduated in 1942, and
later in that year took and passed the five-day District of Columbia bar
examination. Incidentally, I was promoted to lieutenant (JG) by the middle
of 1943 and had never been on a ship or boat bigger than a rowboat.

2. The Atlantic Theatre
About this time, my conscience began to bother me just a little. Here I was
single, in good health, no dependents, and doing military service by working for an organization drafting hundreds of thousands of the same kinds of
guy into a fighting army. I was also living in an essentially civilian setting,
not on any military base or subject to the usual military constraints. I was
through law school by now and would have to remain in the military service
anyway until the war ended. I felt I liked the Navy but in spite of my rank I

knew practically nothing about it. I wanted to go to sea, at least for awhile, to get some naval experience to go along with my rank. I didn't want to get killed either but I figured the odds were in favor that I would not.

For some reason, I decided to try to go to the antisubmarine warfare school in Miami, Florida, and eventually serve on an antisubmarine small vessel. These were called subchasers and were operating primarily in the Atlantic because the Germans were sinking a lot of merchant vessels and causing supply ammunition shortages in Europe and these antisubmarine vessels were to counteract that problem. That way I would not end up in the amphibious forces, which everybody knew were sooner or later going to spearhead an assault on Europe, likely France.

When I talked with General Hershey about it and asked him if he would consent to my transfer from his staff as a naval liaison officer he said he would, but offered the opinion that I could remain in the legal division at National Headquarters Selective Service until the war ended, and unless I was going to make the Navy a career it would be better for me personally to remain on duty there.

I nevertheless put in for subchaser duty and after a few weeks with his help was ordered to the officers' indoctrination school in Newport, Rhode Island, for six weeks and then to the Subchaser Officers' School in Miami. The subchaser school was rigorous and the subject matter was about as foreign to me as anything could be. Diesel engines, seamanship, navy regulations, underwater sound gear, and antisubmarine warfare tactics, depth charges, and what have you. I wasn't sure I had made the right choice, and in fact most of the time at the school I had the fear that I might not be able to handle the seamanship, as I was sure I had not had any experience. Besides, as a child I could not go up in a swing without getting sick, and I thought if I did have any extended sea duty that that was probably what would happen. I'd just be sick all the time.

This did not last too long, however, and before the course was completed, a bunch of orders came to the school transferring most of us, if not all, to the amphibious forces! We were shortly moved to Camp Bradford, Virginia, a World War I camp of tents having cement floors and canvas tops. The weather was terrible, it was cold and rainy, and the tents leaked. I was certain my Selective Service luck had run out and I wondered if it would ever again be possible for me to get back there where I really enjoyed the duty.

It was not long before we were shipped to Boston and were quartered in the Fargo Building awaiting transportation to Europe to become the officers of English amphibious ships which were going to be turned over to the United States somewhere in England. Most of us knew nothing about the ships we were to take over and the scuttlebutt about the duty was that they were typically austere British ships which were used effectively as anti-air-

In the Navy

My Crew

craft platforms covering the British soldiers in their humiliating withdrawal from the continent at Dunkirk.

At about Thanksgiving time, in November 1943, we were taken to New York by train along with our crews, which had been formed in Boston and were loaded aboard the *Queen Elizabeth*. The trip was quite an experience. Here was an ocean luxury liner which would normally carry 2,000 to 2,500 crew and passengers, stripped of everything luxurious, including wood, bathroom fixtures, etc., on which there were now about 16,000 troops of the various services and units, including ours, of approximately 1,000 officers and enlisted men, all going to England. The number of officers in a stateroom varied from about thirty or so in double bunks down to ten, depending upon rank; and some of the enlisted men were required to "hot sack" their sleeping area, which meant that the space was shared. That is to say, each would have the space for eight to twelve hours before someone else would take it over. Meals were served continuously and everyone had been given a numbered table and seating time at the time of embarking for eating twice each twenty-four hours. In the stateroom to which I was assigned, normally used by two people, there were about seventeen others besides me. We had to crawl over other bunks to get to the one assigned, and on many occasions I had to ask myself—is this trip necessary?

The *Queen* ran alone without convoy or escort, relying on her speed and zigzag course to avoid submarine attack and about five days later at daybreak we saw an F.W. Woolworth sign as we steamed up the Clyde River in Scotland. It was a small but refreshing reminder that we weren't in a completely strange place after all. Debarking was a painstaking process because of the large numbers of units and troops going in all directions and on all kinds of transport. After awhile, however, our transportation became available. We were transported by trucks to a train station for the trip by train to Roseneath, Scotland. Roseneath was located on the Garelock, not far from Loch Lomond where we were housed in Quonset huts and an old castle.

In about a month, the English ships were turned over to us and we began limited training. The formal turn-over ceremony with bands, dress blues, flags of both countries, and the whole nine yards, took place on January 10, 1944. My ship was the USS LCF 22.

About the first of March, all of the LCFs put out from Roseneath into the Irish Sea headed for Falmouth, England. We arrived in Falmouth a week or so later, which was to be our new port until the invasion of Europe, which nobody knew where it would be or when. The next couple of months were feint departures on occasions and schooling for the crew and a lot of guessing and speculation as to when and where the invasion would take place.

Finally on the night of June second, the group commander brought aboard orders for the invasion which was to occur on the morning of June 5, 1944. The orders weighed at least ten pounds and purported to cover every ship and aircraft involved in the whole Utah Beach operation. There was not much about the LCFs in the orders, except that we were to leave the harbor at 4:00 P.M. the next day, June third, along with the Eighteen, Twenty-six, and Thirty-one. We were to proceed in convoy along with numerous other kinds and types of craft and ships, to Point E, off the coast of Normandy, which was on a chart which had been placed in the orders; then go into Red Beach of Utah Beach with the first wave, which had been scheduled to land at 6:30 A.M. on June fifth. Our general mission was to provide gunfire support for the landings as needed, and particularly support against enemy aircraft which might be present. After the initial landings, we were to cease fire upon the beach and then patrol the boat lanes to protect landing troops against enemy aircraft. We held a general muster, where the orders were explained to the crew and at 4:00 P.M. on June third, we unmoored and steamed out of the harbor in company with the other three LCFs.

The orders also provided that if the code words "post mike one" were received at any time, we were to reverse course 180 degrees and head back to England. The weather was terrible, wind and rain made ship handling difficult, particularly flat-bottomed ships, and the current was so strong and our speed so slow that it was almost impossible to maintain a course. Early in the morning of the fourth, we received the code words "post mike one" and reversed course accordingly. When this happened I had a lot of mixed feelings. I was not anxious to proceed in foul weather or for that matter to be shot at or sunk, in good weather or bad. Maybe a miracle would happen and the whole thing would be called off. On the other hand I realized there would be no miracle and I would just have to go through the same thing again later, which might be even worse. But, there wasn't much I could do about it anyway. All of us knew that it would be General Eisenhower who would make the decision as to whether we went or not and when. I am sure we all felt confident that he would not expose us to any more danger than he had to.

After making the turn and getting back to Weymouth Bay, I was really quite relieved when we got the word that D-Day was changed from the fifth to the sixth and the convoy was ordered to again set out for France.

The weather continued bad, but on the night of the fifth, it seemed to abate slightly, and it had improved considerably by the morning of the sixth. When we arrived at what we thought was the transport area and somewhere near Point E marked on the chart, but which in no way was marked on the water, it became light enough to see hundreds of ships of all types and kinds, including battleships, cruisers, landing craft, transports, and jillions of small boats with troops in them, milling about the transports. There was open sea to the west and a long way easterly appeared to be Normandy. We could see gunfire coming in our direction from what appeared to be pillboxes, so we headed for what we presumed to be Utah Beach. There was no

The Captain at his Desk

One of the Guns on our Ship

way to tell whether or not we were in a boat lane which had been swept of mines. We hoped and prayed we were. A few minutes after 06:30, we observed a black smoke signal, which meant that our troops were on the beach and firing should cease. But there were still several machine gun nests which appeared to be continuing their fire so we continued on our course to the beach in the direction of the nests, shooting our guns, until we could no longer see fire. German 88 shells were dropping in our vicinity, but we could not tell exactly where they were coming from. We were as close to the beach as we could get even with our flat-bottom ship, although it was still quite a ways. We knew that we were going to be in trouble if we got any closer because several times we had hit the sand and had to back away and move out just a bit further. From time to time as we made a turn to go along the beach we fired at what we believed to be machine gun nests. We anchored in the transport area at about 11:30 P.M., having been at general quarters (battle stations) for twenty-three hours. It was quite a long day.

On the seventh, eighth, ninth, and tenth, there was sporadic German firing by shore batteries into the transport area and a few enemy aircraft were able to strafe parts of the beach and the landing areas. Ships were sunk from time to time by mines or gunfire and an occasional enemy aircraft was shot down or otherwise crashed in the transport area. Then and since I have thanked my lucky stars many times that the Luftwaffe had been practically destroyed before D-day, otherwise our small gunfire crafts would have had a much rougher day.

We didn't know how the war was going on Omaha Beach or the British and Canadian beaches, Sword, and Juneau. They were too far away to see. We did know that the landing of troops and equipment was continuous on Utah Beach almost from the beginning, and things appeared to be going well, although numerous ships, some loaded with troops, struck mines from time to time and sunk. From our standpoint, after the first few days at Utah Beach mines were much more of a problem than enemy activity.

Beginning on June nineteenth, everything came to a screeching halt. The weather turned bad and for the next several hours a terrific storm struck the beach, sinking or damaging hundreds of landing craft, pontoons, and causeways. The LCF-22 suffered irreparable damage, losing our fuel tanks and steering capability, and suffering severe hull and other damage. We were blown onto the beach during the storm and when it subsided on the early morning of the twentith, we were high and dry on the beach with a long barge directly to seaward blocking our path to the water, even if there was any, which there wasn't.

While on the beach high and dry the beachmaster came along and told me that Patton's Third Army was going to land on the beach in a few days and if I didn't get the ship off the beach by some ridiculous time, they would dynamite it—I told him that was okay with me as it belonged to the British anyway. But we would do what we could if he would get us a bulldozer and tug boat.

We stayed on the beach until spring tide on the fourth of July, some two weeks after the storm, when we were floated into the water with the help of a bulldozer which cut a small channel from the water line to the boats. Pyrotechnics were shot by the ships in the beach area to celebrate the fourth of July, which also seemed appropriate for our success in getting off the beach and we didn't mind sharing the celebration.

The USS LCF 22 never again ran under its own power. Within a few days, a U.S. tugboat towed us back to England and we moored to a buoy at Southampton. In a way, it would have been safer if we had stayed in Normandy. Essentially the beach fighting had ceased and things were relatively calm. All the shore batteries too had been silenced so that we didn't have any immediate danger from those. In Southampton we now had to endure the buzz bombs on a regular basis. Those were the Germans' last-ditch effort at England. They did considerable damage to the civilians in Southampton, but from a military standpoint they were ineffective.

When John Hollandhorst of KSL interviewed me at Utah Beach on June 6, 1994, fifty years after D-Day, he asked me if there was a "lot of confusion." My answer was no, not that much. And he said that that was surprising because everybody he had talked to said there was. I told him that fifty years was a long time and I might have to rethink the matter. Since then I found the original ship's log, which I didn't even know I had, and which has enabled me to be fairly accurate as to dates, places, and major happenings. Besides, I didn't know enough about the operation as a whole to be confused.

Based upon the log, and rethinking the occasion, my personal feeling is the same as I expressed to John. Of course, we weren't sure of our exact position and we couldn't tell red from green as far as the beaches were concerned or that there were or were not guns on it, but we knew that it had to be Utah Beach and we knew it was our job to help the assault troops get on the beach. From our perspective, it didn't matter much whether we were exactly in the boat lanes or not or whether we were landing on green beach or red beach or whatever, we were simply assisting the assault troops, which we thought would know where they were supposed to go better than we, and besides there was less chance of us hitting a mine if we stayed in the boat lanes. The problem was to discover where the boat lanes were. The lanes supposedly had been swept by mine sweepers two or three hours before H-hour, but I was never sure whether we were in a swept lane or not.

The buzz bombs which I indicated we encountered at Southampton, were motorized, unmanned bombs launched from Germany and aimed primarily at Southampton. They came mostly at night when they could not be seen, but the motors could be heard. When the motors stopped that meant the bomb was heading down. The louder the motor, the closer the bomb

SUPREME HEADQUARTERS
ALLIED EXPEDITIONARY FORCE

Soldiers, Sailors and Airmen of the Allied Expeditionary Force!

You are about to embark upon the Great Crusade, toward
which we have striven these many months. The eyes of
the world are upon you. The hopes and prayers of liberty-
loving people everywhere march with you. In company with
our brave Allies and brothers-in-arms on other Fronts,
you will bring about the destruction of the German war
machine, the elimination of Nazi tyranny over the oppressed
peoples of Europe, and security for ourselves in a free
world.

Your task will not be an easy one. Your enemy is well
trained, well equipped and battle-hardened. He will
fight savagely.

But this is the year 1944! Much has happened since the
Nazi triumphs of 1940-41. The United Nations have in-
flicted upon the Germans great defeats, in open battle,
man-to-man. Our air offensive has seriously reduced
their strength in the air and their capacity to wage
war on the ground. Our Home Fronts have given us an
overwhelming superiority in weapons and munitions of
war, and placed at our disposal great reserves of trained
fighting men. The tide has turned! The free men of the
world are marching together to Victory!

I have full confidence in your courage, devotion to duty
and skill in battle. We will accept nothing less than
full Victory!

Good Luck! And let us all beseech the blessing of Almighty God upon this great and noble undertaking.

Dwight D. Eisenhower

U.S.S. LCS(L)(3) 67

and then after a few seconds of silence, an explosion. Fortunately we were not hit or damaged by any while most of them struck the civilian areas of Southampton.

We remained at Southampton for awhile and were then towed to Salcomb, where we remained powerless except for one generator which furnished light and cooking heat. Numerous efforts were made by shore personnel to weld the fuel tanks which had been damaged in the storm at Normandy, but all to no avail. Painting and cosmetic repairing and some leave occupied the crew until the ship was turned back to the British about the first part of September. The crew were taken off and reassigned by Navy personnel officers and returned to the States. I received orders to proceed back to Boston via the *Bayfield*, a troop ship, and proceed to Solomons, Maryland, for further training and reassignment. Thus ended my service in the Atlantic Theatre. I was awarded the Navy Commendation medal for the efforts of the ship to be of help to the assault troops, but it could have just as easily been the award of a court martial if the gunfire we were shooting at turned out to be gunfire of our own troops.

3. Pacific Theatre

When I got back to the States from England and after a few days delay en route to visit New York, I went to Washington, D.C., on my way to Solomons, Maryland. I thought seriously of going back to the Selective Service Headquarters and asking General Hershey to get me reassigned on his staff, but decided against it for some reason which I can't remember now. I did go visit him, however, and we had a great visit, but he didn't ask me if I wanted to come back so I never broached the subject. At Solomons I found out as soon as I got there that I was going to be the CO of the U.S. S. LCS(L)(3)67, and the ship assigned to Flotilla 4 consisting of thirty-six ships, which was being built by the Albina Engine and Machine Works in Portland, Oregon. The crew had been formed and the officers and the crew had been training together for a few weeks at that base. Lieutenant John Palmer Murphy, from New Jersey, had been the CO and when I came he became my executive officer. He and I became very good personal friends. He died about fifteen years ago and until his death we kept in touch through Christmas cards, letters, and occasional telephone calls. We once had a reunion of sorts with three other of the officers and our wives at the Hilton Hotel, New York, and had a grand time.

The original mission of the LCS, of which a total of 130 were built, was to provide close in fire support for assault troops, much as at Normandy. There were two big differences, however, and they were that the LCSs were ocean-going vessels with a typical ship's pointed bow, whereas the LCFs were not seagoing and had square bows. More importantly, the LCS's were much faster, though still slow (fifteen knots) when compared to a destroyer, and had more fire power than the LCF, including beach pulverizing rockets. They were flat-bottomed, like a landing craft, but did sit down in the water further than did the LCSs. Smooth sailing, however, was not an LCS characteristic because of the shallow draft. Almost as soon as I got processed at Solomons, our crew and two other crews, a total of about 200 officers and enlisted men, were sent to Portland on a troop train on the Northern Pacific Railroad. Because of my rank, I was military officer in charge of the train and what a chore. It was winter time, extremely cold, and the train lost its heat. Some of the enlisted men got hold of some booze and got into a scuffle and one smashed his hand through a window, cutting it quite badly. I asked the conductor to wire ahead to Albert Lea, Minnesota, where we were scheduled to stop for about five minutes, to have the military police meet us and take him off the train. I don't remember any place ever being as cold as it was in Albert Lea the night we stopped. When I got out of the train to converse with the military police, it was as though razor blades were being sucked in as I breathed. With no heat on the train and cold food, the trip was not a pleasant experience. At Portland, the enlisted personnel were taken to a Navy housing base and the officers were billeted in the old Portland Hotel. The 67 was assigned office space in a building near where the ship was being constructed and we were able to monitor the progress and become familiar with the plans. To that time I had never seen or been on an LCS.

After the ship was completed and launched on January 18, 1945, a civilian pilot came aboard and with the pilot and one other LCS, captained by my very good friend, Joe Cardamone, a young lawyer like myself from Ithaca, New York. We sailed down the Willamette River into the Columbia and across the bar at Astoria to the Pacific. The pilot then left the ship on a small boat and we proceeded down the coast to San Diego for "shakedown" and training. A few weeks later on March third we left in a convoy of twelve LCSs for Pearl Harbor and ultimately to Okinawa.

Our utilization at Okinawa turned out to be quite different from what it was in the assault on France. The landings had already taken place when we got there and we were immediately made a part of a radar picket force around the island. In a piece written by my executive offer, Murphy, after the Japanese surrender when we were at Tokyo Bay, he graphically described the LCSs and their mission. Excerpts from the writing, which is entitled "Well Done Mighty Midgets," are as follows:

> In all, during the Okinawa campaign the Japanese sent and lost about 1600 aircraft against the U.S. forces, losing a pilot per plane. The Kamikaze did, in fact, inflict terror from the sky, sinking 32 ships and damaging 368 others with a loss of life of 4,900 men and nearly as many more wounded. But even with the terrible damage they inflicted

upon the U.S. Navy, the Kamikaze (Divine Wind) was not able to change the outcome Okinawa, nor did they drive the Navy from the seas around Japan.

People back home probably couldn't describe one, even if they heard of one. They don't have names; they are of the large assorted group of miscellaneous Navy ships that have numbers. When sunk or damaged, the Navy's communique groups them among the "light units."

But Vice Admiral Richmond Kelly Turner called them "our mighty midgets"; Fleet Admiral Nimitz called them "resolute ships" in praising their "valor and gallantry"; Admiral Raymond A. Spruance expressed his pride in the "magnificent courage and effectiveness of these vessels"; the late Lieutenant General Simon Bolivar Buckner praised their "cheerful efficiency" and "heroic degree of courage"; Admiral Halsey singled them out for commendation.

And the Japs knew them—and feared them. "Miniature destroyers" they called them.

They are the LCS(L)(3)s—Landing Craft Support, Large. The "large" is a relative term, for they are larger than their predecessors, but still only a third of the size and a sixth of the tonnage of a destroyer.

When they made their debut in the invasion of the Philippines they were something new. They began flexing their muscles at Iwo Jima. At Okinawa they reached their majority, slugged it out with the best the Japs could throw against them, and won.

Originally built as rocket ships to provide close in bombardment of invasion beaches just in advance of the first wave of landing troops, the Navy soon found they could be useful in other ways between invasions. They made ideal fireboats, and were given fire-fighting equipment equivalent to that of five pieces of metropolitan fire apparatus. It was found they could be used to advantage as anti-aircraft ships. Their shallow draft made it possible for them to support underwater demolition teams close inshore. They were equipped to do salvage work. They had sufficient speed and firepower to be useful as escorts. Small enough to move about crowded anchorages without causing too much confusion, yet big enough for good-sized loads, they could be used to advantage in the many inter-ship necessary dealings. They could do reconnaissance, investigate suspicious objects, rescue downed aviators, sink drifting mines, and patrol inshore waters.

All of this they were called upon to do at Okinawa, and they did it, but their chief job was out on the radar picket lines, forty or fifty miles from the fleet and transport anchorages, where they were the road block on "Bogy Highway," outside the anti-submarine screen where they got the title "bogy bait," and where they met the Japanese Special Attacks Corps (Kamikaze), and destroyed their suicide planes, boats, and swimmers. Here they, with their destroyer partners, set the amazing record total of 490 planes destroyed during the 82 day campaign, but at a cost of over 1,000 casualties.

A regular "radar picket team" consisted of two, sometimes three destroyers or destroyer escorts, minesweepers, and three or four LCSs, with an LSM (Landing Ship Medium) often filling in for an LCS in the early days of the campaign. There were about sixteen picket stations at strategic intervals around Okinawa and the outlying smaller islands, at distances ranging from twenty to eighty miles from the anchorages and from the bombardment stations of the big ships. One station was within ten miles of the Japanese-held island of Kume Shima.

These ships were originally there to warn the ships at the anchorages and the troops ashore of the approach of enemy planes. But it soon developed that the Jap pilots, sighting the small groups well out to sea, spent their force on the pickets. With magnificent, courageous, and selfless support from the Marine pilots of the Combat Air Patrol in their Corsairs, the pickets took them on, and splashed them or drove them back.

The LCSs would spend ten to twelve days on such patrols, plodding back and forth over a five-mile area, and would then return to the main fleet anchorage for three or four days to obtain provisions, ammunition, fuel, water, mail, and similar necessities. During these days in the anchorage, the ships were called upon for many other duties: to form an anti-aircraft screen to seaward by day, to patrol against suicide boats and swimmers, to provide smoke cover for the battleships and cruisers at anchor or engaged in bombarding the beach, or to perform salvage and firefighting operations either afloat or ashore.

An LCS resembles a ship more than do most landing craft, and the absence of bow doors or ramps gives her an almost streamlined appearance when compared to her sisters of the amphibious fleet. With a top speed of a little better than 13 knots, powered by General Motors Diesel engines, an LCS, at cruising speed, can travel over 5,000 miles without refueling. She has a mean draft of 5 foot 8 inches, loaded, and a displacement of 385 tons. A good part of her weight is made up of guns (almost all automatic machine guns) and ammunition—the greatest amount of fire power per ton of any ship in the fleet. And they are "rocket ships," well laden with those powerful new weapons which will pulverize an invasion beach. One hundred and fifty seven feet long, with a 23-foot beam, they carry no armor plating on their 3/8 inch hull and it has been said that "two more coats of paint and she would stop a .22 caliber pistol slug."

The complement of these ships was 6 officers and 65 men, over half of whom were specialists in one branch of naval warfare or another; 13 types of petty officer ratings are carried, with approximately half the crew being rated men. Originally all LCSs were commanded by senior-grade lieutenants, but in some cases where commanding officers were casualties, junior-grade lieutenants were given commands.

Led by the LCS 84, which rescued 328, the ships of Flotilla Four (consisting of 36 LCSs) rescued a total of 1290 survivors, shot down 55 aircraft, got 6 probables, assisted in the destruction of 34 more, destroyed 16 suicide boats, engaged in six landings, took part in 18 salvage operations, captured 41 Jap prisoners. Thirty-nine officers and 34 men had been recommended for medals and awards for actions during the campaign, and 15 ships had been recommended for unit citations. (Commander Bullock was awarded the Bronze Star with Combat "V.")

General Buckner sent this message:

On behalf of all members of the Tenth Army I desire to express appreciation of the splendid service rendered by crews of radar picket boats of CTF 51 in contributing to the anti-aircraft protection of our forces at Okinawa. Without their skill in warning and guiding our planes, our forces would have suffered heavily in life and equipment. Although the bulk of enemy air attack was directed at them, resulting in their suffering serious casualties, they performed their hazardous duties with cheerful efficiency and displayed a heroic degree of courage. They are fully deserving of the highest commendations.

From Fleet Admiral Nimitz:

> The Commander in Chief Pacific Fleet shares with the entire Navy the admiration expressed CTF 51 for the valor and gallantry of the resolute ships on radar picket duty who are contributing magnificently to the successes being achieved by the current campaign.
>
> The "mighty midgets" of Flotilla Four had good reason to be proud of the part they had played when they steamed into Tokyo Bay early in September and took their places side by side with Admiral Halsey's battleships, cruisers, and carriers, ready for the occupation of Japan.

The Okinawa operation was the last battle of the war, and it is generally agreed by navy historians that it was the greatest sea-air battle in the history of the U.S. Navy. It was also the most costly. Nearly 5,000 sailors were killed and 4,824 were wounded in the 3_-month campaign. Thirty-six U.S. ships were sunk and 368 were damaged. Twenty percent of all navy casualties in WWII occurred at Okinawa. Of a total of 1,321 ships massed for the Okinawa campaign eighty-six were LCSs. Again, as in France, Lady Luck, the stars, or the Almighty saw to it that we suffered no injury to the ship or crew.

When Okinawa was secured around the middle of July, we left with other LCSs to go to the Philippines, there to stage and train and prepare for the invasion of Japan itself. Scuttlebutt had it that we were to make the first landings on Honshu and we were to make ready for that in the Philippines. We arrived on July eighteenth, encountering a typhoon en route, and were mighty glad to drop anchor in Leyte Gulf.

On August 6 and 9,1945, atomic bombs were dropped on Hiroshima and Nagasaki and Japan surrendered on August fourteenth. When the official announcement of the bombing and the Japanese surrender were made, most if not all the ships in the anchorage fired their pyrotechnics in celebration. When they ran out of pyrotechnics they used 20mm tracer bullets from the machine guns and in some cases, even larger shells were used. It was quite a show for a short time, but extremely dangerous to the ships and personnel in the anchorage. My thoughts were first how wonderful it was that the war was over, but then what a great tragedy it would be if the shooting caused casualties to our own forces which the Japanese with their kamikazes had been unable to inflict upon us throughout the entire Okinawan campaign. Fortunately the ships in the anchorage, including the sixty-seven, got control before any serious damage to ships or personnel occurred.

On September third, we departed Leyte Gulf in company with entire Flotilla Four, consisting of thirty-six ships, and proceeded to Tokyo Bay, arriving on the eleventh for duty with the occupation forces.

4. Occupation
On September 4, 1945, we departed Leyte Gulf for Japan, arriving at Tokyo Bay on the eleventh. Within a few hours liberty parties were permitted to go ashore. As far as the eye could see, Yokohama was rubble. But as we walked around, it was evident that there was much underground and surface makeshift housing, such as sheets of tin propped up against a wall or with posts or something of that nature. There were also myriads of underground living quarters, which would have posed serious problems for any invasion of that area. We carried side arms, but the Japanese were not in any mood to create any kind of incident. They bowed and scraped as we would walk past them, but you had an uneasy feeling that if given the chance they would become hostile. Somehow you wanted them in front of you rather than behind.

On the Ginza, which is the main street in Tokyo and is to Tokyo much as Broadway is to New York or Market Street is to San Francisco, there were thousands upon thousands of people just milling around and rubble and debris on the streets and where the buildings had collapsed and it was just a big general mess. There were no cars on the street and only an occasional bus-type vehicle fueled by a charcoal fire burning in the rear. My thoughts were that someone needed to take charge and get the people to work just cleaning up. Even if they had no tools it appeared that much could have been done by just simply hauling off the rubble and debris in the streets and putting it in piles some way by hand.

Our duty consisted primarily of taking liberty boats to and from the big ships to a shore pier and otherwise we acted as a carrier between ships, such as mail, etc. We had considerable shore leave and on one occasion my exec, Murphy, and I, and a couple of other officers from another ship made a trip to Fuji. It was a first-class Japanese hotel, but even the first-class hotels did not have beds, they had a straw mat to lie on and the toilets were simply places cut in the floor under which there was a big crock pot which was periodically emptied.

In October I was promoted to lieutenant commander and therefore had too much rank to remain skipper of an LCS. So I was relieved of command of the 67 and made group commander of Group 11, consisting of twelve ships. I hated to leave the 67 and especially the officers and crew, but there would be no further contact with her since she was in Group 12.

About this time, the Navy circulated a notice stating that reserve officers were invited to apply for extended duty and if interested, they should go aboard the Wisconsin to talk with the recruiters. I thought seriously of staying in because I liked the navy and I didn't have a job to go back to. Senator Adams had died, so I decided to at least make inquiry about the possibilities. I had enough points to warrant my separation at that time and I knew I would not have to stay long in Japan. I wanted to go back to the States and get started on a law career, since by now it had been about three and a half years since my graduation from law school. Furthermore, I was single, about thirty years old, and if I wanted a family I would have to get started pretty soon or it would be too late.

The recruiters told me that the Navy would undoubtedly accept my application and that I probably could transfer from the reserves to the regular navy if I wanted to. However, when I asked if I could be returned to the States and be reassigned there, they told me "no," that I could not do so. "They needed officers to remain in Asia." So, I did not apply, but I thought I might do so after I got back to the States.

In about a month I was relieved of command of Group 11 and ordered to report aboard a destroyer for transport to San Diego to be discharged. After arriving in San Diego I was rerouted to San Francisco near Christmas in December 1945. I was released from active duty in San Francisco, to be effective March 1946. I still thought I might apply for the regular navy some time before the effective date, but never did, and in retrospect I am glad I did not. I would have had an entirely different life than the one I have had. I would not have practiced in Provo and probably would not have had the judicial career, which I enjoyed so much. More importantly, it is likely I would not have met Ethel and would not have had the wonderful family that I have and that would have been tragic.

J. Robert and Friends

Commander J. Robert Bullock

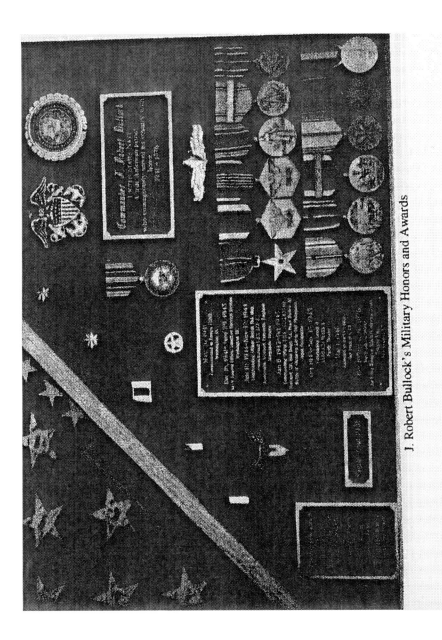

J. Robert Bullock's Military Honors and Awards

C.J. (BUD) HARMON

WEIGHT ?? 136   ?? MAY
Ft. WORTH ?? TEXAS   1944

HARMON, C. J.   2nd LT

THE LIFE OF C.J. "BUD" HARMON

A Compilation of Oral Histories and Written Documents
edited by Mary Ann Harmon, granddaughter
December 10, 1997

Foreword and Acknowledgments:
This is a history of my grandfather, C. J. "Bud" Harmon. Because of the
breadth and depth involved in a life history, it is my ambition to bring to
light significant life events and stories which trace his course through
time. To borrow the words of a famous German historian, Johann Droysen,
this history is not the light—the complete, objective truth of the past—
but "a search therefore, a sermon thereupon, a consecration thereto."[1] It is
a tribute to a great man whose life influenced the lives of many, especially his family.

Grandpa Bud was a singular figure of strength in our family. He passed
away on February 2, 1997. This separation was a difficult thing for many of
us to accept. His memory is written upon our hearts through the great work
of love and endurance he performed here. It has been a great source of
esteem to have been with him for the past twenty years.

Many thanks to contributors Ruth A. Harmon, Paul L. Harmon, and
MacNeil Boyter. Additional thanks to cousins, aunts, and uncles, and my
parents for their help in obtaining information for this history.

The Life of C.J. "Bud" Harmon

Clarence Jesse Harmon was born in Provo, Utah, on December 11, 1922, to parents Clarence Holman Harmon and Sarah Myrl Lewis Harmon. He was delivered in a hospital on 200 South and 100 East in Provo, Utah. He had one brother, Paul, who was three years his elder. Six years later his sister Colleen was born, who completed the family in 1928.[2] His early years were spent in a modest home on 136 West 500 North in Provo. His father, Clarence, had inherited the home from his father Jesse Martin Harmon, after Jesse passed away in early 1922, suffering from what was termed "abdominal cramps," which may have been something akin to appendicitis. According to Bud's brother Paul the home consisted of "a bath and a half and five bedrooms." The home no longer stands due to land development.

Previous to C.J.'s birth, Clarence and Myrl (as Sarah was called) had spent a few years on a ranch in a small town called Colton, in Spanish Fork Canyon. After returning from service in the armed forces in World War I, Clarence and his brother Appleton had migrated to Colton in search of work. They prospered there in Colton with their sheep, cattle, and large mercantile store. It was upon their return to Provo a few years later that little "Buddy" entered their home.

Paul and C.J., or "Buddy" as he was called, grew up together under the tutelage of their mother, who was an elementary schoolteacher, and father, who taught them how to work. Paul remembers that in the evenings they would gather together and Myrl would have them read something from a ten-volume "Book of Knowledge" which she had sacrificed for and saved to purchase for their family. In addition to his introduction to reading and intellectual pursuits, Bud vas also taught work ethics. As young boys, both Paul and Buddy were assigned a newspaper route. Paul claims that neither liked to deliver papers, but "Bud protested [the paper route] more than I did so he finally got off the hook." Despite Bud's aversion to the paper route, Paul affirms that Bud was dependable and could be counted on to do it.

One Christmas when Bud was maybe ten or eleven years old he received a BB gun with which he was delighted. Paul, being his older brother, would remind Bud that he was responsible for taking care of his BB gun and should bring it inside after he was finished playing with it. Despite Paul's warnings, Bud left the gun outside on the fence. It rained and the gun was rusted. After Paul made a full report of Bud's carelessness to their mother, she gently reminded Paul that Bud was only a boy and he needed his help to take care of things. In the tender spirit of childhood, when Bud realized what he had done he claimed defensively, "I didn't like the BB gun anyway. That BB gun won't hit anything."

Bud, or "Buddy" as he was called at the time, was appointed to be class president in the seventh grade for the Brigham Young Junior High. There are several entries in his seventh grade yearbook written to him by fellow class-mates which compliment him on his year as their class president. In his 1936 "Wildcat" yearbook, one young woman named Polly Taylor wrote, "Dear Buddy, You have made a very good president and classmate." Another class-mate, Helen Martin, wrote, "Dear Buddy, You have been a swell class presi-dent for this year." It seems that Bud found favor and was respected by his peers during his school years.

Bud made many friends during his school years. As his brother Paul recalls, "Bud liked to socialize with people and have a lot of fun. He was a good dancer and the girls liked him." However, there was one thing at least that Bud did not care for and that was acting. During his junior year of high school, one teacher, Ms. Stella Rich, decided that Buddy and his classmates would enact the stabbing of Julius Caesar, requiring the participants to wear long draped cloth for clothing after the Roman tradition. Bud refused to wear a sheet to recite lines in front of classmates. He was not about to have anything to do with that "sissy stuff," so Ms. Rich found someone else to take Bud's part in the play. Brant Harmon, Bud's son, recalls that Bud would often talk about a Ms. Anna Boss Hart, a high school English teacher enam-ored of poetry and Shakespeare, and that Bud "just couldn't care anything about all that stuff." Bud was a pragmatic young man, a characteristic that remained throughout adulthood. He was a person of thrift and worked hard to attain financial security for himself and his family.

Bud was an excellent athlete in high school. He was involved in both tennis and basketball. In fact, Buddy's basketball team was the first team from Brigham Young High to beat their arch-rivals, Provo High, on Provo High's court. Brigham Young High School, a private school, had a very small student body in comparison to Provo High. Therefore, the pool of athletes was considerably smaller for BY High and this victory was a considerable achievement. Bud was a tall young man, reaching about six feet, two inch-es, and he was an excellent guard. Paul remembers that, "In those days we used to play man to man [defense] and they assigned a man to Bud and he might as well [have] been under a cloud...he wasn't going to make any bas-kets with Bud watching him." Not everyone appreciated Bud's athletic excel-lence. In a letter written to him by his grandmother Sarah Holman Harmon, on occasion of his graduation from Junior High, she begins by commending him on his graduation with honors and then continues, "I am afraid I don't appreciate your accomplishments in tennis and basketball, will you[r] activ-ities along this line help you to make a living later on?"[3]

It was during his high school years that Bud first began to court a beau-tiful, dark-haired young woman named Ruth Ann Ercanbrack. They first became acquainted in junior high school. He was about one year older than she, and although she went to Provo High School while he attended Brigham Young High, they continued to date off and on throughout their late teenage years. She would later become his gracious wife and lifelong companion.

When Bud was twenty years old he received his patriarchal blessing. It was at this same time that World War II was raging in Europe and parts of Asia and American troops were being sent over by the thousands to halt the work of the German war machine run by Hitler. He was promised in his patriarchal blessing that he would return safely if he entered the war:

> If you go into the service of our country for the purpose of fighting for liberty and freedom, our Father in Heaven shall bless you and you shall have the privilege of returning home to your relatives and friends and you shall receive no permanent injury, but you shall become a stronger man both spiritually and mentally. You shall always be able to grapple with the problems that come in your way and be able to solve the same; and while you are in the service dear brother, you shall not remain a private but you shall [have] commissions placed upon you and you shall have power to carry these responsibilities that come with these commissions in an honorable manner. And you shall be honored and respected at all times among the people you come in contact with be they friend or foe.

These promises were fulfilled as Bud enlisted in the United States Army Air Force shortly thereafter and returned home two years later physically unharmed.

Bud endured grueling hours of training before he entered the war overseas at an army air base in Texas.[4] He told me once that many days they would spend nearly eighteen hours in flight training, and because of the strain on his eyes, he could barely see the next morning. Many of the recruits "washed out" because of the stress and did not complete their training, but Bud endured and graduated from flight school as a second lieutenant. He was later promoted to a first lieutenant overseas. He was stationed near a little town called Hethel, England (about forty-five miles north of London) as a pilot of B-24 and later B-29 bombers, navigating dangerous air missions over Germany, strategically targeting industrial centers. In describing one of his more intense combat moments during the war, Bud stated the following:

> I had my engines shot out more than once. My crew maintained that I could land on three engines better than I could land on four. The incident I remember most distinctly was when we were sent over to bomb the German gen-

eral staff headquarters on the south side of Berlin. It took the absolute range of our B-24 to fly over there, which was twelve hours. They [the Germans] had it very heavily protected with anti-aircraft guns and when I had just begun my bombing run, I looked around me and could count thirteen B-24's going down at the same time all around me. One guy bailed out in front of me and instead of going straight down, he got caught in the propwash of all the planes and was going straight backward. I don't know if he survived or not.[5]

This experience is from one of eleven missions which Bud flew during the war. It took strength and stamina on the part of those crews to stay focused on the war effort. One of C.J.'s gunners, "Pop" Williams,[6] remembers that towards the end of the war, while Bud and his crew were flying over Germany, the German transport trains were so crowded that men were standing and sitting on top of the train cars en route. Bud was such a good pilot by that time that he would fly directly over the trains very close to the top of the train cars, and the men would jump off, believing that he was coming straight for them.

Grandpa Bud once showed me a small picture of the grand cathedral in Cologne, Germany, which was taken from the turret of his plane during the war. At first glance the small pocket-size photo looks quite normal; he then pointed out to me something unusual—all of the large, stained-glass windows from the cathedral are missing. The Germans had removed them to prevent their possible destruction during the war, and they replaced them after the war was over. Years after the war while he was traveling through Europe, he contemplated showing the picture to a German tour guide, but then thought the better of it and kept the memory to himself.

The crew of a B-24 bomber consisted of seven or eight men, including navigators and gunners. After the Allied victory in Europe in May of 1945, Bud's crew members had developed such a respect for Bud and a feeling of unity, that they volunteered to stay with Bud in the continuing war against Japan if he was to enter that conflict. Bud flew back to the States to prepare to fly over to Japan, but the conflict ended shortly thereafter through the deployment of the atomic bomb on the Japanese cities of Hiroshima and Nagasaki. The war was over and Bud was a part of the first group of veterans to return to civilian life.

After the war, Bud returned to Provo and began his studies at Brigham Young University in business and he also resumed his courtship of Ruth. They were engaged in December of 1946 and married on February 14, 1947, in the Salt Lake L.D.S. temple. When asked why they chose Valentine's Day for the wedding, Ruth replied, "Well I told him [Bud] 'we'll get married on

Valentine's Day and then you can remember when it is and you won't forget our anniversary.' The next thing he said was, 'Well, when is Valentine's Day?'" The marriage was a joyful occasion. Ruth's mother, Fern, and her friends pooled together their wartime sugar stamps rations to make goodies for the reception. Ruth and Bud both graduated from Brigham Young University later that year, Ruth with a degree in English and Bud with a degree in business and banking. Bud spent about three months after that in Flint, Michigan, at a GM automobile dealership school. Bud and Ruth sold their car upon his return so he could start his own automobile dealership working out of a small service station in Spanish Fork, Utah, where he was initially only able to bring in about two new cars a month. He lived in Provo and commuted to Spanish Fork for about seventeen years. He later purchased an automobile dealership on 100 North and 500 West in Provo, originally called United Sales and Service, and changed the name to Harmon's Incorporated. The business, which was first owned by his father Clarence, has continued in the family since 1936 and is currently run by his two sons Brant and Mark Harmon.

Bud was well respected by his employees and he had good friends in Spanish Fork and Provo, which helped him in his early years of business. One gentleman in Spanish Fork by the name of George Hawkins came to Bud when Bud was first starting out and told him of about seven or eight individuals in Spanish Fork with whom he should avoid business transactions. Bud followed Mr. Hawkins's advice and it saved him money and undue trouble. Reportedly, one of these men who bought a car from another dealer would bring it in frequently with new complaints. Bud had good friends who looked out for him.

At another time, Bud caught a young man going through his cash register attempting to steal money. Bud went to the city judge and was told that he should file a complaint. Instead of letting the moment slip idly by, Bud went over to the home of the delinquent young man with the judge and gave the boy a speech, letting him know that what he had done was wrong. He let the boy know that he was starting his life off on the wrong foot. The judge told him later that boy would never forget that speech.[7]

Bud and Ruth were blessed with a family of five children, three boys, Brant, Mark, and Hal and two girls, Linda and Gina. His son Mark remembers, "My father always seemed to be doing his best to keep his family together. If he thought your hair was too long, he said so. If he thought you weren't working hard enough, he told you. But, in his heart and in his love, he was always accepting of us."[8] Bud spent a great deal of his life providing for his children and his wife. He was a dedicated husband and father.

Bud loved to fly, and with his wartime training he was able to fly many private planes. He finally sold his *Cessna Skylane*, a small passenger airplane, when he was about sixty-five years old, after he could no longer pass the flight physical because of his deteriorated eyesight. A friend and longtime employee, Mac Boyter, recalls flying with Bud on many occasions. One time when they were trying to fly out of Southern/Central Utah into Utah Valley, a huge storm front came up quickly to the north. Bud was extremely wary because of the possible dangers of turbulent air and downdrafts in the canyon. He stayed in the air waiting for a break or an opening in the storm front. Bud kept reassuring Mac and asking him if he was all right while calmly realigning the plane. Finally he saw a hole in the storm and he took off toward it. They broke through and he landed them safely in Provo later in the hour. Bud was calm under pressure and was able to handle difficult situations with a sense of personal conviction.

Mac worked for Bud for many years and sincerely believed that Bud had a good relationship with his employees. Mac observed that Bud did not fraternize with his employees or "play favorites." He supported them in their distinctive roles. Many of Bud's employees stayed with him for years.

Bud also loved to hunt. One thing he asked Ruth to promise him before they were married was that he would still be allowed to go hunting. She assured him that it would be all right with her if that was what he wanted. Some of the game that Bud hunted included deer, pheasant, sage hen, and antelope. Bud loved the deer hunt and went on several hunts arranged by Brick Sorensen, a friend who owned the Dollhouse Restaurant in Salt Lake City. Bud would often go on hunting trips with family and friends.

Bud truly was a great man and a leader in our family. He led a life of honor, and he made us feel we were truly worth something. In a letter he wrote to me while he was in Arizona on March 12, 1996, about one year before his death, he stated in the closing paragraph, "[I] Will be coming home to Provo on April 7th. Hope to see you then and have some time to tell you about my life history. I did not have a grandpa to talk to so I would like you to know what your ancestors did…"

Bud, you have left a great legacy for us. Thank you.

NOTES

1. From *Stern's Varieties of History*, 144.
2. One other child was born to the family in 1932. It was a baby girl, given the name Myrl Harmon, who died at birth.
3. An excerpt from a letter most likely written by Sarah Ellen Holman Harmon, his father's mother, in about 1938.
4. He spent some time in flight training in Georgia also. Much of the information presented here is taken from an interview entitled "A Pilot's Story," conducted by Kelly Larsen, a grandson, with Bud Harmon in 1994 about his experiences in World War II.
5. Taken from "A Pilot's Story" by C.J. Harmon, p. 3.

6. They called him "Pop" (like father) because he was the oldest man of the crew, possibly about twenty-eight or twenty-nine at the time. This story was shared with me by my father Brant Harmon.
7. This account was related to me by Paul Harmon during an interview on November 14, 1997.
8. Excerpt from "A Tribute to Dad," an address given by Mark Harmon at C.J. Harmon's funeral, February 8, 1997.

Bud Harmon, First Lieutenant in World War II

Bud once said, "The only time I ever saw a tear in my Dad's eye, was when he sent me off to war. He had been in World War I, and so he knew what it was all about."

Clarence H. Harmon, World War I (left)
Camp Lewis, Washington

A B-24 bomber like the one Bud flew during the war.

The Cathedral in Cologne, Germany (right). This
photo was taken from the turret of Bud's B-24 during
the war.

WORLD WAR II INTERVIEW WITH GRANDPA BUD
MAY 15, 1996

CLARENCE JESSE HARMON

by
Robbie Harmon

1. Why did W.W. II start?
    Because Hitler convinced people that he could take over the world and that they Were superior.
2. What was the most harsh battle of the war for you?
    Lead pilot, S-67 bomb. England bombing Germany and later the B-29's.
3. What training did you go through to prepare for the war?
    Very concentrated training required to pilot four engine planes and intense physical training. We never had less than sixteen hour days.
4. Where did you serve most of your time?
    Flying B-24's in England.
5. What were living conditions like at your camp?
    We lived in a tin hut that looked like half of an irrigation pipe. Used a tiny stove for heat and burned cardboard packages from the bombs for fuel. Our beds were flat boards with one blanket. If there was ever a time that a soldier did not return, everyone tried to get his blanket to use for cushion underneath or a little more warmth.
6. Who was the worst enemy, Germany or Japan?
    They were both equally bad. Both committed atrocities. The Japanese caught his friend and cut off his urination organ.
7. What kind of plane did you fly?
    B-24's
    B-29's
8. How many crewmembers were in your plane?
    B-24 = 10
    B-29 = 5
9. What were the responsibilities of each member?
    B-24 = Co-pilot, navigator, Mickey man, radio controller, gunners, engineer, two waste [waist] gunners, two tail gunners
    B-29 = Co-pilot, engineer, navigator, radio controller, one gunner
10. Describe the kind of clothing worn while flying a mission?
    B-24 = long underwear, wire suit for heat, sheepskin, silk, wool, leather gloves, throat mike, goggles, helmet
    B-29 = not as cold
11. How many years did you serve?

3 1/2 years

12. Were you drafted or did you enlist?

Enlisted. His father was head of the Draft Board and said, "You better enlist or I'll have to draft you."

13. What was the greatest hazard facing pilots?

To be shot down or run out of fuel. Each time we took off in a B-24 from England to Germany, there was a 50 percent chance that we would be killed.

14. How long did you have to train?

One year and four months.

15. What company made the planes and engines?

Ford Motor Company.

16. What was the name of your plane?

No name on his. It was the B-24 M Model.

17. How many different planes did you pilot?

Ten.

18. Did the government pay you to serve in the war?

Yes. Time and a half. B-24 pilot was the most hazardous job in the war.

19. How old were you when you first enlisted?

Nineteen years old.

20. Was it hard to communicate with your family?

No.

21. What were your family's feelings about you going to war?

His dad was in WWI. The only time he saw a tear in his dad's eye was when he got on the train.

22. What kind of bombs did your plane carry?

Whatever type of job they were assigned determined what kind of bomb was to be used. Jellied gas to 2000-pound blockbusters.

23. What kind of guns were on the plane?

B-24 = 50 cal. machine guns

B-29 = 20 ml. cannons

24. How large was your plane?

B-24 = 4 X 1200 horsepower engines

B-29 = 4 X 1600 horsepower engines

25. Were you ever hurt or injured during the war?

No, never injured, nor any of my crew.

26. What do you think brought the war to a close?

The atomic bomb and the fact that the Germans and Japanese nations were defeated.

27. Do you think there will ever be another World War?

It's possible. If so, it will be in the Middle East.

28. Tell me about your release?

He was one of the first to come home because he was in the middle of more training in Atlanta, so he was sent directly home instead of back to England.

Thomas S. Taylor

A TRIBUTE TO DAD

by Mark L. Harmon

February 8, 1997

We appreciate our friends and family members that have joined us this afternoon. I know Dad would be greatly pleased that you have come here today. This last week I wondered what would be best for me to tell you about our dad, and I believe it is important we simply pay tribute to him for the type of person he was.

There are certain people that seem to be beyond the bounds of this life. The scope of their presence is so significant, that others begin to build their lives around them. People rely on them for strength. Others seek their advice and counsel. They become almost an institution, rather than just a member of their community. These special men and women create a "legacy" in their own time. I believe you can find people like this in most family lines. Some of them existed in generations past, and some of them have lived in our time. Dad was indeed one of these people. He was not just our father, he was the "patriarch" of our family. He was truly our protector.

The legacy Dad left our family, and how we can use his legacy to bless our lives in the future, will be the focus of my remarks this day.

As his son, I would have to say I don't remember Dad ever being a negative or pessimistic person. His attitude and countenance radiated positive enthusiasm. He was always happy and full of zest for any and all opportunities. In fact, the only times I ever noted a hint of discouragement in his demeanor were in his later years, when health problems seemed to plague him continually. But we all knew Dad would be okay, because he just always seemed to bounce back. Dad was a fighter, he always won his battles, and we just seemed to think that Dad's tremendous energy level and the power of his enthusiasm would carry the day. His legacy of a positive attitude is something that should never be forgotten!

My father always seemed to be doing his best to keep his family together. He was our leader and very stern at times. If he thought your hair was too long he said so. If he thought you weren't working hard, enough, he told you. But in his heart and in his love, he was always accepting of us. I believe it was hard for him to see problems in his family and not try to become directly involved with fixing them, but he never intruded, and tried to discreetly help in any way with support, encouragement, and counsel. His goal was to keep everyone together so his family would stay strong and unified. He believed families should communicate with each other regularly. To that end he spent hours on the phone calling all over the country, but ironically he seemed always concerned when we would call and talk too long on the phone. Dad spent the last two years of his life planning and building a new ranch home in the South Fork of Provo Canyon. It was his hope and desire this new home would be a continual gathering place for his children and grandchildren. He wanted us to stay together. In today's world of broken marriages and troubled homes, his legacy of family unity is more important than ever.

As a child in his home, I was blessed with the gift of "unbridled dreams." I can honestly say there was never "a time in my youth when fear, money, criticism, or discouragement had dashed my hope for the future. I had a clear understanding he would be there to help me achieve anything I wanted. My dad was my champion. He was there when I needed him. Fathers should be the protectors of the hope of their children. At this, my dad was an expert. His legacy of hope for a bright future will never be lost in the memories of our father.

Those of you that knew Dad well know that he was a worker. He always seemed to have boundless energy for whatever tasks he set out to accomplish. This work ethic was instilled in Dad in his early years by his father, and then reinforced by his military training. He often spoke of the sixteen hour days required of him while training to become a pilot in the Air Force. During the war, this training was so intense and exhaustive that over 50 percent of the men enrolled with him washed out before completion of their pilot's training. Not only did Dad complete this training, but he finished first in his class and was therefore given the first opportunity to fly solo in their P-19 training aircraft. This was an honor for him; and Dad noted in his journal that it created some jealousy among the other candidates in officer training. Dad also noted that he didn't care about this jealousy because he was much stronger then and could whip any of those other guys if he needed to. Dad was known as the "Mormon" among his peers there. He didn't drink, he didn't smoke, and was very naive as to things of the world at that time. As a young man he had led a clean life, and this helped him excel in this rigorous training.

After the War, dad started his first automobile dealership in Spanish Fork. He sold his 1946 Pontiac to get some operating cash and borrowed the rest from a banker there in town. Dad would leave early in the morning from Provo, drive to Spanish Fork, and stay late into the evening doing his own accounting and bookwork. He told me that he would often be so tired when driving home that he couldn't see clearly and would have to pull off the road to rest his eyes. This hard work soon paid off, and his business became successful to the point that he was able to purchase the much larger dealership from his father and uncle in Provo. Dad was a self made man. His work ethic and keen mind brought him great success through the years. I believe more than any thing else this legacy of hard work has been the trademark of his life.

As I observed Dad through the years something else in his life has made an lasting impression on me. Dad was one of those guys that always seemed to know something about everything. This is not to say he was a "know-it-all," but that the breadth of his understanding and knowledge of an amazing variety of topics was at least to me quite amazing. He often counseled me on the importance of listening to those who are more knowledgeable than yourself and acting on their counsel. Dad could carry on an intelligent conversation about everything from African gazelles to jet engines. He never, and I mean never, wasted his time. Instead of watching television, he was always reading the *National Geographic* or carefully studying some other periodical. Dad was a voracious reader and was always making an effort to improve his understanding of new concepts and ideas. He had an uncanny ability to be able to fix things and enjoyed working with his hands. He loved to figure out how things worked and had an amazing grasp on the engineering and design of mechanical devices. A legacy of learning and seeking after those things in life that increase our understanding of the universe in which we live was clearly one of my dad's attributes.

My father's entire life was marked by thrift and self-control. He could have built a mansion, but chose instead a modest home. Because of business, Dad always had a new Cadillac in his driveway, but in his later years he was just as comfortable in his old white Pontiac. Dad took great delight in repairing, restoring, and cleaning broken things to make them look good and function properly. He loved to take an old car and fix it up for his personal use. There was just a certain satisfaction in this for him. I would tell him to just get something new, but his nature was to conserve and restore something old. He believed in owning something of quality and then caring for and properly maintaining it, rather than purchasing something of lesser quality then replacing it when broken. Dad believed in being thrifty. He saved in any small or large way he could and has now left his family a legacy of a strong and secure financial foundation.

Although strong-willed and forceful at times, Dad in his own way was a very kind man. He discreetly helped his family and others in many, many ways that no one will ever know about. Dad gave freely to those who were justly in need and responded generously when called upon for help. While still in high school and working part time at the dealership, I remember noticing a young woman in my father's office that had purchased an automobile from him several months earlier. She had trusted my dad and obviously felt his strength of character. She told him she was in trouble and needed help. She asked my father if he could arrange, as she termed it, a "good strong blessing." The young woman had breast cancer and had recently undergone a complete mastectomy. She could not afford to continue her chemotherapy treatments that each time also required a trip to Salt Lake City. Her husband had left her and she just needed some help.

Dad arranged to have two of his older friends come to Provo, meet this young woman, and the three of them gave her a blessing. One was a bishop and restaurant owner, the other a doctor. They all chipped in and gave the woman enough money to cover her needs, and the doctor was able to arrange to have the rest of her chemotherapy treatments done at no charge. Approximately a year later, the young lady returned to my dad's office. She looked great and told my dad she was free of the cancer at that time.

In my mind, I believe my father had the gift of healing. If someone was direly sick, Dad's presence in the hospital room seemed to always guarantee a better outcome. Dad just seemed to know what to do, and I knew that when Dad arrived, things would eventually be okay. This was a unique gift he had. I don't know whether it was a spiritual thing or just the ability to organize things properly for the desired outcome. In any case, my father blessed many in this fashion. His legacy of healing strengthened my testimony of the power of the priesthood.

"For meritorious skill and courage in the face of enemy opposition." These words were written on the citation from the Air Force when Dad was awarded the "Air Medal" at the conclusion of World War II. Bud Harmon was a brave man. Anyone who knew him knew he was courageous. Not only did he demonstrate his bravery as a twenty-one-year-old bomber pilot during the war, but his bravery in life was always evident in the way he faced adversity. He was always very hesitant to discuss or complain to any of us regarding his health concerns. Only occasionally did I notice a sense of discouragement and worry in his voice, but he was always more concerned about what he could do for me and never asked for help for himself. Dad taught me to face life bravely. He would say to us that life was not made to be easy, so just get a "thick skin" and don't let it worry you. "For meritorious skill and courage in the face of enemy opposition." This was yet another legacy he left to us all.

In conclusion, I would like to speak directly to Dad's grandchildren. As I said earlier, Grandpa left you a legacy for the future. A legacy to build and strengthen your characters. A legacy to shape your lives for good. Remember carefully the importance of a positive attitude and cheerful countenance, remember above all that family unity creates a bond that spans the eternity, don't ever forget that there is hope for your futures and that someday as parents you must protect the hope of your children, you must never forget that a strong work ethic is the basic foundation for success. Always strive to increase your knowledge of the world in which you live, and seek after those things that are good in life. Be thrifty with your resources. Save your money for the future and care properly for your possessions. Like Grandpa, you also can be blessed with the gift of healing, and will someday be called upon to exercise this gift. Finally, don't ever forget to be brave in the face of life's challenges. It just wasn't supposed to be easy for you, so get thick-skinned and move on. Your grandfather has left you a proud legacy, and now he is gone. So it is your turn in life to chart your own course. Set your sails for your own life's journey, and let the legacy of your grandfather guide you. Remember how your granddad was a fighter. He spoke strongly for his beliefs, and he never gave up on his goals. May the legacy of his life continue in yours.

Dad was my mentor, my teacher, and my hero. Even in his death he was teaching us. At his hospital bedside we learned the depth of true compassion, we learned the virtue of long suffering, and the importance of hope. In this final moment he unified us again in our love for one another.

There is now only one survivor of the ten crew members on my father's plane in WWII. Pop Williams was my Dad's waist gunner; we called him last week to inform him of Dad's passing, to which he replied, "Oh no, our skipper is gone." Like Pop Williams, I too have lost my skipper. He guided me in combat and always brought me home safely. I will dedicate myself to the honor of his name, and I say it in the name of Jesus Christ. Amen.

Iceland 1945

Enroute home, Iceland 1945

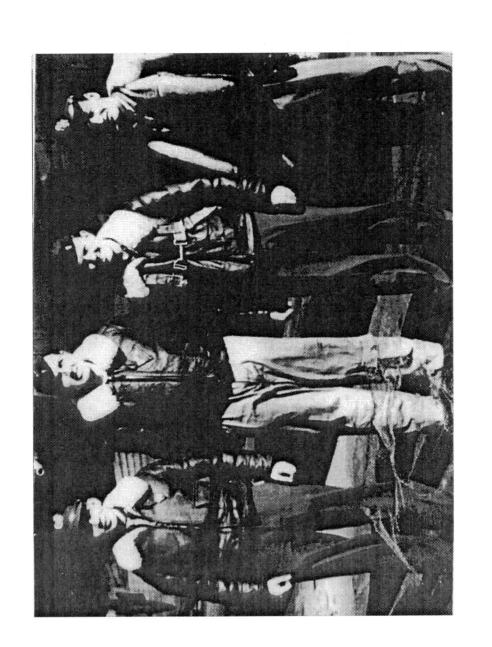

England 1944-45; C.J. "Bud" Harmon holding dog

C.J. "Bud" Harmon

Forgiving Others: Sacred and Secular Perspectives
Aaron Dalton
Oak Hills Second Ward   Provo, Utah
March 12, 2006

1. INTRO: ABOUT US

a. Provo, Minneapolis
b. Met in this chapel. Both undergrads at BYU but didn't know each other there, even though we discovered later that we had several mutual friends, most of whom were her boyfriends, guys who, I have come to learn, are evidently much cooler than I remember them being.
c. We moved here six years ago from Cincinnati, where I went to graduate school
d. LHM; Aegis
e. We both enjoy serving in the primary, where Elise inspires your children through the Spirit, and I coerce them into singing loudly.
f. Two kids, Eliza who's six years old and enjoys skiing, and Wesley who is two years old and enjoys life
g. Elise and I enjoy the ongoing process of refining our skills in forgiving each other, which relates to the topic I'll be speaking on today.
h. Specifically, I'd like to take a brief look at the *spiritual* necessity of our forgiveness of others as part of our own repentance, and also consider the growing *secular* case for forgiving others as a requirement of our own well-being.
i. So be forewarned that we will be mingling some of men's philosophies with scripture, but I hope that it will be of value.

2. FORGIVENESS STORY: THE BIEHLS

In 1993, Amy Biehl, an idealistic white American college student who was about my age at the time, won a Fulbright Scholarship to travel to South Africa to assist the anti-apartheid movement. Caught in a race riot, she was murdered by a black mob.

Her killing stunned that country and made international headlines, but more shocking for many people was the response of her parents, Peter J. and Linda Biehl.

Following years of various failed attempts to overcome their grief through what are to western society the traditionally accepted methods, the Biehls gave up their fashionable upper-middle class California lifestyle and moved to South Africa to try to complete the work their daughter started. They dedicated their lives to work full time on racial reconciliation in that troubled land.

The Biehls not only met two of the young men who killed their daughter but, learning of the chaotic circumstances of the riot and the heartfelt remorse of the killers, testified in favor of their political amnesty. The young men asked if they could atone for their crime by doing public service for a foundation the Biehls established in Amy's name. For two years they worked with Amy's parents daily, and eventually became close enough that they addressed Linda Biehl as "mom."

What lingers from this story is that the elder Biehls reported that they felt happier, more at peace, and liberated after forgiving their daughter's killers.

3. WHY IS THERE NOT MORE FORGIVENESS AMONG US?

Given cases like the Biehls' (and there are innumerable others, all of them beautiful, some of which we've heard from this pulpit recently), why is there not more forgiveness among us? I see two reasons, one societal, and the other personal.

a. **Societal:**

KINDS OF

   i. The problem with forgiveness has been that of all acknowledged good acts, it is the one we are most suspicious of. "To err is human, to forgive, supine," punned humorist S.J. Perelman. In a country where the death penalty has been a proven vote getter in recent years, forgiveness is often seen as effete, wimpy and irresponsible. Sometimes it seems to condone the offense, as noted centuries ago by Jewish sages who declared, "He that is merciful to the cruel will eventually be cruel to the innocent."

   ii. As quoted by President Hinckley in his recent book *Standing for Something*, American General Omar Bradley, for whom the Bradley Fighting Vehicles were named (irony intentional?), laments that "We have grasped the mystery of the atom and rejected the Sermon on the Mount... Ours is a world of nuclear giants and ethical infants. We know more about war than we know about peace, more about killing than we know about living." (end quote)

   iii. We live in an age and a society in which the collecting of grievances and nursing of grudges is elaborately and systematically encouraged, while forgiveness is largely looked down upon as a quaint and obsolete relic from *Little House on the Prairie*. Entire industries have at their very foundation the encouragement of men and women to view themselves as wronged by various forces real or imagined, to get angry, and to get even.

   iv. Recent years have seen the flourishing of an entire genre of television and radio programming dedicated almost exclusively to the spewing of venomous grievances and the extracting of revenge, usually among family members and other close relationships.

   v. Such "culture" doesn't lend itself to a culture of forgiveness.

b. **Personal: Three reasons**

   i. It's hard

      1. Far from being the recourse of sissies, forgiveness is the hardest course of all. Gandhi: "The weak can never forgive. Forgiveness is the attribute of the strong."

      2. Although it involves decisions made in split-seconds, forgiveness is not in itself a moment, but a process, and often an arduous one, requiring grit and determination. C.S. Lewis observes that forgiving a "single great injury" is one thing, but that the greater challenge lies in forgiving "the incessant provocations of daily life," especially when those provocations come at the hands of those nearest to us.

      3. And I, for one, struggle with the daily grind of forgiveness, but have found invariably that when I forgive, I don't lose face, I don't lose control, and I don't lose satisfaction. In fact, I lose nothing but a burden.

      4. Forgiveness is also hard because the transgressed may be relying on the initiative of the transgressor, before the forgiveness process can get underway. And this initiative, if in fact it comes, may not come in the way that best lends itself to actual forgiveness between transgressor and transgressed. I'll explain: An important distinction can be drawn between seeking forgiveness and offering an apology. Forgiveness requires an act of contrition. When asking for forgiveness, the penitent transgressor willingly opens a dialogue that may lead to rebuke before it achieves reconciliation. But when we have wronged and just say we're sorry, case

closed, we can simply be shrugging off the offense rather than allowing for the necessary shared healing.

   ii. It's messy

      1. Sometimes we may fear that forgiving an act condones it the act. Archbishop and Nobel Peace Prize Laureate Desmond Tutu, who knows a thing or two about forgiveness, speaks of forgiveness within the African concept of "ubuntu" - that a person is only a person through other people, and he clarifies that "Forgiveness is *not* to condone or minimize the awfulness of an atrocity or wrong. It is to recognize its ghastliness but to choose to acknowledge the essential humanity of the perpetrator and to give that perpetrator the possibility of making a new beginning." (end quote) In no way does forgiving mean that we're saying that what happened is OK. Forgiveness doesn't require that we accept or tolerate evil. It doesn't mean that we ignore the wrong or deny that painful things occurred. Having a forgiving character or being predisposed toward forgiveness does not mean being predisposed toward being a doormat or a fool. It doesn't mean that the transgressed cannot experience a negative catharsis prior to a positive one, or that there will be no consequences for the transgressor. "Forgiveness is *in advance of* justice," said President John Taylor, (end quote) not exclusive of it. After all, the forgiveness we receive from the Father is possible because the Son *satisfied* the demands of justice. Those demands weren't ignored. Forgiving somebody who lies to you doesn't mean that you necessarily believe her next promise. "Turning the other cheek" doesn't mean that a wife who has forgiven her husband of alcohol-related abuses is required to stick around the house if he relapses and comes home drunk six months later.

      2. Furthermore, forgiving is a messy proposition because it's not the same as excusing. Something that has a *justifiable* excuse doesn't conflict with justice, and therefore, doesn't require forgiveness. Again, I quote C.S. Lewis: "Real forgiveness does not require that a case be made out in the transgressor's favor. That would not be forgiveness at all. Real forgiveness means looking steadily at the sin, the sin that is left over without any excuse, after all allowances have been made, and seeing it in all its horror, dirt, meanness and malice, and nevertheless being wholly reconciled to the person who has done it. That, and only that, is forgiveness. To excuse what can really produce good excuses is not Christian charity; it is only fairness. To be a Christian means to forgive the inexcusable, because God will forgive the inexcusable in you." (end quote)

   iii. It's awkward

      1. As Christians and Latter-Day Saints specifically, having been so thoroughly schooled in the ways of personal repentance, we may be more comfortable playing the part of the transgressor than that of the transgressed. When offended, we may be hesitant to broach the subject with our offender, possibly out of fear of being rebuffed, dismissed, or accused of condescension, but *more* likely out of fear of "judging," even though our Lord has instructed and our doctrine dictates that we reprove when moved upon by the Holy Ghost (D&C 121:43), that we go to the one who has offended us, reproach him or her, and then be reconciled (Luke 17:3, Matthew 5).

         a. I have a bad habit – actually, I have several, but we'll stick to the one that's most relevant to the topic: As I develop relationships, I tend to be formal for a long time, and then swing abruptly from formal to casual. A professional colleague responded to something that I said recently: "That hurt my feelings." Struck by the simplicity and stark honesty of the statement. Wasn't couched in normal business jargon. His initiative in this mild rebuke led to a reconciliation that has strengthened the relationship beyond what it was prior to the offense.

4. THE SPIRITUAL CASE FOR FORGIVENESS

To a large segment of society, the forgiving actions of Linda and Peter Biehl might seem preposterous. And, really, as a practical matter, who among us, given their extraordinarily tragic circumstances, would have questioned them had they pursued a vendetta, allowing their lives to burn with hatred for the transgressors? But the Biehls' choice is overwhelmingly endorsed by our Christian perspective, because we know that our forgiveness of others is a condition of the forgiveness that we seek, through our own repentance.

    a. Nibley: Two-fold purpose of life is to learn to repent and forgive.

    b. Doctrinal case for our forgiveness of others is tight:

        i. "For if ye forgive men their trespasses, your heavenly father will also forgive you. But if you forgive not men their trespasses, neither will your Father forgive your trespasses." (Matthew 6:14-15) "Inasmuch as you have forgiven one another your trespasses, even so I, the Lord, forgive you." (D&C 82:1) "...forgive us our debts, *as* we forgive our debtors" (Matthew 6:12) "Forgive one another your trespasses." (Mosiah 26:31) "Even as Christ forgave you, so also do ye." (Colossians 3:13) "Ye ought to forgive one another, for he that forgiveth not his brother his trespasses, standeth condemned before the Lord, for there remaineth in him the greater sin. ...Of you it is required to forgive all men." D&C 64:9-10

        ii. There is no ambiguity: in the Lord's position on the matter; regarding our obligations, as those seeking forgiveness, to forgive; in the blessings we stand to gain from it.

5. THE SECULAR CASE FOR FORGIVENESS

Throughout history, such truths showing the "benefits," if you will, of forgiveness to the forgiver have remained largely the domain of the sacred. Whether specific social or philosophical movements served to galvanize this association, I'm not sure. But even when touching on forgiveness themes, great art and literature (which served as the *Dr. Phils* of past centuries) have most often shown the benefits that forgiveness gives to the forgiven, not necessarily the forgiver. And given the deep historical association, there was an assumption that forgiveness can only be motivated by faith, and that its benefits are not to be enjoyed by the forgiver during this mortal sojourn. But recent developments and rediscoveries in the medical and social sciences are supporting the idea that forgiveness, long considered the "extra mile" of mercy toward the offender that is required from a believer, is in fact a creative human faculty for overcoming estrangement, and that Christ's counsel wasn't only the pronouncement of a holy philosophy or the spelling out of a condition of salvation—he was, rather, giving practical advice for living. Forgiveness is spreading from its acknowledged domain in religious thinking and practice into the scientific community, where research has shown impressive results, and some practitioners are developing enthusiasm for its wide potential.

    a. Background on this "Forgiveness Movement"

    For the better part of its existence, modern psychology focused almost exclusively on the negative. It observed behavior that was considered sick, destructive or otherwise abnormal, and sought first to understand and then to remedy it. By one count, during the 20th century, there were 8166 scholarly psychological articles published on the topic "anger," versus 416 on "Forgiveness." The presumably encyclopedic *Encyclopedia of Human Emotions*, for many years a standard reference book for clinicians, listed page after page of detrimental emotional states, but contained no entry for "gratitude." The *Diagnostic and Statistical Manual*, another standard feature in professionals' libraries, detailed fourteen major psychoses and dozens of neuroses and other psychological maladies, but neither it nor any comparable publication codified in a similar fashion the positive conditions that psychologists should try to encourage. Then in the1990s, a "positive psychology" movement took root in the field, seeking to figure out just why it was that some people became altruistic, honest, loyal or noble. Central to the findings and tenets of this movement is the role of forgiveness in living a contented life.

Today, forgiveness is one of the hottest fields of research in clinical psychology, and is used to treat a number of anger-related ills in a totally secular context.

It has a growing body of scholarship, including reams and reams of published, peer-reviewed studies, citing its unrivaled benefits for dissipating anger, mending marriages banishing depression, and, yes, prolonging life.

There are university programs dedicated to it, and not just at the types of universities that would first come to mind. There is a Stanford Forgiveness Project, housed within that university's Center for Research in Disease Prevention, with the stated objective of "training forgiveness as a way to ameliorate the anger and distress involved in feeling hurt. This can have important implications for the prevention and treatment of cardiovascular and other chronic diseases." (end quote) Harvard Med School has hosted seminars on the topic, featuring lectures with titles such as:
   "The Power of Belief and the Role of Forgiveness in Healthcare"
   "The Role of Spirituality and Forgiveness in Health and Illness"
   "The Spiritual Assessment: Forgiveness As A Tool for Use with Patient Populations"

The movement even has its own generously-endowed foundation, A Campaign for Forgiveness Research, which has as one of its stated aims "to propose an alternative method for treating anger other than medication."

b. This movement suggests that to forgive is no longer *just* divine, and points to two primary ways in which forgiveness benefits the *forgiver*:
   i. The first, and more subtle of the two, and relates to research showing that people with strong social networks—of friends, neighbors and family—tend to be healthier and live longer than loners. Someone who nurses grudges and keeps track of every slight is obviously going to burn through some relationships over the course of a lifetime.
   ii. The second reason is more overt, and relates to the forgiver's physical and mental well-being
      1. Negative Effects of Nonforgiveness
         a. Studies have shown "robust" physiological differences between nonforgiving and forgiving states. Subjects' cardiovascular systems inevitably labor when they remember the person who hurt them. But stress is "significantly greater" when they consider revenge rather than forgiveness.
         b. People who do not forgive tend to have negative indicators of well-being: More stress-related disorders, lower immune system

function, higher blood pressure, and higher rates of arterial plaque and cardiovascular disease than the population as a whole.
2. Positive Effects of Forgiveness
   a. Forgiveness reduces depression and anger. Increases self-esteem and hope.
   b. Yields sounder sleep and happier marriages.
   c. Gives a greater sense of individual power, enhanced capacity to trust, freedom from compulsions to exercise subtle control of individuals and events of the past, and increased feelings of love.
   d. One study found that elderly women who scored well on a test of forgiveness traits had fewer episodes of anxiety than those who scored poorly on the same test.
   e. A prominent researcher in the field gave a weeklong forgiveness training session for a group of Catholics and Protestants from Northern Ireland who had lost a family member to sectarian violence. By the week's end, all but a few of the participants reported a rise in feelings of forgiveness. Symptoms of stress (dizziness, loss of appetite, headaches and stomachaches) fell by 35 percent.
   f. Other studies link forgiveness and: Less pain, depression and anger in patients with chronic back pain; Fewer relapses in women in substance abuse programs
3. Key Underlying Points
   a. The positive effects in these studies hold true not only for cataclysms, but also the everyday reconciliations that so many of us struggle with.
   b. Lack of forgiveness doesn't just affect the aggrieved; it affects those around him/her.

6. ONE GREAT WHOLE

a. In this context of the sheer *health* benefits of forgiveness, consider closely the words of our prophets:
   i. Brigham Young once compared being offended to a poisonous snakebite: "There are two courses of action to follow when one is bitten by a rattlesnake. One may, in anger, fear, or vengefulness, pursue the creature and kill it. Or he may make full haste to get the venom out of his system. If we pursue the latter course we will likely *survive*, but if we attempt to follow the former, we may not be around long enough to finish it."
   ii. More recently, President Hinckley has taught us that "[Forgiveness] requires a self-discipline almost greater than we are capable of. The application of this principle of forgiveness [is] difficult to live but wondrous in its *curative* powers..."
b. Indeed, as they pertain to our obligation to forgive others, we see that the true words of the prophets and the professionals can be circumscribed into one great whole.

7. [OPTIONAL STORY IN CLOSING: FIGARO]

Mozart's (supposed) musical nemesis, Antonio Salieri, on witnessing the fourth act of *The Marriage of Figaro*, in the 1984 Academy Award winner for Best Picture, *Amadeus*: "A wonder was revealed. One of the true wonders of art. The fourth was a miracle. I saw a woman disguised in her maid's clothes hear her husband speak the first tender words he has offered her in years, only because he thinks she is someone else. I heard the music of true forgiveness filling the theatre, conferring on all who sat there a perfect absolution. God was singing through this little man to all the world – unstoppable. What shall I say to you who will one day hear this last act for yourselves? You will – because whatever else shall pass away, this must remain."

I cite this not just because it is perhaps my favorite forgiveness story in all of the Arts, but because it distills a key point: Whether the Count's contrition is sincere or just a product of the duress of the "hand in cookie jar" moment is a debated topic among musicologists and opera buffs. Surely Mozart and his librettist, Lorenzo Da Ponte, both infinitely sensitive to the nuances of human behavior, were aware of this possibility, and yet they allowed for it. Why? The music and its effect, described so perfectly in Salieri's quote, make it clear that independent of the Count's own repentance, his wife's forgiveness is real, is valid, and is healing, *for her*. Among mortals, forgiveness is more about the transgressed than the transgressor.

8. CONCLUSION

   a. While the secular case for forgiving others is a compelling one, it is, at the end of the day, based largely on selfishness. And although the sacred case for forgiveness is not altogether devoid of self-interest (in that our own forgiveness and, consequently, salvation depend upon it), it is, in the final analysis, about glorifying God, loving his children, and exercising, as gods in embryo, the divine power to forgive. And by failing to forgive, we punish ourselves.
   b. Why, then, as I asked earlier, is there not more forgiveness among us? Are we afraid that if we approach our transgressor to provide an opportunity for reconciliation, that we'll be rebuffed? Not if it's done in a spirit of edification, accompanied by an even greater outpouring of love. Are we afraid that by raising another through the act of forgiving, we are somehow diminished? We are not. Forgiveness is not a zero-sum proposition, in which one party's gain is the other party's proportionate loss. Christ's "grace is sufficient for all men" (Ether 12:26).
   c. I pray that we, and myself especially, can be better purveyors of the Balm of Gilead of which we sung in the opening hymn, that we can better allow the atonement to work *through us* and allow God's hand to move molecules of peace and goodness *through us*, as we forgive others, so that we, as the transgressors and the transgressed, will feel its sweetening, curative and saving effects.

Sources

Carson, James. "Correlates of Forgiveness & Preliminary Results from a Loving Kindness Meditation Intervention for Low Back Pain Patients." Duke University Medical Center: April, 2003. Cited at http://www.medicalnewstoday.com

Easterbrook, Gregg. *The Progress Paradox: How Life Gets Better While People Feel Worse.* New York: Random House, 2003.

Hinckley, Gordon Bitner. *Standing For Something: 10 Neglected Virtues That Will Heal Our Hearts and Homes.* New York: Times Books, 2000.

Lewis, Clive Staples. *Fern-Seed and Elephants, and Other Essays on Christianity.* London: Fount, 1977.

McCullogh, Michael E., et al. "Vengefulness: Relationships with Forgiveness, Rumination, Well-Being, and The Big Five." University of Miami (FL): April 2000. http://www.psy.miami.edu/faculty/mmccullough/Papers/McCullough.pdf

Sorenson, Elder David E. "Forgiveness Will Change Bitterness to Love." General Conference of The Church of Jesus Christ of Latter-Day Saints. Salt Lake City: LDS.org, April 2003.

Witvliet, Charlotte Vanoyen. "Forgiveness and Health: Review and Reflections on a Matter of Faith, Feelings, and Physiology." *Psychology and Theology:* Vol. 29, 2001. http://www.questia.com/PM.qst?a=o&se=gglsc&d=5002422544

Online articles from sources including:
The Atlanta Journal-Constitution
The Christian Science Monitor
ForgivenessWeb.Com
Forgiver.Net
Forgiving.Org
The New York Times
Newsweek Magazine
The Philadelphia Inquirer
Time Magazine
USA Today

Some content has been reproduced (extensively, in a few cases) verbatim in this talk from the above sources, without direct citation – unacceptable for academic or professional use, of course, but OK for a Sunday morning.